PENG

THE STAR S

Naomi Jackson is the author of *The Star Side of Bird Hill*, which was nominated for an NAACP Image Award and the Hurston/Wright Legacy Award, longlisted for the National Book Critics Circle's John Leonard Prize and the Center for Fiction's First Novel Prize, and named an Honor Book for Fiction by the Black Caucus of the American Library Association. A graduate of Williams College, Jackson studied fiction at the Iowa Writers' Workshop and traveled to South Africa on a Fulbright scholarship, where she received an MA in creative writing from the University of Cape Town. Jackson was born and raised in Brooklyn by West Indian parents.

* * *

Praise for *The Star Side of Bird Hill*

"The evocation of the island is romantic and alive. . . . Jackson renders [the characters'] inner lives effectively."

—*The New Yorker*

"Once in a while, you'll stumble onto a book like this, one so poetic in its descriptions and so alive with lovable, frustrating, painfully real characters, that your emotional response to it becomes almost physical. . . . [A] wrenching debut . . . The dual coming-of-age story alone could melt the sternest of hearts, but Jackson's exquisite prose is a marvel too. . . . A gem of a book. A."

—*Entertainment Weekly*

"Jackson's evocative, lyrical writing . . . makes Barbados come to life, and she's comfortable with both humor and pathos. . . . A lovely [book], and Jackson seems likely to have a distinguished career ahead of her."

—NPR.org

"Moving . . . [Jackson] has delivered a novel of remarkable strength and beauty as she chronicles the sojourn of two sisters to their mother's homeland of Barbados for the summer. . . . This is a story of sisterhood and tough, unbreakable love. This is a book that asks: What happens when you go home and find the answers you didn't know you were looking for?" —*Gawker*

"*The Star Side of Bird Hill* is, at its core, a story about mothers and daughters. But the rich and colorful world Ms. Jackson renders on the page moves well beyond that, too, setting itself the task of exploring so much more. . . . Ms. Jackson has a deft hand with characterization—all of the people she creates feel utterly human. . . . Naomi Jackson vividly delivers two entirely different worlds and a whole range of experiences that taught me a little bit more about how to be a better human."

—*Pittsburgh Post-Gazette*

"From Maryse Condé to Edwidge Danticat to Tiphanie Yanique, contemporary Caribbean writers have produced an exquisite literature of diaspora and affirmation. . . . Now Naomi Jackson joins their ranks with *The Star Side of Bird Hill*, a serious yet effervescent debut. . . . More than a coming-of-age novel, *The Star Side of Bird Hill* evokes the intractable forces that tear at families and cultures."

—*Minneapolis Star-Tribune*

"[A] keen-eyed debut . . . A lush and sensitive read with a setting well matched for a sultry summer afternoon."

—Oprah.com

"Naomi Jackson is our new favorite writer." —*PureWow*

"*The Star Side of Bird Hill* moves forcefully between Barbados and Brooklyn in this plangent coming-of-age debut novel about two sisters torn between their absent father's reappearance and their strong, matriarchal island family." —*Elle*

"A winning coming-of-age tale with Caribbean flavor."
—BBC.com

"A heartbreaking coming-of-age story, *The Star Side of Bird Hill* is ultimately about the choices we must make about love and family, and what it means to go home." —*Buzzfeed*

"Holy cats, this novel is wonderful. . . . Lyrical, a really stellar debut." —*BookRiot*

"The writing is especially fine, with even minor characters benefiting from Jackson's lyrical descriptions. . . . [*The Star Side of Bird Hill*] recall[s] Toni Morrison's *Love*."
—*Library Journal* (starred review)

"A bittersweet coming-of-age tale of heartbreak and loss . . . The themes she touches on—mental illness, immigration, motherhood, sexual awakening—are potent and deftly juggled, anchored in the vivid locale of Bird Hill yet universally relatable. Readers will be turning the pages to follow Phaedra and Dionne's memorable journey." —*Publishers Weekly*

"*The Star Side of Bird Hill* reads as if we're let in on a sometimes wonderful, sometimes thrilling, sometimes terrible secret. It's the unwritten history of women without men, of girls in conflict with themselves, and the damage—and healing—that can come from the same place: family."
—Marlon James, author of *A Brief History of Seven Killings*

"Naomi Jackson packs a hell of a lot of love and death and magic into this wonderful debut. *The Star Side of Bird Hill* travels between Barbados and Brooklyn, telling the story of a family, and a people, who move between worlds and worldviews. But really this is the story of one young girl named Phaedra who is trying her best in a world that doesn't always see the best in her. There are touches of Jamaica Kincaid and J. D. Salinger here, but Naomi Jackson is an artist all her own."

—Victor LaValle, author of *The Devil in Silver*

"Jackson has written a first novel full of heart and heartbreak, a novel about going home, about the ties that bind three generations of women across years and despite absence. It is a bittersweet lesson in learning to recognize love."

—Ayana Mathis, author of *The Twelve Tribes of Hattie* (Oprah's Book Club 2.0 selection)

"Naomi Jackson has written a tender novel exploring the complexities of motherhood and childhood. *The Star Side of Bird Hill* holds together opposing elements—the book is quiet in the telling, but the story being told is sharp and vibrant. It is as much a story of the fears of childhood as it is a story about welcoming old age with optimism. A book that knows death and discovery. A book laced with pain but shimmering with hope. With care, the narrative addresses huge issues such as mental illness, mortality, sexuality and, at its very core, what it means to love another person as they are."

—Tiphanie Yanique, author of *Land of Love and Drowning*

The Star Side of Bird Hill

NAOMI JACKSON

PENGUIN BOOKS

For my sister, Shari
For my mothers, Cheryl and Sadie
For my grandmothers, Lily, Oriel, and Ruth

PENGUIN BOOKS
An imprint of Penguin Random House LLC
375 Hudson Street
New York, New York 10014
penguin.com

First published in the United States of America by Penguin Press, an imprint of Penguin Publishing Group, a division of Penguin Random House LLC, 2015
Published in Penguin Books 2016

ISBN 9781594205958 (hc.)
ISBN 9780143109167 (pbk.)

Printed in the United States of America
10 9 8 7 6 5 4 3 2 1

Designed by Michelle McMillian

Summer 1989

⁂

Bird Hill
St. John, Barbados

THE PEOPLE ON THE HILL liked to say that God's smile was the sun shining down on them. In the late afternoon, before scarlet ibis bloodied the sunset, light flooded the stained glass windows of Bird Hill Church of God in Christ, illuminating the renderings of black saints from Jesus to Absalom Jones. When there wasn't prayer meeting, choir rehearsal, Bible study, or Girl Guides, the church was empty except for its caretaker, Mr. Jeremiah. It was his job to chase the children away from the cemetery that sloped down behind the church, his responsibility to shoo them from their perches on graves that dotted the backside of the hill the area was named for. Despite his best intentions, Mr. Jeremiah's noontime and midnight devotionals at the rum shop brought on long slumbers when children found freedom to do as they liked among the dead.

Dionne Braithwaite was two weeks fresh from Brooklyn and Barbados's fierce sun had already transformed her skin from its New York shade of caramel to brick red. She was wearing foundation that was too light for her skin now. It came off in smears on the white handkerchiefs she stole from her grandmother's chest of drawers, but she wore it anyway, because makeup was her tether to the life she'd left back home. Hyacinth, while she didn't like to see her granddaughter made up, couldn't argue with the fact that Dionne's years of practice meant that she could work tasteful wonders on her face, looking sun-kissed and dewy-lipped rather than the tart her grandmother thought face paint transformed women into.

Dionne was sixteen going on a bitter, if beautiful, forty-five. Trevor, her friend and eager supplicant for her affections, was her age mate. Although Dionne thought herself above the things the children on Bird Hill did, she liked the hiding place the graveyard behind the church provided. So it was that she and Trevor came to the cool limestone of Dionne's great-grandmother's grave, talking about their morning at Vacation Bible School, and imitating their teacher's nasal Texas twang.

"Accepting Jesus Christ as your Lord and Savior is the only sure way to avoid eternal damnation," Dionne pronounced, her arms akimbo.

Trevor grinned, his eyes caught on the amber lace of Dionne's panties as she walked the length of the grave.

"What do you think happens when you die?" Dionne asked Trevor.

"I don't know. Seems to me it's just like going to sleep.

Except you never wake up. Why do you think so much about death anyways?"

"We are in a graveyard," Dionne said. She traced the name of her ancestor while Trevor's hand worked its way beneath her dress and along the smooth terrain of her upper thigh. She liked the way it felt when Trevor touched her, though she hadn't decided yet what she'd let him do to her. She'd let Darren put his hands all the way up her skirt on the last day of school. But here, where girls her age still wore their hair in press and curls, she knew that sex was not to be given freely, but a commodity to ration, something to barter with.

Dionne squeezed Trevor's wrist, halting his hand's ascent, and then crossed her arms at her chest, which was testing the seams of her dress. After a few weeks of eating cou-cou and flying fish, her yellow frock fit snugly and rode up on her behind. Dionne was a copy of her mother at sixteen—her mouth fixed in a permanent scowl, her slim frame atop the same long legs, a freckle that disappeared when she wrinkled her chin. She hoped that one day she and her mother would again be mistaken for sisters like some of the flirtatious shopkeepers in Flatbush used to do back when her mother still made small talk.

Dionne's and Trevor's younger siblings, Phaedra and Chris, played tag among the miniature graves of children, all casualties of the 1955 cholera outbreak. Nineteen girls and one boy had died before the hill folks abandoned their suspicion of the world in general and doctors in particular to seek help from "outside people." This was just one of the stories that Dionne and Phaedra's mother summoned as evidence for why she left the hill the first chance she got. "They're clannish. They wouldn't know a free thought if it smacked them on the behind," their mother would hiss, her mouth specked with venom.

Chris and Phaedra darted between the tombstones, browning the soles of their feet, losing track of the shoes they shook off on the steps at the top of the hill. They had become fast friends since Phaedra and her sister arrived from Brooklyn at the beginning of the summer. Phaedra was small for her ten years; even though they were the same age, her head reached only the crook of Chris's elbow. Her skin had darkened to a deep cocoa from running in the sun all day in spite of her grandmother's protests. She wore her hair in a French braid, its length tucked away from the girls who threatened her after reading about Samson and Delilah in Sunday school. Glimpses of Phaedra's future beauty peeked out from behind her pink, heart-shaped glasses, which were held together with Scotch tape.

Hyacinth tried to get Phaedra to at least cover her head and her feet, saying that she didn't need any black-black pickney in her house, and that, besides, good girls knew how to sit down and be still, play dolls and house and other ladylike games. Phaedra had never been one for girls in Brooklyn, and she didn't see herself starting now. At the beginning of the summer, a whole gang of girls her age filed through her grandmother's house to get a good look at her. They drank the Capri

Sun juices Phaedra begrudgingly offered them from the barrel her mother sent. They chewed politely on the cheese sandwiches Hyacinth made and cut into quarters. Once they'd asked her all the basic questions (Where did she live in New York? What year was she in school? How old was her sister?), there was little left to talk about. They papered over the awkward silences by staring dumbly at each other and then promising to stop by soon. But by the time VBS started, none of them had come over again.

Phaedra knew that these friendships were doomed the moment she met Simone Saveur, the ringleader of the ten- and eleven-year-old girls because she towered over them and spoke with a bass the boys their age didn't yet have in their voices. On her first and last visit to Hyacinth's house, Simone Saveur sat down and started looking around, taking mental notes, collecting grist for the gossip mill. Because while Hyacinth could safely say that she had been into almost every house on Bird Hill, whether to deliver a baby or visit an old person who was feeling poorly, or just to sit for a while talking about who had died and left and been born, only a handful of hill women could say that they had seen Hyacinth's house beyond the gallery where she sat with guests. All of them had at one point or another been invited to admire Hyacinth's rose garden, which in her vanity she sometimes showed off, going on about how they bloomed, the insects that troubled them, her pruning techniques. It could be said that Hyacinth's rose garden, which she tended to like another set of grandchildren, was an elaborate fortress whose beauty so thoroughly enchanted its visitors that they never questioned why they'd never been invited inside.

When Phaedra saw Simone looking around, she suddenly felt protective of Hyacinth and her house and everything in it: a pitcher and glasses with orange slices etched into them that had been around since before Phaedra was born, the open jalousies and the white curtains that lapped against the girls' faces, the lovingly carved archway that separated the front room from the dining room, just barely fitting a dining table and a hutch, the pictures of Phaedra and Dionne and their mother, Avril, lining the walls. Where their apartment building in Brooklyn was marked with just a number, 261, Phaedra loved her grandmother's house because of the question "Why worry?" written in blue script above the front steps. Everything in Hyacinth's house had been touched by those she loved, and so it was Phaedra's and Dionne's in a way that their apartment in Brooklyn never would be.

Once, when there was a lull in conversation, Simone Saveur's roving eyes settled on Phaedra. Simone tried to explain the concept of cooking a dirt pot, but Phaedra was not at all interested in cooking, not even for play, much less near her grandmother's outhouse, which she was still too chicken to use, even when Dionne was taking forever in the inside bathroom, and she was dying to go. She knew she wouldn't be playing any such game, or spending time with girls who thought this was a good time. Phaedra's mouth corners turned down and soon everyone was saying their good-byes. Phaedra's mother said that her daughter's gloomy face could rain out a good time. In this case, Phaedra thought the force of her foul mood came in handy; it encouraged a quick end to what had been an uncomfortable, bordering on unpleasant, afternoon.

That summer, Chris and Phaedra were inseparable. Phaedra could barely trouble herself to remember the other girls' names, having put them in the category of "just girls," which was the same as dumping them into the rubbish bin of her mind. With Chris, there was ease to their play, a rough-and-tumbleness that she welcomed. Chris made Phaedra most happy by not asking her too many questions. Because while most of the Bird Hill girls were too polite to ask, she knew they most wanted to know about the thing she least wanted to talk about—her mother.

Phaedra liked to look at Christopher, who had the same sloe-eyed gaze as his mother's, an ever-ready smile, and pink lips that made him seem more tender than other boys his age. Now she watched as he stuffed the stocky fingers of his eternally ashy hands into his pockets and surveyed the land below the hill, mimicking the firm stance he'd seen his father take in the pulpit.

From where they stood, Phaedra and Chris could see the fishermen's boats at Martin's Bay, the buoys bobbing up and down in the blue-green water. Further east, a riot of rock formations, vestiges of an island long since gone, jutted out at Bathsheba. It was Phaedra's first summer in Barbados, and she wanted more than anything to feel the sand between her toes and to look at her feet through the clear-clear water. With its natural beauty, Barbados was far superior to Brooklyn; you were more likely to find a syringe than a seashell on the beach at Coney Island. She stood next to Chris, looking out at three rocks at Bathsheba that she and Chris had nicknamed the Father, the Son, and the Holy Ghost. It was hard to explain, but she had a feeling, standing there, that she'd never felt before in Brooklyn, not that she owned these things, but that she was somehow part of them. When Phaedra went on a class trip to the Empire State Building and looked down at the city from 102 stories above the sidewalk, she didn't have that feeling. The city was beautiful in its own way, but it wasn't hers. She didn't try to explain how she felt to Chris. What she most liked about their friendship was how much space there was for silence, the kind of quiet she'd never found with girls her age.

Chris turned his back to the sea, toward Phaedra.

"Touch it," Chris said. He dared Phaedra to touch the grave of her namesake, her great-aunt Marguerite Phaedra Hill, who had died from cholera like the others.

"What if I don't want to touch it?" Phaedra said.

"Then I'll make you."

Chris picked up an enormous rock and threw it at Phaedra. It opened her right temple in the same place where she had a dime-sized birthmark she had seen the Bird Hill girls looking at and straining not to ask about. The force of the blow knocked Phaedra off her feet.

The dull thud of stone against skull roused Dionne and Trevor from their mischievousness. Dionne ran to see what happened and gasped when she saw her sister lying prone on the grave, blood running down the side of her head.

"But what happen here?" Dionne said, breaking into the patois that usually lay hidden beneath her tongue.

"Why did you do that?" Trevor asked Chris.

"Mummy say wail woman head can't break," Chris said incredulously, over and over again, as blood seeped out of Phaedra's head and commingled with the hill's red dirt. Phaedra didn't know what wail women were yet, but Chris leaned on those two words in a way that made it clear to anyone within earshot that being called one wasn't a compliment.

Dionne took off up the hill with Trevor trailing behind her. She pressed her hands to her breasts to still them as she ran. (She'd already outgrown the bras that she brought with her; the homemade ones her grandmother had sewn lay unused at the bottom of her mother's old chest of drawers.) She swept past the church and stopped at the rectory, a white clapboard house with a view of all the other houses on the hill.

Chris's mother was where she always was, sitting on her veranda, listening to Jamaican rockers on her radio. The way that Mrs. Loving stared out for hours over the hillside, unmoving, reminded Dionne of her own mother.

"Phaedra got hit in the head by a rock in the cemetery," Dionne blurted out before she made it to the veranda steps.

"Oh dear," Mrs. Loving said. She went running behind Dionne, moving unexpectedly fast.

Hill women were busy putting laundry out on the line, picking okra for cou-cou, humming along to the grand old gospel of salvation on family radio. They formed a circle at the hill's bottom, looking on.

"Christopher Alexander Loving, what have you done?" Chris's mother bellowed as she walked toward him. Upon hearing his full name, Chris would usually have run to hide. Instead, he stood at Phaedra's feet, shading her from the noon-high sun. He looked down at Phaedra, transfixed, mumbling to himself.

Mrs. Loving took Phaedra's head into her lap and let the blood soak her dress. She slapped gently at her face. "Come now, child, don't let sleep take you."

Finally, Phaedra opened up her eyes. "Mommy, what happened? Everything's starry."

"Hush, child, hush. Mummy's not here, but she soon come," Mrs. Loving whispered.

Phaedra looked up at Chris's long shadow and then at Mrs. Loving above her. She was struck then, for the first time, by the heaviness of her head, the aching there, and the oddness of someone other than her mother trying to comfort her.

DIONNE HATED MOST THINGS about Barbados, especially the weather. She disliked the cool damp of the mornings, followed by the unforgiving heat and insistent afternoon rains that drowned any hopes of going outside. During the long, wet days when she was forced to keep watch over her sister, Dionne felt like one of the sick and shut-in from the church bulletin. Maybe this is what growing old was like, she thought. Maybe the world gets smaller and smaller until there's nothing but the walls around you to show you where you end and the rest of the world begins.

The weather was just one thing on a long list of gripes that Dionne kept in her head, and occasionally wrote in the margins of the fashion magazines she'd brought with her from Brooklyn. Chief among her complaints was that there was nothing to do to entertain herself. The days just seemed to drag on and on. She sometimes looked up at the clock thinking an hour must have passed, when in fact it had only been a few minutes. And while she always resented the long list of things she had to do back in Brooklyn—prodding her mother, Avril, to get up and bathe each day, making sure Phaedra was dressed and her hair decently combed, cooking dinner and packing lunches for herself and her sister—in Barbados she felt like she had been demoted back to childhood, asked to put on a pair of too-small shoes by being responsible only for herself.

Hyacinth believed that idle hands were the devil's playground, and so she gave the girls chores to do and signed them up for not one but two sessions of Vacation Bible School. Still, Dionne felt a restlessness welling up in her. Dionne thought Bird Hill was provincial, far too small a stage for a girl like her. There was a flash of excitement when a talent scout for the Miss Teen Barbados pageant came to Bird Hill. For a brief moment, something like joy washed across Dionne's face when the other girls pushed her forward, saying that she would surely win. But when the scout heard her accent, the woman—whom Dionne later pronounced both too fat and too ugly to be scouting for a beauty pageant—asked whether she was of both Barbadian heritage and Barbadian citizenship, and she'd had to admit that she was in fact an American citizen. Just like that, Dionne's dreams of emancipation from the lot of the fatally dull girls in Bird Hill were dashed.

How she longed for her best friend, Taneisha, who could make a walk to the corner store exciting, stopping every few steps to say hello to the boys who were hypnotized by

Taneisha's green eyes and something else, not aloofness, exactly, but a way of broadcasting magnetism without need. Whenever Dionne tried to emulate Taneisha's cool, she ended up seeming standoffish or mean. After years of being on the periphery of the popular girls at her school, she had finally broken through because of Taneisha, whose tongue never got thick in her mouth when she was nervous the way Dionne's sometimes did. It helped that Dionne had scored Darren as her boyfriend, and that soon after they started dating, flesh and muscle started to fill out her lanky arms and bust and behind. The spring when Dionne and Darren started going together, there was a temporary pouring in of sunshine through the cloud that generally hovered over Avril, and she asked which boy was touching Dionne's bubbies under moonlight. Dionne was taken aback by her mother's directness, but then she answered that she didn't know any boys who would be touching her like that. Some part of Dionne was annoyed by how quickly Avril dropped the issue, ready as she was for a fight, and desperate as she was to feel the unfamiliar prick of an adult's concern.

Dionne didn't feel bad about lying to her mother. She knew intimately the precarious nature of their life, the way that it depended on a series of carefully constructed lies, the ones she told to get meat on credit at the butcher at the end of the month when her mother's money ran out; the ones she told to fend off her and Phaedra's teachers' suspicions; the ones she told to keep her friends from coming over to her house, and seeing her mother. Avril didn't move around much, so Dionne knew she could probably get away with shepherding any visitors into the back bedroom she shared with Phaedra. But there was still the problem of the smell—the scent of eucalyptus from the humidifier Avril kept going all day and all night, the stench from the stinking bush teas Avril bought from some woman on Church Avenue and that she was convinced might heal her, although months and then a year had passed and Avril still showed no signs of getting better. Dionne and Phaedra held their noses every time they came home, lest they choke on their mother's sadness. The more lies Dionne told to protect her mother and herself and her sister, the easier it was to lie to her mother, to anyone, really. And by the time Dionne arrived in Barbados, lying was less a moral dilemma than a means of getting by.

Despite the difficulties of life back in Brooklyn, Dionne preferred the predictable chaos of life there to the monotony of life in Bird Hill. To say that she was disappointed to be spending the summer in Barbados would be an understatement. She was furious. On this particular afternoon, Dionne was contemplating the relative virtues of a quick death—a plane crash, a car accident—over a long drawn-out one, exacerbated by a church's prayers that held you precariously in the land of the living. Today, the radio was looping a story about the death of Barbados's oldest living man, at 113 years old. While everyone on the radio marveled at his fortitude, Dionne couldn't help thinking that 113 years was just too many years to live, especially here. She sighed to herself, and went back to the book she was reading to Phaedra.

Phaedra was lying in the bed she shared with her grandmother, draped in her favorite bluebird bedsheets while Dionne read to her from the well-worn pages of her favorite book, *Annie John.*

In my small room. I lay on my pitch-pine bed, which, since I was sick, was made up with my Sunday sheets. I lay on my back and stared at the ceiling. I could hear the rain as it came down on the galvanized roof. The sound the rain made as it landed on the roof pressed me down in my bed, bolted me down, and I couldn't so much as lift my head if my life depended on it.

Phaedra fancied herself like Annie John, sick for days upon days, coming in and out of dreams while her body repaired itself. She sighed and nestled herself further into the sheets. Overhead, the ceiling fan whirred slowly, swirling air thick with the smell of rain.

Dionne marked her page, and then stretched the paperback across her knees.

"So how long are you going to work this sick thing?"

"What do you mean? I am sick," Phaedra whined.

"I had some patience and even some sympathy for you before. But it's been a week now. And you look fine to me."

"You're just mad because you can't use me as a cover anymore for your rendezvous with Trevor," Phaedra said. She sat up in the bed.

Dionne closed the bedroom door and moved until she was

within an inch of Phaedra's face. She knew she would only have a few minutes before her grandmother asked which grown people lived in her house and were bold enough to lock her doors. The people on the hill held privacy as a luxury not to be extended to children.

"Phaedra Ann Braithwaite, what business is it of yours what I do with boys?" Dionne said. Her hot breath formed a bridge between her face and her sister's.

"I know what I see. And you know Mommy said that if you don't keep your pocketbook shut tight, you're going to find yourself in the family way soon."

"I swear to God, Phaedra, I will cut your bony ass in two."

"I'll tell Granny about how you curse at me and sneak out of the house at night."

Phaedra paused to let the force of her threat land.

"What do you want from me?"

"Bring me Chris," Phaedra said.

Dionne flung the book at Phaedra, catching the very center of her right breast, which was budding in a way that their grandmother called force ripe. On the hill, becoming a woman was like that—shared with all the women who witnessed you coming into yourself, becoming one of them. Phaedra pressed her hand to the tender place where she'd been hit, but did not grant Dionne the satisfaction of seeing her cry.

"COME, NUH," DIONNE SAID, nudging her sister awake. Dionne was dressed in her only pair of Lee jeans and an orange-and-white-striped tube top she found in the back of her mother's closet, a treasure trove of risqué clothes Avril hid from her mother when she was living there. Dionne smiled when she found it, struck by how similar it was to the stash of clothes and makeup stashed beneath her bed at home. When the girls landed at the airport that June, Hyacinth took one look at Dionne in her miniskirt, leggings, and tank top and said, "Lord, Jesus, please have mercy on my soul. I don't know how me and this child going to make out." Dionne pretended to be annoyed when her grandmother said that Dionne seemed intent on giving her the same series of heart attacks Avril had given Hyacinth when she was a teenager. But secretly she liked the steadiness of Hyacinth's concern for her, which was comforting after so many years of Avril's absentmindedness. She enjoyed hearing stories about the troublemaker her mother was and how much Hyacinth loved her despite her antics.

Dionne complained at first about sleeping alone in the back room that was once her mother's bedroom. No matter how many times Phaedra wet the bed or thrashed during her nightmares, Dionne took comfort in having her sister's body beside hers in the room they shared in Brooklyn. Right around the time that Avril began her downward spiral, Dionne started double-checking all the doors before she went to bed at night; she couldn't sleep if the closet door in her bedroom was open even an inch. Avril had been gone to them for some time by then, a ghost who sometimes left a jar of peanut butter open on the kitchen counter or feces floating in the toilet or who abandoned a knitting project she'd gotten excited about in the middle of the night that was an unsalvageable mess by morning. As Avril retreated more and more into herself, Dionne took comfort in the familiar annoyance of Phaedra's moaning, tossing, and turning, her body dampening the bedsheets. Between her sister's nocturnal theatrics, the bass that pumped from the club across the street, and the garbage trucks that rumbled up Flatbush Avenue as dawn peeked through their apartment's windows, in Brooklyn Dionne had noise to lull her to sleep and, more important, to distract her from the insistent worry that she'd wake one morning and find her mother gone, and not just for a trip in her mind.

Eventually, Dionne came to be soothed by her grandmother's heavy snores, which rose above the walls that stopped just short of the ceiling to let the breeze pass through. It was a comforting layer of sound alongside the frogs that chirped and croaked and occasionally made the nights in Bird Hill seem louder than the nights in Brooklyn. Soon, Dionne enjoyed having her own room, which was impossible in Brooklyn, where everything that was hers was also Phaedra's.

Now, Dionne nudged her sister again, pressing her bony knee into Phaedra's rib cage, which was puffed up with sleep.

"What?" Phaedra moaned. She felt for her grandmother in the bed bedside her, but her spot on the bed was cool. Phaedra was startled at first, and then she remembered that she'd sometimes stir in the middle of the night and find Hyacinth gone, or wake in the morning to find her grandmother deep in sleep well past sunrise.

"Get up. Don't you want to see Chris?"

"What time is it?"

"Don't worry about the time. Just come."

Phaedra took in the time on the digital alarm clock, 3:05, and looked up again at Dionne, whose figure she could make out better as her eyes adjusted to the dark. She pulled on her favorite pair of black jeans, an indigo t-shirt, and a sweater she'd brought for chilly nights, but hadn't yet worn.

They walked to the back of the house. Dionne undid the locks on the door that led to the backyard. Once they were outside, the chickens started to rustle their feathers, but stopped when Dionne sprinkled feed for them. The girls skirted the edge of their grandmother's garden, wetting their ankles with hydrangea dew. And then they found the road.

The night was brighter than Phaedra expected, brilliantly lit by the full moon and stars that seemed close enough to pluck from the sky. Phaedra stuck close to her sister as they rounded the first ring of the hill road. She wanted to reach for Dionne's hand, but she knew she was too big for that now.

The girls passed a pink chattel house that Phaedra knew was the halfway point between her grandmother's house and the church. The hairs on Phaedra's arms stood up. Suddenly, she felt a hand grab her right elbow. She yelped and her sister stopped a few strides ahead.

"What kind of time you looking tonight?" the voice rasped in Phaedra's ear.

Phaedra could feel the man and his breath and then his grasp as he ground his hips against her.

"Let me go," Phaedra said in a voice that was half whisper, half scream.

Dionne stepped between her sister and the stranger and said, "What exactly do you think you're doing?"

"I just want a dance," the stranger said. Dionne could see the man's glassy eyes and smell the liquor on his breath.

"Does she look like she wants to dance with you?" Dionne asked.

"All right, all right, all right. No need to get upset. I was just trying to have a good time."

Mr. Jeremiah let Phaedra go and stumbled down the hill, in the opposite direction of his house. He sang, his voice rising above the cricket chorus, "Long time we no have no nice time. Do you, do you, do yah think about that?" He punched the air for emphasis on "that" and Phaedra and Dionne stood watching his retreat until he was too far gone for their eyes to follow or their ears to hear.

"Next time walk closer to me," Dionne said.

Phaedra nodded. She was too focused on the damp rings of sweat Mr. Jeremiah's hands had left on her wrists to speak.

The front steps of the church at the top of the hill were always lit for travelers on their way home. Phaedra felt some of her fear drop away as they approached it, her heartbeat descend back to her chest from where it had taken residence inside her eardrums. When they came closer to the Lovings' house, the rectory next to the church, Phaedra felt her heart quicken again. Trevor leaned against the metal gate and Chris did the same, imitating his older brother's ease. The girls met up with the boys and then split off into their usual pairs, Dionne and Trevor holding hands, Phaedra's and Chris's arms grazing.

Phaedra and Chris climbed over the railing that enclosed Phaedra's great-aunt's grave. Chris pulled out a flashlight and a handkerchief to wipe the dusty wet. Then, he indicated that Phaedra should sit down. Phaedra, suspicious of this extra attention, chose to stand.

"It's cold," Phaedra said. She felt the cool of the night's small hours travel beneath her layers and make contact with her clammy skin.

"You want my jersey?" Chris asked.

"No, I do not want your sweater, Christopher. What I do want is a reason why you thought it would be a good idea to try and kill me with the biggest rock you could find."

"I just wanted to know."

"Know what? Know what I looked like lying unconscious? What exactly is so interesting about that?"

"I'm not saying that. I just was curious about . . . you know."

"No, I do not know. What are you talking about?"

"I wanted to know if it's true what people say about your family. If it's true that you can't die."

"Who told you that?" Phaedra grabbed the flesh on Chris's arm and pulled, wringing it until she felt his skin grow hot.

"Nobody. Nobody told me," Chris said, trying to wrestle out of her hold.

"Besides, how could you even believe that when we're sitting on the very real grave of my very dead great-aunt? How stupid could you be?"

Phaedra waited for Chris to say something. When she heard nothing, she turned to step out of the grave, which was enclosed by a knee-high ring of intricately wrought iron. She tripped and Chris caught her before she fell.

"You all right?"

"I'm fine. Glad that it was my own two feet that tripped me this time and not you."

"Come on, Phaedra. You're fine now."

"Tell me who told you."

"It's not just one person. Everybody knows."

Phaedra felt the weight of this truth as another blow to her already fragile sense of belonging. She shook her head, not wanting to believe that she was as much an outsider here as in Brooklyn.

"I'm leaving."

"Wait. I wanted to give you these," Chris said. He pressed three blue marbles into her palm.

"Why?"

"I wanted you to have something of mine . . . something almost as beautiful as you."

Phaedra grunted, a sound that was halfway between dismissal and thanks. Then she closed her fingers around the marbles.

Phaedra and Chris used the beams from Chris's flashlight

and the murmurs of Dionne's and Trevor's voices to lead them to their siblings' hiding place. Chris cleared his throat as they approached, giving Dionne and Trevor a chance to untangle themselves from each other. If she'd been on the hill longer, Dionne would have known that years of experience had taught Chris not to interrupt his brother's flow with girls who let him touch them. But Dionne was new to the hill, and her relationship with Trevor depended on her believing that she was his first or, at least for this summer, his only.

"Yes?" Dionne said from the cocoon of Trevor's arms.

"I'm going to walk Phaedra home," Chris said.

"You know the way?" Dionne asked, although she was unlikely to leave the comfort of Trevor's embrace to give directions or lead them anywhere.

"Of course," Chris said.

"I'm only letting him walk me because he asked," Phaedra said.

"That's my boy," Trevor said. He went to give his little brother a high five, but their palms missed each other in the dark.

"That's my sister, you ass," Dionne said, and then started play-punching Trevor.

Phaedra, who knew that, for Dionne, anger was often a prelude to affection, understood that they'd been dismissed. She tugged at Chris's elbow to indicate it was time to go.

Chris lit their way back onto the main road. And although Phaedra told Chris that she could find her way home from here, thank you very much, when they reached the rectory, he continued to shine his light at their feet. Just as they rounded the last ring of road at the hill's bottom, there were footsteps on the path in front of them. They ducked into a sugarcane field, afraid to be caught by an adult or, worse, met by a jumbie. Phaedra had always been afraid of ghosts, and being in Barbados hadn't done anything to lessen that fear.

In the night, Hyacinth was a rustle mostly of air, hurrying along without the aid of her walking stick, like she had important business to attend to. Gone was the white turban that she wore; shocks of kinky platinum hair stood up all over her head. She was freer, too, her hands hanging loosely about her, her gait that of a much younger woman. If hill women had been watching, they might have said that Hyacinth looked freer than before she was baptized.

Phaedra, upon seeing her grandmother, backed up so far into the cane that she hit upon a well. She remembered her mother's warning that, despite how enticing they seemed, sugarcane fields were as rank as New York City subway platforms and as dangerous too. The year before, a girl was found dead in one of the wells just up the road from Hyacinth's house, her body disposed of in the countryside by a scorned boyfriend who thought nobody would look for her there. Avril had said, "You think the cane pretty? Well, think so from far. If you must have some cane, then take some from the outside part. You hear me, child? You hear?"

Phaedra recalled the way that rage creased the corners of her mother's eyes, and she was glad she wouldn't be seeing her for a couple more months at least. She shook her head, trying to push the thought, which she knew was disloyal, away from her. It was nice, Phaedra thought as the cane scratched her, to have a break from defending her mother, from the pressure to do as Dionne commanded and keep their family business to herself. Where Dionne found ease in making things up to get along, lying about Avril and their life strained the limits of Phaedra's earnestness. What a relief it was, Phaedra felt, to be somewhere where she didn't have secrets to keep.

Chris pushed through the thick stalks of cane, looking for Phaedra. "How you find yourself all the way here?" he said when he saw Phaedra backed up against the well like it was holding her up.

"Move from me, Christopher. I'm ready to go now. Stand up in this field too long and soon I'll have leptospirosis."

"What's that?"

"Rat pee poison."

"Oh. That could kill you?"

"Dead."

"I wouldn't like that, Phaedra. I wouldn't like it at all if you died."

"What kind of foolishness you talking? Don't confuffle your head and think that I'm paying you any mind, Christopher Loving."

"I like it when you try to talk Bajan," Chris said.

Phaedra was so mad then that she couldn't speak; she could only draw in air to make one of the epically long suck-teeth sounds she had learned from Avril. Chris was lucky it was dark, so he couldn't see just how much Phaedra tried to dislike him in that moment.

When both their hearts started beating slower, they left the field and made their way back to the road. Chris walked Phaedra back home, not leaving until he heard all the latches lock.

THE NEXT MORNING found Phaedra nestled in the bluebird bedsheets she loved and her already long face stretched to its limits. The swelling on her head had all but gone away, but the wound was a crescent moon on the right side of her forehead, indigo at its heart with shades of lavender at its edges. A new clover of bruised flesh blossomed on her behind where she'd backed up against the well in the sugarcane field the night before.

Unlike the other hill women, Hyacinth woke up well past cock's crow and left her bed only when the spirit moved her. Phaedra found it odd that her grandmother would sleep in. But having known her mother, whose quiet struck in the late hours of the evening, Phaedra knew that the Braithwaite women were anything but predictable, and that it was best not to disturb her grandmother's sleep. Phaedra was nothing if not an expert at making herself small for the sake of other women's need for peace.

It was well past daybreak when Hyacinth came into the room she shared with Phaedra, bringing her scent of nutmeg, mint, and the cherry chew sticks she kept posted in her mouth's corners. Phaedra rubbed the sleep from her eyes and searched her grandmother's face for traces of the woman she'd seen the night before. But there she was, exactly the same as the daytime Hyacinth with whom Phaedra was becoming familiar, dressed in white from the turban on her head to the socks on her feet. Hyacinth pressed a heavy, moist hand to Phaedra's forehead and neck, checking to see if the fever that rose when Chris hit her had finally broken.

Phaedra took in their room, noticing the table in the corner where she and Hyacinth dashed cold water on their faces each morning. She felt some pride in having finally figured out how to draw water so that she didn't hold up the line while the other children laughed at her, the Yankee girl who didn't even know how to make water flow from the standpipe. Hyacinth insisted that Phaedra wash the night off her face and brush the evening off her teeth as soon as she got up each morning. This never made sense to Phaedra since she just got dirty all over again when she ate her breakfast of salt bread and cheese and the Ovaltine Hyacinth made her drink, even when the sun was already high in the sky and pouring heat through the windows, because she said that she needed to have something hot on her belly. Hyacinth said that it was a gift to greet a new day, and that you needed to meet it in a way that showed how grateful you were to have your life spared. Phaedra wasn't sure what Hyacinth meant, exactly, but she did like the routines and rituals they had, the way they made a kind of container so her mind could wander to the things she thought and felt and dreamed about. The sameness of the days in Bird Hill comforted Phaedra as much as it rattled Dionne.

"You vex with somebody, Phaedra? Or somebody vex with you?" Hyacinth asked, drawing her palm away from Phaedra's cool brow.

"No, Granny. Why would you say that?"

"Just the way I see you lying down here still in bed. The Phaedra I know would have already had her breakfast and tea, and be bringing me mine by now."

"I still don't feel quite like myself," Phaedra said. Despite everything she knew about the women in her family, Phaedra still hoped that her sickness might elicit sympathy.

"Cuhdear. Well, I don't think that all that late-night walking about is helping your case."

Phaedra hesitated, weighing her options. She considered denial, protest, blame, then settled finally on projection. "Well, what were you doing out there? I was surprised to see you out on the road like that."

"Sometimes I need nightfall to hear myself properly."

Hyacinth pulled back the sheets to reveal the street clothes Phaedra had slept in.

"Oho. So the thief in the night was too busy to even change her clothes."

"I was so sleepy when I came in last night."

"Don't worry, darling. Just more proof that it's time for you to get out of the sickbed. You practice being one kind of thing too long, and soon enough that's who you become. Besides, don't you want to go play with your friends?"

Hyacinth's use of the plural, "friends," was generous.

"The one friend I had did this to me," Phaedra said, pointing at the bruise.

"Boys are like that. I had one boy who would punch me every day in primary school. When I finally hit him back, he told me that he liked me but he just didn't have the words to tell me so."

"Well, I have enough words to say that I am done with Christopher Loving for good."

"What did he do to you?"

"What do you mean, what did he do to me? He's the reason why I look like this."

"That much I know is true. But the way you're going on, I know that there must be something else there. Something that wound you below the skin."

Phaedra considered whether to tell her. "Chris said that I'm like you and my mother, that no matter what I do, I can't die."

"So that's what has you so upset?" A small laugh escaped from Hyacinth's generous mouth.

"Don't make fun of me. I'm tired of everyone treating me like such a baby."

Hyacinth sighed. Her ample bosom heaved as she pushed Phaedra from her perch and started stripping the sick-sheets from the bed. "People say we can't die, but there's no man who won't go when God calls him home. That's just people trying to make sense of something they don't understand. Let's make a deal. You go out and play. Soon, I'll start to show you what it all means."

"Really?"

"You have my word. Now, out!" Hyacinth said. She pushed her granddaughter out into the bright of day.

PHAEDRA WAS WALKING to the back of the house when she glimpsed her sister in the mirror through the open bathroom door, her feet planted firmly and a pink toolbox full of makeup and hair-related paraphernalia splayed open on the toilet seat. After her breakfast, Phaedra wanted badly to pee. She knew her sister would tell her to use the outhouse or stop being so scary and just pull the curtain in front of the toilet while Dionne fixed her face. But Phaedra had inherited her shy bottom from her mother so she liked privacy when she used the bathroom. Besides, she wasn't in the mood to beg Dionne for anything.

"You think those goats are going to milk themselves?" Dionne said, with a bobby pin clenched between her teeth. It was hard to tell what hairstyle she was fashioning, but knowing Dionne, even though she didn't have anywhere special to go that day, it would be elaborate.

"I'm going to milk them right now."

"Well, nobody's stopping you. And I don't need an audience," Dionne said, noting the fact that Phaedra was still standing inside the door frame.

"You sure about that?" Phaedra asked.

"Will you please stop ugly-ing up my mirror and do what you're doing before I tell Granny it's been days that I've been doing your chores for you while you pretend to be ill?"

"Do you know how many hours of your life you'd get back if you stopped spending your time on that mess?"

"It takes time to look this good."

"I'm just saying, you could be reading a book or painting or—"

"Ahem. Is Phaedra Ann Braithwaite, tomboy of tomboys, trying to give me beauty advice?"

"I didn't say that. I'm just saying that—"

"Go say whatever you're saying to the goats. They look like they might listen to you."

Phaedra felt sweat drench her face the minute she opened the back door. She put her hand to her forehead and looked out from the top of the three steps that led down into Hyacinth's garden. She was relieved to find Abigail where she expected her, lying on her side in the galvanized tin lean-to; the blue tarp they pulled down when the rains came flapped above the shed. Abigail the goat, which Mr. Jeremiah mated with his goat King David, had had six babies the week before Phaedra and her sister came to Bird Hill. Phaedra was sad she hadn't been there to witness their birth. The kids liked to roll around in the dirt to stay cool and they enjoyed being chased around the yard with the hose that Phaedra sprayed them with after she watered her grandmother's garden. Phaedra descended the steps and approached Abigail calmly, remembering what Hyacinth had told her about animals greeting humans with the same spirit in which they were approached.

"Here, girl," Phaedra said. She knelt down and gave Abigail a few pieces of pineapple. No matter how much Dionne told Phaedra that she was spoiling the goat and Hyacinth insisted that she wasn't cutting up fruit for any animals once Phaedra went back to Brooklyn, Phaedra insisted that the goat was easier to handle after she got what she wanted. Abigail sniffed the fruit and then ate it lying down, making it clear that she would get up when she was good and ready. She stood finally and her kids came running from the cool hiding spot they'd found beneath the house. Phaedra watched the ease with which they latched on and drank their mother's milk, and she was reminded of Avril. Her grandmother's words, about how if you practice being one kind of thing too long, you become that thing, were stuck in her head. Maybe that's what was wrong with Avril, she thought. Maybe it was a matter of her pretending to be sick at first and then, when it was time for her to be well, she didn't know how to be that way anymore.

Phaedra watched the goats eat and remembered feeding her mother ice cubes and pressing cool washcloths to her forehead the summer Avril took to her bed. In the beginning,

Phaedra believed her mother when she said that she just couldn't take the heat in New York, and that's why she stopped going to work at the hospital. She went to a round of doctors, none of whom could find anything wrong with her, but soon she was on medical leave, and then she didn't have any job at all, just checks from the government that came the first of every month like clockwork. Phaedra held out hope that when the fall came, Avril's mood would lift, but she and Dionne went back to school and Avril stayed home, and, after a time, the new state of affairs was old news, and then it was almost normal.

Phaedra was starting to understand how you could become someone else, even if you didn't intend to at first. She never imagined she'd be milking goats every morning and throwing boomerangs in the field behind Ms. Zelma's house with Christopher in the afternoons. The shape of her new life surprised her, and even though it had only been a little while, Phaedra already felt herself becoming a girl from Bird Hill; she could feel herself shedding the armor she needed in Brooklyn.

The baby goats scattered. Phaedra pulled the pail from its hook in the shed and dragged a well-worn stool beneath her. Phaedra got into the rhythm of tugging at Abigail's teats and pressing the milk out with her fingers like her grandmother had taught her. The pail filled at a laborious rate, but Phaedra didn't mind. She liked to be alone with her thoughts and the familiar, musty smell of the animals and Hyacinth's herbs and vegetables and flowers.

Maybe Chris does like me, Phaedra thought. Her hand jerked and milk that was meant for the pail squirted into her right eye and dribbled onto her t-shirt.

"Damn you, Abigail," Phaedra said. And then she remembered what her grandmother had told her when she kept dropping the clothespins onto the ground while they were hanging clothes out to dry. "When you're doing your work, you have to be really doing it, and not dreaming about something else, child." Phaedra had nodded, but kept dropping things anyway, and Hyacinth had simply shaken her head and wondered aloud where this child had inherited this habit of daydreaming.

Abigail looked at Phaedra and sat down. No amount of prodding would lift her off the ground. Phaedra gave up and poured milk from the pail, barely filling the bottom of the bottle she'd pulled from a crate on the back steps. At least she'd tried, she thought, which was more than she had been doing the last few days. She walked back to the kitchen in search of something else that might soften up the goat.

ON HER WAY to the kitchen, Phaedra felt Dionne's fingers grab the soft flesh at the top of her arm.

"You believe all those old-wife tales Granny tells you?" Dionne said.

"Old-wife tales?"

"All those stories about working roots and spirits and death and so on. I heard you begging Granny to reveal the secrets of the universe earlier."

"Yeah. So what, you're saying that her stories aren't true?"

"I thought that you were smart enough not to believe everything you're told."

"I don't see any reason why Granny would lie."

"Let me ask you this. If Granny knows so much, why can't she fix what is wrong with her own daughter?"

"You don't think she at least tried?"

"Well, if she did, clearly it didn't work. One month in Barbados and already you're turning into a ninny who believes everything they hear. Not everything is just a matter of walking by faith."

"I need to pee," Phaedra said. She tried to push past her sister into the bathroom, but Dionne planted herself in the door frame.

"You think you know everything. It's complicated. And I know more than you do."

"Did you hear something from Mommy?" Phaedra asked, a tense crackle in her voice where her certainty would usually be.

Dionne pulled her sister into the bathroom, an echo chamber where sound bounced off the walls but didn't travel to the other rooms. It was the closest thing the girls had to privacy.

"I heard Granny talking to Ms. Zelma yesterday. She said, 'Something tells me that my child is coming home soon,'" Dionne said in her best imitation of Hyacinth's voice. She closed the toilet seat so she could sit down.

"When?"

"She didn't say when. Granny heard me coming up behind her so she stopped talking."

"You really think she's going to come?" Phaedra asked, forgetting momentarily that Dionne was her tormentor.

"Of course she will, of course," Dionne said.

Dionne pulled Phaedra close and felt her sister's tears start as a pulsing in her chest. As Dionne held her, Phaedra smelled her sister's new scent, a combination of salt from the corn curls she was always eating, sticky fruit juice, and something else, something their mother smelled like, neither entirely sour nor exactly sweet. Held in her sister's embrace, Phaedra was reminded of a picture where Dionne was holding her on her hip. She was two and Dionne was eight, and you could tell that Phaedra was too heavy, but Dionne was determined to carry her. Avril was in the background of the photo, staring off into the distance, transported. Phaedra always thought it was strange that she'd only seen pictures of Dionne holding her, never her mother. But she still knew what being held by her mother felt like. At least she thought she remembered.

"If she's coming, why doesn't she at least call or send a letter?" Phaedra said.

"Mommy is very busy. She's looking for work and a new apartment for us, one with a window seat like you like."

Phaedra smiled, remembering the bay window where she sat daydreaming after school until her mother yelled at her to change into her home clothes.

"How do you know that?"

"Granny gets letters from her every week, and she reads them to me."

"Why just you? How come nobody ever tells me anything? And if Mommy's sending you letters, how come I've never seen any of them?" Phaedra asked.

"Because you whine like that," Dionne said. She walked out of the bathroom in a huff.

Phaedra watched her sister as she left, the lavish spread of flesh between her thighs and lower back, her hair that had become unruly, the thick curls standing up and off her head before sticking straight out over her neck. The windows of her sister's openness were getting smaller and smaller with each passing day.

Phaedra stopped for a moment to consider what her sister had said about their mother, the way she had insisted Avril was not an absent mother but a busy one. She wondered whether there was a difference and, finding no distinction she could discern, focused on the relief of finally using the bathroom instead.

IN BROOKLYN, Barbados was bimshire, a jewel that Bajans turned over in their minds, a candy whose sweetness they sucked on whenever the bitter cold and darkness of life in America became too much to bear. Avril, while she reserved a healthy amount of disdain for Bird Hill and its people, still felt something like love for her country, and she wanted at the very least to keep up with what was going on there. Almost twenty years into living in the States, she had no illusions of moving home and starting over again like the other women she knew who went home every year, packed barrels and kept up with phone calls, went to the meetings of the old boys' and old girls' clubs of their high schools where fattened, impoverished versions of themselves showed up in the harsh lights of church basements in Brooklyn, picking over the grains of famous stories from the old days and new stories about who had done well or not well at all in what they liked to call "this man country." In the same way that Avril had never been a good West Indian girl when she was home, she was not a good West Indian woman abroad, not given to cultivating a desire for and a connection to home that smacked of devotion. Still, she told Dionne and Phaedra that no matter what she felt about Bird Hill, it was important that they spend time with their grandmother, and get to know the place without which they would still be specks in God's eye.

Phaedra got her sense of what it might mean to go home one evening in Brooklyn. She was seven when she made the mistake of complaining about having to eat chicken for dinner every night. Avril's eyes turned from their usual doe brown to the shiny black beads they became under the influence of brandy or the winds of a changing mood. "You think life's hard here? Try life at home," she said.

Phaedra knew better than to respond to what she knew was not a question. She went back to pushing withered chicken strips around on her plate. And then she felt her chair give way beneath her. Suddenly, she was on the floor and the full heat of her mother's rage was on top of her. Avril hovered over Phaedra, seething, trying to decide what to do with her.

"You think people at home eat meat every day?" Avril asked. She dragged Phaedra down their apartment's long hallway, holding her by the flesh at the top of her right arm, talking the whole way. "You want to go home to live with Granny? Let's send you home and see if you like it there."

Avril flipped on the light in the girls' bedroom and rifled around in their closet for suitcases. Phaedra didn't dare offer to help by telling her mother that they were stored beneath the bunk beds. Avril found one eventually, a red valise coated in a thick layer of dust.

"Let's see what you should bring. You'll only need light clothes there," Avril said.

She climbed a step stool and pulled down the bin with Phaedra's and Dionne's summer clothes, then emptied its contents into the suitcase and zipped it closed.

"You want to go home?"

"No, Mommy," Phaedra said, hoping her lesson would end there.

"Too late now," Avril said. She shoved the suitcase toward Phaedra, then unlocked the door to the apartment. Avril pushed Phaedra and the suitcase into the cold hallway, all the while repeating her classic line, "Who don't hear will feel."

"Please, Mommy, I'll be good, just let me come inside," Phaedra said to the closed door, even after she'd heard her mother turn up the volume on the television to drown out her noise.

Phaedra stood at the doorway for the better part of an hour, shivering. Neighbors—a man with a pregnant wife who looked like she was about to give birth to a fully grown person any day—passed by. The man asked if she was OK and

Phaedra just nodded at the wonder of his wife's belly and turned toward the door to hide the holey shorts and thin tank top her mother had pushed her outside in. Phaedra sat down on the suitcase. Each time she heard the strains of the elevator, she prayed that no one would get off on their floor.

Phaedra's tears had dried by the time Avril finally came to the door to let her back in. Avril didn't say anything, not about dinner or what she'd done. From then, it was impossible to separate the idea of going to Barbados from the stark memory of Avril's anger. Bird Hill was for Phaedra, at first, as much a place to be banished to as a place to call home.

For Avril, the island loomed large whenever a tropical storm bore down on the Caribbean, and she called Hyacinth to make sure one of the young fellas battened down the windows, and she and the girls watched anxiously as the hurricane turned colors on the television news and usually spared the island. It was there when Barbados Independence Day came and with it a feast of Bajan food and overly enthusiastic greetings at their church's Saturday night dinner dance and Sunday service, celebrations Avril and the girls had missed since Avril took to her bed. It was there in the *Nation*, the Bajan newspaper Avril bought each weekend from the newsstand on Nostrand Avenue and read with more regularity than the local newspaper, piling issues high before using them to pack away dishes and the few fine things they had left for their imminent move.

As Avril became more lethargic, her commitment to moving out of their apartment, which she more often than not referred to as "this stinking place," became more strident. Sometimes, when she couldn't hold sleep long enough to find rest, Avril would go through fits of packing, never mind that she'd done nothing to find a new apartment besides saying that she wanted one, and despite the fact that being packed with nowhere to go was at best delusional, and at worst depressing. For Avril, staying on the move, or assuring herself that she would be leaving soon, was one way of trying to outrun her feelings.

Like many of the other West Indian women she knew in passing—because Avril was not the kind for fast friendships—upon moving to the States, she had gone from being a teacher at home to becoming a nurse there. She'd started working at Kings County, the city hospital just a few blocks away from the apartment she shared with Errol and the girls. Avril ended up at St. Vincent's after Phaedra started day care. In the time she was there, seven years in total, Avril saw the hospital go from treating people with what they were calling GRID, or gay-related immune deficiency, to calling what consumed them AIDS, and the thing that caused it HIV. Regardless of what its name was, Avril witnessed the way the disease tore down young men in the prime of their lives who checked into the hospital, once, twice, maybe more often for the frequent fliers, and then never checked out again.

As Avril got pulled deeper into her work at St. Vincent's, Errol—who had always wanted nothing less than his wife's full attention, who was the kind of man who would have taken pride in having a wife who didn't need to work, who couldn't understand why she would want to leave her good-good house to put herself in the company of men he considered less than dogs—had questioned how she could choose her work over her family. What he'd said actually, in the argument that Avril understood as the point of no return, was, "I don't know how you expect me to trust a woman who would risk bringing that nasty disease home to her husband and her two young kids." And it was this misunderstanding, and not Errol's empty dreams or Avril's foolishness in following him, that undid them in the end. Avril, for all her faults, was nothing if not someone who wanted to be devoted to family, and she knew that she couldn't love anyone who only saw the ways she fell short, and not her desire to be a good mother and wife. Errol, for his part, not hearing a response to his question, which was really, "How much do you love us?" knew that it really was over, that she would keep choosing her work and the sadness and stress it brought her over him and the girls.

If Avril made any good friends since leaving her best friend, Jean, and Mrs. Loving behind in Bird Hill, at least one of them was death. Some men passed after just a few days of struggling against the disease on the ward where she worked, which was nicknamed the Sevens. Avril felt each of their deaths keenly. But during the late-night and early morning shifts that she worked, she also felt a sense of purpose, a feeling of working against something that she still believed could be defeated.

Besides, being surrounded by the remains of other people's lives in the hospital made it a fitting place to mourn the person she thought she'd become in the States, the family she thought she would have, the husband she thought would love her unconditionally, the children she thought she would raise.

Avril wondered sometimes if she wouldn't have preferred teaching rude American children in the public schools, or wiping old people's behinds in a nursing home, but once she'd committed to her work, she couldn't stop. It was her gumption (and being told that she couldn't do it by a coworker at Kings County who was a refugee from the death and dying at St. Vincent's) that drove her right into the open arms of the plague. There were the men, some with their rooms fitted out like the Waldorf, others with little more than the clothes on their back, some with so many piercings and tattoos it was hard to make out the contours of their skin. There were their chosen families of friends—lovers and madmen, Avril liked to call them. There was one couple she remembered, two women who looked more like boys, who would come after late nights of clubbing and climb into bed with their friend, a dancer who was larger than life onstage, they said, but never agile enough to navigate the wires and tubes that engulfed him.

And then there was that man's lover, a tall man with gorgeous dark skin the color of eggplant who put her in mind of Jean. Because he reminded her so much of Jean, when he looked confused about how to keep up with the regimen of meds the doctor prescribed when he took his lover home to die, Avril gave him her home phone number. And so she was the first one he told that the symptoms that had cropped up in his lover now had come to wreak havoc on his body too.

The night he called was a night like any other night; the girls were doing their homework at the kitchen table when the phone rang. Avril had made dinner, and it was Phaedra, who was usually the sweeter of her two girls, who asked her why they always had to eat the same thing. Avril had not quite landed at home yet; she was still in the world of the ward, the tubes and the flickering lights that she knew would go out for the one person whom she'd allowed to become a sort of friend, when she heard Phaedra's question. She was angry, and that was why she came down on her child, talking so hard and fast about what home would be like, because what she really wanted more than anything at that moment was to go home to her own mother, to be held by Hyacinth, to be told that the death that had come to sit down beside her would eventually take its leave and go. What Avril wanted more than anything then was the gift of a gentle lie, someone to tell her that her friend would beat this, unlike so many others who had not. Not finding someone who would do her that small favor, she turned to destroy the closest, smallest thing outside herself, which just happened to be Phaedra.

After that night, the sadness that had been crouching at the corner of Avril's eyes consumed her face, and then her body. She called in sick to work the next day and never went back. And then she was down. Without the daily dramas of either the hospital or the hill, Avril was floating, anchorless. A kind of freedom she'd always wanted, but didn't know what to do with when it came.

"Just like my Jean, he was," Avril would say over and over again.

Dionne knew that a cup of milky black tea could calm her mother. And so she'd brewed countless cups until the box of PG Tips was empty and there was no money to buy more.

"Just like him," Avril kept saying. And then, "You remember Jean?" she'd ask Dionne. At first, Dionne would shake her head. But Avril insisted that Jean had held her when she was a baby, that he'd come to visit and she'd laughed and played patty-cake with him until Jean's arms were tired. Eventually Dionne went along, repeating stories Avril had told her about Jean, because it made her mother smile, and Dionne had learned that some things were worth the price of dishonesty.

Once Avril was home for good, anything that was out of its designated place would be lost to Avril's packing fervor. And it was for this reason that Dionne pared down her clothes to just a few items. She hid them beneath her bed because she knew Avril wouldn't trouble them there—three pairs of jeans and five tops, a few dresses, two pairs of shorts, two bras, and seven panties. The danger was not in loving something too much, Dionne thought, but in loving anything more than what you could carry in your pocket or on your back. Dionne had learned to make the objects of her affection small—designer jeans, a certain kind of pencil whose eraser released a scent when you used it, a new lipstick.

Loving another person, she knew well from watching and knowing Avril, was the most dangerous thing of all. Loving a country besides the one you lived in was a recipe for heartache.

For Dionne, Barbados was at best an inconvenience. As far as she was concerned, being born in Barbados had never benefited her in any particular way. She did know that Barbados was the one thing that her crazy mother and absent father had in common. Which is to say that for Dionne, Barbados was at the root of what she thought was wrong with her family, and not anywhere she wanted to spend an extended period of time.

Dionne once had another idea entirely about how she would celebrate her sixteenth birthday. She and her best friend in Brooklyn, Taneisha, had their hearts set on a party hall on Church Avenue. Everybody was going to be there: Taneisha's Trinidadian cousins and uncles and sisters, their friends from school (mostly Taneisha's), and Darren, the boy who Dionne had been going with since he'd moved up from Jamaica three years before.

Dionne was drawn into the school yard romance with Darren by girls who said "it would be cute if y'all went together" because of the way that Dionne's chestnut skin played off Darren's hazelnut eyes, the same eyes that had every girl from Vandeveer to Erasmus fantasizing about Darren looking at them. As Dionne got to know Darren on their bus rides home together, her affection for him had deepened, fulfilling the vain promise that had brought them together. Since she'd arrived in Barbados, Dionne thought of Darren often in spite of herself, though she knew that attachment was the first step on the road to disappointment.

After her father left, Dionne witnessed a parade of men her mother entertained for as long as they would stick around. But while she could attract men, draw them into her web, Avril had trouble keeping them. In the last relationship, the one that ended the year before Dionne started high school, Dionne wanted to believe her mother's conviction that her boyfriend, Musa, would marry her. But something happened once her mother made her intentions for Musa clear, and every time he came over after that, he was always just about to leave again, as if her mother's desire for him had propelled him in the opposite direction. By his last visit, Musa wouldn't even take his coat off, just brought the books he'd promised to Phaedra and the *Vogue* fall fashion issue he'd promised to Dionne, kissed their mother, and left. Dionne had learned from her mother that if you wanted to keep a man, he should love you at least a little bit more than you loved him.

Avril's plan to send the girls back home for the summer, announced just one week before they left, had messed up everything—the party, working at V.I.M. to save up money for school clothes, Dionne's hopes of going into the city on Saturday nights with Darren and Taneisha and her girls. So, here she was in Bird Hill on her birthday, Saturday, July 16. And as her grandmother Hyacinth would say, nothing at all go so. There would be no DJ making special shout-outs to the birthday girl, no adults hovering in the back alley smoking joints, drinking beer, squeezing past each other to heap their plates high with curry chicken and roti skins. No girls dancing front to front on boys, winding their waists as if their whole lives had made them move this way, talking afterward about the boys whose dicks had gone hard, then soft on them.

Back in Brooklyn, the outfit that Dionne put on layaway—white jeans with a question mark in gold thread on the back pockets, a matching white top and jacket—still had $20 to go before it was paid off. Instead of wearing it, Dionne was sporting the new dress her grandmother made for her with "room to grow," a maritime number with a boat collar, white trim, and heavy navy fabric. Dionne thought that the dress was more fit for a box of powdered milk than a girl like her, with legs that started just below her neck, arms made for hanging on to boys rather than pounding nutmeg, and hands more fit for finger-snapping than housework of any kind.

Buller Man Jean was the one to whom most of the hill women turned to get their clothes sewn and, in a pinch, their hair done. He owed Dionne's grandmother a favor and so he gave Dionne a relaxer before the party that left her hair not quite straight. A night of sleeping in hard plastic rollers had given Dionne a neck ache and tight curls that didn't brush her shoulders the way she liked. But it would have to do. A lifetime of watching her mother closely had been nothing if not a tutorial in resignation and making do.

Now Dionne looked around for Jean. She searched first for the elastic hair bands he wore like bracelets around his wrist, and then for his skin that was the color of a ripe plum. She wanted to catch Jean's eye so that she could register her disdain about her hair with him, but she couldn't find him in the crowd. She took note of the fact that she had never seen Jean at church or a church function, which in Bird Hill was a way of saying she had never seen him out. The church, more than being just a place to worship the Lord, was the place where the fabric of the community was woven, public dramas played out and put to rest, subtle lines of hierarchy drawn and redrawn again. If the hill were a quilt made up of its families, Jean and his mother Trixie's patch was one the quilter forgot beneath her bed.

The party, if it was fair to call it that, was a joint one with Clotel Gumbs, a girl who wore glasses with lenses as thick as breadfruit skin, crinoline dresses that reached her ankles, and a mouth that seemed to open only to correct grammar or to quote Bible verses. Dionne thought Clotel rather unfortunate. And though in summers past the girls played together and ran as far as the hill women saw fit to let them, now it was clear that they had nothing in common besides a birthday. Where Clotel envisioned a life as a schoolteacher and homemaker, Dionne saw herself working in a fashion house on Fifth Avenue, selecting trends for the next fall collection. In Dionne's mind, her summer job selling sneakers and clothes at V.I.M. on Flatbush was a humble but legitimate step toward her career in fashion. Being stuck in Barbados, a place she might have described as sartorially challenged, was another step a world away from the life of glamour Dionne wanted for herself, a life full of style and free of the burdens of her mother's and sister's needs. These differences, simply matters of style when Dionne and Clotel were younger, were now big enough to constitute a wall neither of them could see over.

Nevertheless, Clotel and Dionne entered the church hall hand in hand. And both feigned surprise when the lights came up over pink streamers, balloons, and a sign that read HAPPY BIRTHDAY, YE CHILDREN IN CHRIST. The next day, in church, the congregation would sing to them, "Happy Birthday, Dear Christians." But on this night, both young women were glad to be spared a song as they were overwhelmed by the smell of food in the church hall. There were the legendary fish cakes women from Bird Hill were known for all over the island, and which no small number of less-favored women bought at the bottom of the hill on Saturday mornings. Dionne could smell the yellow cakes with pineapple filling and frosting and the milk-soured mouths of the children who ran circles around their mothers. The church hall doors remained open behind Clotel and Dionne; the sweet stink of the guava trees, which were planted when an ugly woman named Cutie died and left her small fortune to the church, wafted inside.

Both girls were new to the high heels that bore blisters into their feet. Dionne was painfully aware that she'd finally turned sixteen, the age at which Avril said she could start wearing heels, and her mother wasn't there to see her wobbling or to show her how to walk in them. Dionne and Clotel shifted their weight as Father Loving said an interminable prayer, during which Dionne fluttered her eyes open to find the reverend wiping his brow and studying her breasts, which pressed insistently against her dress. After his incantations, Father Loving offered them each a new leather-bound King James Bible. Clotel seemed genuinely excited to accept her gift while Dionne took hers reluctantly. She mumbled thanks to everyone for their gifts and kind words, all their variations on wishing her the best of life in Christ. Then she steeled her shoulders, readying herself for the inevitable conversations on one of two topics—books or baptism.

"So, now that you turn sixteen, are you going to give your life over to the Lord in service?" Mrs. Jeremiah asked, her rheumy eyes taking Dionne in. She clutched Dionne's elbow between two firm fingers. The younger woman felt that Mrs. Jeremiah's conviction about Christ could break bone.

"Yes, God willing," Dionne said. Her voice cracked. God's name felt like a word in a language she'd never learn.

Dionne looked over the jaunty red feather in Mrs. Jeremiah's hat and her gaze landed on her grandmother and Phaedra. She felt keenly the absence of her mother, who was in no small part responsible for her birthday turning out like this and should, she thought, at least be there to witness the disaster. The women kept bringing more and more food in aluminum pans out to the blue-flame burners. And Dionne kept expecting her mother to walk through the church hall's front door.

The people on the hill were Christians, and seriously so, but that didn't mean that they didn't like to have a good time. Lyrics like "get something and wave for the Lord" were made for Bird Hill, where any news was reason to have a party, and parties could start in the late afternoon and put the stars to bed the next morning. The Soul Train line sent women hobbling back to their seats with sweat on their brows and complaints on their lips about their old bones, the small children rubbing their eyes and seeking their mothers' laps.

Dionne and Trevor, who had been keeping each other at a respectful distance until then, came together in the back of the church hall. They agreed to slip out separately and meet at their usual rendezvous location, star side. They'd named it that because of the way the moon and stars bathed the graves in the cemetery that sloped down behind the church in light, eliminating the need for flashlights that might lead prying eyes to their hiding place. "We'll call this our special place," Trevor whispered the night they named it, and Dionne, desperate for space that was not her sister's, not Avril's, not Hyacinth's, just hers, nodded, thinking he could give her what she needed.

A couple hours later, when the sun had long since set and the murmurs of good-byes filled the church hall, Dionne went to find Trevor. It was hot outside, as if all the heat that had gathered during the day decided to stay the night. Sweat collected in Dionne's bosom, plastering her cotton bra to the top of her dress's wide collar. She'd worn the dress all evening with an air of self-sacrifice, but now, in the open air, she tugged at its buttons. She took a seat on Trevor's forbearer's grave with the gift Bible tucked firmly beneath her, making a show of trying not to dirty her new clothes.

"You having fun yet?" Trevor asked.

"Define fun."

"C'mon, Dionne. You have to admit that seeing Sister B. do the pepper seed was fun."

"Yeah, I guess you're right." Dionne laughed. She remembered the old woman's shaking shoulders, the way that everyone was genuinely concerned about her teeth rattling out of her mouth.

"What do you think his life was like?" Dionne asked.

"Whose life?"

"His life. Trevor Cephus Loving. July 14, 1928–July 21, 1973."

"Probably the same as my father's. Baptisms, weddings, funerals. More food than you could ever eat in one lifetime."

"Same as yours? Do you want to be a reverend?"

"I guess I never thought I had a choice."

"Everything in life is a choice. It's not like you just wake up one day and suddenly you're Father Loving the third."

"Well, it's not like in the States, where you just decide what you're going to be and then you go to school and become that thing. Here on the hill, who you are is who your people have been. I was born the same day my grandfather died. Everyone said that was a sign I was coming back as him."

Dionne felt the door close on anything substantial between her and Trevor, but then also the urgency of their closeness. Dionne knew that any man whose life was already decided for him couldn't be hers. But here, where her spirit felt only halfway home, anchorless without Avril, she wanted something familiar to be close to, somewhere to land.

"Have you ever noticed that all these people died close to their birthdays? It's almost like the earth remembers them and knows it's their time."

"I don't know how your mind works, Dionne, but I like it. What would you do if you knew this was your last birthday?"

Dionne turned to Trevor and whispered in his ear. Trevor was shocked that what he had been begging for all summer was finally being offered freely. He tried to stay cool. He placed a fiery hand on Dionne's thigh and did away with her blue panties with the deftness and care that indicated he knew that at any moment she could decide differently.

"Go slow," Dionne said, warning. She used her hands to guide him inside her.

Trevor made love to Dionne by moonlight, her bare feet planted on the crumbling gravestone while he entered her with sweetness she didn't know he could muster. Dionne remembered the roughness of Darren's hand inside her and braced herself for what Taneisha told her would feel like a pinch and then like the ocean opening inside her. She sighed, taking in the heat of him at her neck and the damp of the night air.

When they were done, Dionne took her panties in one hand and her new Bible in the other and let the breeze when it came touch her where Trevor had before. She felt wiser somehow, and looking at the church lit up above, thought that maybe this kind of pleasure could be her religion.

AFTER THE PARTY, Phaedra helped Hyacinth out of her brassiere. She unhooked all sixteen eyelets until the sandwich of flesh on the older woman's back parted, and marveled at her grandmother's unlined skin. Phaedra was going to find a book to lull herself to sleep with when Hyacinth told her that she should come to the back of the house.

Hyacinth opened up the top half of the back door to let the night air in. Then, she undid the locks of the sea-green cupboards with keys she fished out of her nightgown. For weeks, Phaedra had been dying to know what her grandmother kept there. Whenever Phaedra begged her to open the cupboards, Dionne told her that curiosity killed the cat. Phaedra was annoyed that Dionne, who was generally unafraid of trouble, wouldn't help her. Phaedra bet Dionne that Hyacinth hid a secret cache of Shirley biscuits there and her sister just shook her head, saying it was probably something boring, like mothballs or detergent.

Both of them were wrong. When Hyacinth opened the cupboard doors, she revealed herbs of all varieties in glass jars, each labeled in her careful fourth-grade print.

"What is all this, Granny?" Phaedra asked.

"Roots."

"You mean to do obeah with?"

"Dear heart, labels are for things, not people. I don't work obeah any more than Father Loving does when he says that a couple drops of holy water on a sick man's forehead can make him well. There's all kind of magic, some for daytime, and others for the night."

"So, it's all just different ways to make people well?"

"You could say that. All different ways to help the body do its work. Now, we need to find roots to make a tea."

"What kind of tea?"

"The same tea I gave your mother to drink."

"To make her strong?"

"To make her womb weak."

"What do you mean, weak?" Phaedra asked.

Hyacinth turned the full force of her gaze on Phaedra, the way that she did when she wanted to be heard. With Hyacinth looking at her, Phaedra felt naked, as if her grandmother could see what was beneath her skin, the sturdy parts and what she was ashamed of too.

"A strong womb carries a healthy baby. A weak womb lets go of the baby before it grows."

"So why would you want to give Mommy that to drink?"

"I gave it to her when she started tumbling big with you," Hyacinth said, releasing Phaedra from her gaze so suddenly that Phaedra felt herself slip.

"You mean Mommy didn't want me?" Phaedra grabbed the clothesline where she and Dionne hung their clean underwear after they washed them in the shower, but she felt it give, wavering where she wanted support.

"Sweetheart, it's not to say Mummy didn't want you. She was facing down the facts of her life and couldn't see where another child might fit. I told her myself that if she thought life was hard with her and Dionne and that husband, she would understand what hard life really was with another one pulling at her. If she'd seen just one bit of the sparkle you have now, she would have been trying to bring you out sooner. One day you will see that what must be born will be born. Everything else will find another way."

"Why would you tell me that?"

"Sweetness, the only thing that has power over you is what you can't say, even to yourself."

Phaedra considered this for a moment, letting the night frogs fill the silence between them.

"Everything hurt needs sun and air to heal it," Hyacinth added, hearing what Phaedra had not said.

"So what you're saying is that it's not that she didn't want me, but that she didn't see how to make it work."

"You could say that. I can tell you one thing, though. No matter what she did, her belly just kept growing and growing. You were determined to come."

Phaedra touched the dime-size birthmark nestled inside her bruise's faded half-moon. "Is that where this came from?"

"She tried one last time with the doctor but you would not come out no matter what he did." Hyacinth bent down and kissed Phaedra's scar, leaving a wet imprint of her lips that the breeze soon dried. Phaedra was hard-pressed to recall the last time she'd been kissed by her grandmother. She wished their closeness would last a moment longer than it did.

"Now help me make this tea. Granny's eyes not so good anymore."

"Yes, please," Phaedra said. For the first time, it felt less awkward to say, "Yes, please," which her grandmother had taught her to reply with, and which the Bird Hill girls said without issue.

Phaedra pulled down the jars from the cupboard as Hyacinth called their names—nettles and burdock for cramps, peppermint and gingerroot for an upset stomach, pennyroyal and tansy leaves for hastening the menses. She scooped the herbs in the quantities Hyacinth specified into a pan, and then into seven tea bags.

"Who's the tea for, Gran?"

Hyacinth's lineless face was obscured by the glass jar of

chamomile she held up to the light. "Your sister," she said, nonchalantly.

Phaedra already knew the answer to the question forming in her mind. She steadied herself with the work of alphabetizing her grandmother's roots.

THE SECOND SESSION of vacation Bible School began just as July in Bird Hill was yawning toward a close. Going back for round two was particularly hard for Phaedra because now she didn't have the benefit of ignorance about what VBS entailed to make it seem exciting. Just when Phaedra had conquered the steep ascent from the beach to her grandmother's house, just when her latest rereading of *Harriet the Spy* was getting really good, just when she had learned how to launch boomerangs with Chris in Ms. Zelma's backyard—she was thrust again into the tyranny and tedium of VBS.

Vacation Bible School always followed the same schedule: a prayer when they arrived, morning activities, lunch, afternoon activities, and a prayer before dismissal. Phaedra's favorite things were praise song and Bible Jeopardy because these were the only times when she wasn't being scrutinized, teased about her accent, asked about what her life in America was like, and, occasionally, interrogated about when her mother was coming to collect her and her sister.

The one area where Phaedra excelled, even though she didn't necessarily enjoy it, was memorizing Bible verses. The prospect of wresting the Bible verse memorization championship crown from her nemesis (and three-time winner) Angelique Ward motivated Phaedra to go to VBS even when she didn't want to. Well, that, and the fact that Hyacinth insisted that she was not going to let the good money Avril had spent on VBS go to waste because the girls would prefer to wear out her furniture with their lazy behinds than to learn about the Lord. During recess, while the boys ripped around and the girls jumped double Dutch or played with each other's hair, Phaedra stood off to one side, repeating scripture she'd committed to memory the night before with her grandmother's help. She was not surprised to learn that she and her mother shared the same favorite verse: "No weapon formed against me shall prosper."

While Phaedra flailed against the injustice of being forced to go to VBS, Dionne sucked up whatever feelings she had about it. Her mounting disinterest in Trevor meant that she sought him out infrequently, but VBS guaranteed that she saw him every day. Dionne simply dried up her remaining affection for him and threw herself into a role she knew well—taking charge of the little sixes and sevens who came for the morning program. When Trevor asked Dionne why she no longer had time for him, she told him that she had plans with her friends. Even he could see that she was becoming popular with the older girls on the hill, who had gone from seeing Dionne as an oddity to claiming her as an asset, asking her opinion on boys, their hairstyles, clothes. It wasn't unusual that summer to walk onto the netball court in front of the church and find Dionne holding forth to a group of rapt girls about, for example, how to rock leg warmers in spite of the warm weather.

Before VBS, Phaedra had not had any dealings with white people other than the ones she saw on television. She wasn't sure if she could count as white the Hasidic Jews who lived in her neighborhood in Brooklyn, the ones who rushed past her on Shabbat toward their services. These white people who ran the Vacation Bible School were strange, Phaedra thought, but likeable—big, friendly Texans who roasted themselves in the sun and laughed heartily all the time, as if Christ's glory had a laugh track. Her favorite was her teacher, Tracey Taylor. Phaedra knew from watching television that Ms. Taylor was what some people would call beautiful—blond-haired, blue-eyed, flat-bottomed, and full-breasted. She noticed the way all the men and boys panted after Ms. Taylor, especially her coworker Derrick Boss.

The girls in Phaedra's age group were flexing their last bits of power before they'd be reduced to first-formers when school started back in September. In Phaedra, they found an easy target. It was the first Friday of the second, monthlong session of VBS, right after praise song, when the barrage of questions started.

"A jumbie comb your hair or what?" Angelique Ward drew attention to the halo of frizz that hovered above Phaedra's head, the outcome of Phaedra's tender-headed protest against having her hair cornrowed every week. Dionne was not above chasing Phaedra around the house until she washed her hair and sat down for an hour of oiling her scalp, combing through the knots in her hair, and then braiding it. It was more for Dionne, since she saw Phaedra's appearance as a reflection on her. But Hyacinth cared about different things, and said that she didn't want Dionne acting like anybody's mother, lest she find herself in the family way with some bighead boy's child.

"I thought they had combs in America," Simone Saveur added.

"I don't know where she think she come from with her funny name and her hair flying every which way. What I want to know is who says that light skin and long hair makes you pretty?" Tanya Tompkins pronounced.

The least troublesome of these girls, Donna, was both too round and too timid to join in the teasing. She wore her body like a mistake she hoped to one day be forgiven for. She gestured to Phaedra to follow her inside. Phaedra smashed her fists into her shorts pockets and slid onto one of the church hall's benches beside Donna.

Donna hunched her shoulders as she devoured four tuna fish sandwiches, washing them down with too-sweet Tang, whose flavor crystals stuck to the corners of her mouth. When she'd taken her last gulp, she let out a burp behind her hand and then she turned to Phaedra. Her eyes darted around the room as if she wanted to be sure that no one heard her secret.

"You know, I have an aunt in Queens. Jamaica, Queens. Is that near where you live?"

"No, I don't think so," Phaedra said. She had seen the sign for Jamaica on the taxi ride to JFK earlier that summer. Hearing Donna mention Jamaica, Queens, reminded Phaedra of how confused she'd been when she saw the sign, because the only Jamaica she'd heard of before then was the island Jamaica, and she didn't think you could drive there.

"Maybe one day when you're walking around, you'll see her."

"Maybe," Phaedra said. She was hungry. She looked behind her to see that the pyramid of saran-wrapped sandwiches was gone. When Phaedra had first seen the sandwiches, she'd dismissed them, thinking she could wait until she got home to eat the food she knew Hyacinth was cooking. She was starving now.

"I have an idea. We can be friends. We'll hang out this summer. And then when you're gone, I'll write to you."

Phaedra found it hard to imagine being pleased by running into Donna's aunt or responding to Donna's letters. Still, Donna was kinder than any of the other girls had been to her so far. "That would be nice," she forced herself to say.

Donna offered her second cup of Tang to Phaedra, and she drank it gratefully. She politely declined the bread ends Donna pushed toward her.

Later that afternoon, as they sat cutting pictures of Bible action figures from cardboard, in the same way that the girls had scanned Phaedra for weak spots before pouncing, they pressed the issue of their teacher's potential beau. Angelique Ward hissed the *s* in Ms. Taylor's name until her status as a single woman sounded like a curse. Slowly, because Ms. Taylor had trouble following the rapid-fire patois they spoke, the other girls said how nice she and Derrick looked leading morning prayers together, that they had noticed him looking at her in a way that seemed more than friendly, that his last name, Boss, meant that he would know what to do when the time came.

Phaedra was happy to have the attention drawn away from everything that was wrong with her as they sat talking with the double doors open for breeze. She focused on cutting out a picture of Zacchaeus, the "wee little man" she knew well from praise song, while the other girls weighed in on the possibility of Ms. Taylor's courtship.

And then Phaedra spoke. "Yes, Ms. Taylor," she said. "All now, he could be putting his hands up your skirt."

While the other girls' expressions shifted from shock to judgment, Angelique Ward walked over to Phaedra with her palms planted firmly on her bony hips. She took a deep breath before spitting her words. "Phaedra Ann Braithwaite, it is only your sister who has made herself known for that kind of slackness."

Ms. Taylor, for her part, didn't know what to do with Phaedra's comment or Angelique's swift punishment. After an uncomfortable silence during which the word "slackness" hung in the air, she dismissed all the girls except Phaedra. "Phaedra, is there anything you want to talk about?" Ms. Taylor said. She sat down next to Phaedra on the edge of the church hall's stage, the angle and distance between them perfect for sharing a secret.

"No, ma'am," Phaedra said. Her face strained with the effort of not crying. There was so much that she wanted to say about her mother and her grandmother and Dionne and Chris. But then she remembered what happened when she told her fourth-grade teacher, Mrs. Friedman, about how her mother would disappear for days and that when she was home she would sit looking out the window or staring at the television screen. The sound of the police sirens when they came to take her mother away came rushing back to Phaedra, piercing the hill's late-afternoon hush.

"Are you sure?" Ms. Taylor asked.

Phaedra said "No" again with more force. She walked out of the church hall, leaving Ms. Taylor alone amid the paper cutouts and folding chairs.

HYACINTH'S MOTHER liked to say that even though she never learned to read, never went to college to be a nurse or a midwife or a doctor, that didn't stop her from delivering every baby on the hill. She worked roots for everyone, even for those who said that obeah was backward and against their Christian beliefs, but would still find themselves at her doorstep under cover of darkness, seeking help with a man who suddenly had a hot foot or a taste for another woman's pot, a womb that wouldn't bear children, a son or daughter gone to the States or England and never heard from again. Hyacinth went further than her mother in school and knew enough to write and to read the *Nation* and her Bible. And for her, that was enough. She felt the hill as a magnetic force that pulled her close even when she was outside its bounds. The only safe place to travel was in your dreams, she thought. And despite her daughter spending almost two decades in what Hyacinth referred to alternatively as "foreign," "up there," and "that man country," Hyacinth never stepped foot past Bridgetown. Everything she needed was in her yard.

As soon as Phaedra was old enough to write, she wrote to her grandmother. At first, she just added a few *x*'s and *o*'s at the end of her mother's letters. But soon, she was writing her own short letters every month, catching her grandmother up on what she was learning in school, which psalms she knew by heart, pretending that she'd made closer friends than she had. It was hard for Phaedra to reconcile the hardness in Avril's voice when she talked about Barbados in general and Bird Hill in particular with the peaceful place Hyacinth described. But the different ways Phaedra and her sister saw the world in general and their parents in particular taught Phaedra that two people could feel different ways about exactly the same things, and that they could both be right.

It was Phaedra's grandmother who told her that she should start keeping track of her dreams. Her mother bought her a dream catcher at a powwow out at Floyd Bennett Field, and she placed it above her bed in Brooklyn, hoping to hang on a bit longer to the Technicolor pulse behind her eyes. Avril always told her that dreams were just another world we lived in, different from but related to the waking world.

In her grandmother's house, there was a carafe filled with water on the night table that Phaedra sipped from each morning to help her remember where her dreams had taken her.

There was another glass of water beneath the bed to catch tricky spirits. The carafe was one way Phaedra knew that beauty was not something reserved for the wealthy, but a common, everyday kind of thing that was available to anyone with eyes open enough to see. Phaedra had taken to writing down her dreams, imitating her grandmother, who kept a notebook by her bedside for precisely this purpose.

For days, Phaedra dreamed of schools of flying fish jumping out of the water, not unlike the ones she'd seen on Sunday afternoons after church when Hyacinth let her and Dionne go to the beach with the Lovings. The third day she dreamed of fish, she woke up later than usual, having slept in to savor the feeling of the sun on her skin and the light reflecting the fishes' silver flesh. When she awoke, she wandered into the kitchen, where her sister and grandmother were mixing salt fish and flour together for fish cakes.

"Good morning, Granny," Phaedra said, hugging her grandmother from behind. She felt Hyacinth stiffen at her embrace, but she leaned in further to smell the nutmeg on her housedress.

"Well, hello. I see Sleeping Beauty finally decide to wake. What sweet you this morning so?" Finally too uncomfortable, Hyacinth pulled herself free from Phaedra's grip, making an excuse of reaching for the fish draining in a colander.

"I had the best dream. I dreamed we were all at a picnic at Pebbles Beach and the flying fish were jumping so high it looked like they could touch the sun."

"Hmmm, have you ever thought that maybe you were just dreaming that because we're going to the beach later?" Dionne asked.

"We are?" Phaedra said, the pitch of her voice turning up with excitement.

"Yes, darling. You don't remember the church picnic is today?" Hyacinth looked out at the plants encroaching on the white hydrangeas below her kitchen window. "Looks like a whole army of weeds take over my garden. I don't know how it is that I have two strong girls here with me and I still have to be bending down and cleaning up all the time as if I'm a young person."

"What do the fish in my dreams mean, Gran?" Phaedra asked.

"It means a baby soon come. Take note, darling, and see if your dreams don't bear fruit."

Phaedra looked out through the picture window at the bananas, which she still couldn't call figs like everyone else did. The banana trees she'd imagined stretched their branches high to the sky, not fat and squat to the ground, heavy with fruit that turned purple like Jean's skin before they ripened. Maybe the baby would come just like the fruit on that tree, she thought, upside down and not at all how she expected it.

"So fish mean babies?"

"You dream of fish and a baby soon come. Dream of a wedding and it's a funeral around the corner. Dream of a funeral and somebody's getting married soon," Hyacinth said.

Phaedra jumped when she heard the pop and hiss as Hyacinth lowered the first few tablespoons of batter into hot oil.

"OK, OK, that's all I can remember for right now," Phaedra said.

Phaedra left the kitchen wondering where this child might come from. Her absent wonder almost made her chores go by quickly.

THE BIRD HILL CHURCH of God in Christ 75th Anniversary picnic was a highly anticipated affair. For months before it happened, the head of the church picnic committee, Mrs. Gumbs, made announcements from her seat in the third pew, much to the annoyance of the elders who said they didn't want to strain their ears or crane their necks to hear what she was talking about. Mrs. Gumbs, mother to Clotel Gumbs and four other children with equally stingy portions of character and ambition, stood her ground, saying that she was neither usher nor deacon nor reverend and therefore did not belong in the sanctuary except on Saturdays when she cleaned it with the others from the Women's Guild. It was this kind of obsequiousness that got the gullets of Hyacinth and the other hill women. Phaedra could hear but did not listen to Mrs. Gumbs's long speeches because by then the service had usually gone on for three hours and she could practically taste the cookies from the after-service repast; just the thought of sugar melting against her tongue and the maraschino cherry at the cookie's center, which she always saved for last, made Phaedra ache with longing.

Phaedra marveled at the elaborate headpieces Mrs. Gumbs wore, intricate concoctions with beads and plumes and straw that drew attention away from the massive chest and stomach that she wore with a kind of pride, having appointed herself the mother of the church. Some of the words floated through Phaedra's haze of hunger and boredom—"rousing success" and "pitch in" and "many hands make light work"—but mostly Phaedra was fascinated by Mrs. Gumbs's matronly swagger, which was so different from the kind her mother had. Phaedra looked at the peacock hat Mrs. Gumbs wore on the last Sunday before the picnic and whispered to Chris that he might have to go hold down the bird before it flew off her head. She realized that she was being uncharitable and straightened up a bit when her grandmother shot her a look that Phaedra knew wasn't nearly as deadly as the ones she normally gave her. She'd overheard Hyacinth talking to Ms. Zelma, saying that she was surprised Pauline Gumbs had not yet sat upon and crushed up the little piece of man she called a husband.

Phaedra's stomach grumbled with anticipation on the Sunday before the picnic when she heard all the items on the menu: stew chicken, rice and peas, cook-up rice, flying fish, pudding and souse, yam pie, macaroni pie, potato salad, fried chicken, and Phaedra's favorite, fish cakes. For the whole week that followed, Phaedra imagined the food she'd eat at the picnic. It was easy to forgive Mrs. Gumbs's droning on about the powers of fellowship and the gift of Christian community when she called out the food in a way that made Phaedra see, taste, and touch it.

The day of the picnic came and everyone was at church at the appointed hour, just after eight o'clock when the sun hadn't yet got going. They lined up beside the school buses with beach towels and beach chairs, coolers brimming with ice and drinks, long aluminum pans filled with food, napkins, and paper towels and painkillers, diapers, and changes of clothes. They were wearing outfits they had waited for weeks to show off, only to shrug off compliments with words like "this old thing" and "just something I had in my closet." Looking at the hill people assembled, you would have thought they were leaving on a long journey to see Jesus Christ himself, even though it took at most two hours to drive from Bird Hill in St. John to Folkestone Beach on the west coast.

Trevor offered Dionne a ride in his father's air-conditioned car, but she declined, citing plans to take the bus with her new friends. She was glad she could give them as the reason for saying no, because the truth was that Trevor's pouty, accusing looks annoyed her; and his mother, who insisted that she be driven because she couldn't tolerate noise, was just too much to be around. If she were being honest with herself, Dionne might have said that Mrs. Loving's sullenness reminded her too much of Avril, that she felt naked beneath the microscope of her intense gaze.

Dionne boarded the bus, muscling her grandmother's giant pan of potato salad to the back where the other girls were sitting. Accidentally on purpose, she knocked her sister in the head.

"Ow," Phaedra squealed.

"You know I didn't hit you that hard," Dionne said.

Then Dionne asked Chris, who was sitting next to Phaedra, "And you, how'd you manage to weasel your way out of the family caravan?" Dionne kept walking when Chris started to say that he was there to help Phaedra carry Hyacinth's pan of fish cakes.

The excitement that day was infectious and even Dionne, with her practiced nonchalance, found herself giggling with her new friend Saranne and the hill girls who stuck to them like honey. The teenage girls, minus Clotel Gumbs, who sat next to her mother, huddled together so that they could gossip and squeal when the bus hit bumps and potholes. The girls listened as Saranne spun tales about her boyfriend, a big-time record producer in Port-of-Spain who she bragged not only called her every evening at her aunt Trixie's house, but also had written her love notes every week since she arrived. The girls sighed with envy at each turn in Saranne's romantic fable. And because Saranne—with her eyes spaced far apart in a way that would have been ugly on another girl, her skin the color of wet sand, hair that ran down her back, and slim thighs that never rubbed together like the Bird Hill girls with their legs grown thick by yard work and cornmeal—because Saranne was beautiful and had a Trini accent that made words tumble from her mouth like song lyrics, no one poked holes in her story or mentioned the rumor that this very same boyfriend had gotten Saranne pregnant and that this was the reason her mother had sent her to live with her cousin Jean and her aunt Trixie in Barbados for the summer. Everyone was in a light mood that day, and listening to Saranne's stories, and Dionne's tales of her boyfriend Darren back in Brooklyn, whispered just loud enough so that the girls could hear but the adults could not, made the hill girls feel like they could borrow some of what boys saw in Dionne and Saranne.

The trip ended when the bus rumbled up to Folkestone and let its passengers out in a dense cloud of diesel exhaust. The church people unloaded their things and stood staring at the grove of manchineel trees, two new public washrooms and tennis courts, and beyond them, the sea. Then they seized upon the picnic tables, acting as if someone else were fighting them for space at ten on a Saturday morning. Dionne and her crew stood back, trying to distinguish themselves from the country ways of their mothers and grandmothers and brothers and sisters, until their armor of teenage cool was cut through by threats to break their you-know-whats right then and there if they didn't bring themselves over where they were supposed to be, and promptly.

Once everyone's food and belongings were laid out on the tables, it was time for a prayer. Phaedra hated how holy the hill women and some of the men became when they came together under the auspices of church functions. And this time was no different, as the hill women fell over themselves in an effort to prove their godliness, taking the baseline level of Bajan gentility to a fever pitch. Phaedra thought that Father Loving's prayers to bless the food and the cooks and the church family and the sea and the fishermen and our nation's leaders would never end. Ever since she'd seen Hyacinth and Dionne making fish cakes earlier in the day, her heart had leapt with single-minded focus toward devouring them. And so as she endured Father Loving's endless entreaties to the Father, Son, and Holy Spirit, Phaedra soothed herself by imagining how the oil, batter, codfish, onions, and pepper would explode in her mouth.

Father Loving wound through his prayers, and Phaedra felt Chris fidgeting next to her. Phaedra and Chris were still friends, though sometimes the tension between Dionne and Trevor was thick enough to slice with a cutlass, and that meant that they couldn't all hang out together anymore. Chris had been waging a campaign for closeness during the bus ride, holding Phaedra a moment longer than necessary when the Bird Hill caravan veered too close to reckless drivers on the south coast road. Now Chris slid in when Phaedra was defenseless, her head bowed respectfully. Phaedra felt Chris's leathery fingers creep toward hers, but she swatted him away before he could take her hand in his. When Chris's hands were a safe distance away, she heard Father Loving starting up again with more fervor, this time with a plea that the children of Bird Hill would not forget where they came from, that the blood of Jesus and of their people that was shed for them would not have been shed in vain.

The Bird Hill Church of God in Christ picnic was held every third Saturday in July. If you asked some of the old people, like Hyacinth, they would tell you the real story, that the church had only taken what the original seven men who founded the hill did to celebrate their emancipation, and made it their own. They would also tell you that Bird Hill was once a community of freedmen, born when the local slaveholding family was wiped out by a series of unfortunate events. Pneumonia whipped through the white Braithwaite children like fire in a cane field. A boating accident took the overseer. A mysterious illness rotted the patriarch from the inside, bloating him until one day his belly ballooned to three times its normal size and his lips cracked and eventually stopped letting air pass through. Mrs. Braithwaite found herself without a child, husband, or another white person of her class to talk to. She looked out upon the fields and saw herself outnumbered by big strapping women and men grown strong on provisions and pork fat. Mr. Braithwaite was a firm believer in keeping his property in tip-top shape, and it was not unusual for the Braithwaite boys, as his male slaves were called, to take first prize in running and boxing competitions with the other plantations. Soon after her husband's death, Mrs. Braithwaite was consumed by a rot similar to the one that took her husband, although in her case she got smaller and smaller, well past the slim-waisted figure she cut when she was first married. The disease progressed quickly, and in a matter of days, she emitted such noxious gas that her servants took her commands from well across the room where she lay wasting away. The old-time hill women would tell you that Phaedra and Dionne's great-great-grandmother, a heavy-footed woman with sour sops for breasts named Bertha, spoke the spells that ruined her masters and their progeny, that it was Bertha's daughter who leaned over Mrs. Braithwaite's ailing body and said plainly, "She deading."

In the aftermath of Mrs. Braithwaite's death, there was some debate regarding the circumstances of her passing. But whether she'd died or been killed, there was a whooping that went up when her will was read, as it decreed that all the slaves, including the unborn (because just then Marguerite, Hyacinth's great-great-grandmother's cousin, was inside her mother's belly), would be free. The land on which they lived was passed to them as well. And although it was said that Mrs. Braithwaite was forward thinking, generous, extraordinary even, in her gift of posthumous manumission, she was in fact a woman of her time, having witnessed and survived the terror of Bussa's Rebellion, when the death of even one white slaveholder was enough to threaten the way of life to which she and the rest of the plantocracy had become accustomed. She knew that she couldn't take with her to the grave what she had once owned in life. Like the courage of the women in Phaedra and Dionne's family, the celebration every July had been passed down for generations on the hill. Eventually the festivities were co-opted by the church.

Phaedra had inherited her fair share of fierceness from the women in her family. And so when it seemed like Father Loving was turning down yet another prayer avenue, Phaedra opened her mouth and spoke: "Lord God, Heavenly Father, please feed us with the food the cooks have prepared, especially the fish cakes. Amen." And the hill women, who would normally have gathered themselves on a mission to correct a child speaking out of turn, simply chuckled and said "Amen," because in truth hunger and heat were making close friends of their bellies and their backs.

"From the mouths of babes," Father Loving said. He looked at Phaedra and she saw something like anger flash across his face even as his lips stretched wide across his teeth in a grin. Phaedra turned to Chris and he shrugged his shoulders; she remembered their unspoken pact not to discuss their parents.

In the requisite hour between feasting and going into the water, the adults' heavy eyelids shuttered almost closed and the children who knew what was good for them sat in such a way as to preserve the neatness of their plaits and the pleats in their slacks and dresses. When they couldn't stand it any longer, the children stripped down to the bathing suits they'd worn under their clothes because their mothers, suspicious as they were of germs, preferred the plain air to the public washrooms.

Dionne went off with Saranne to the changing rooms farther up the beach; they switched out of the dresses they'd arrived in and put on polka-dot bikinis, a matching set of swimsuits Saranne's boyfriend had sent from Trinidad when she whined that she didn't have anything to wear to the boring church picnic. Their tops covered the mosquito bumps Saranne had for breasts and Dionne's ample bubbies. Dionne watched Saranne out of the corner of her eye, noting her flat stomach and firm arms. She was reminded of changing with her friend Taneisha for gym at Erasmus, the way she was comforted by her friend's endless chatter that dulled the shame of having to undress in front of strangers. Dionne wondered for a moment what Taneisha was doing. It was Saturday and so it was likely that her mother, who made roti skins and cooked curry goat for women who called in orders from as close as Canarsie and as far away as Long Island, was already pouring oil into her pans and asking Taneisha to get the dough out of the industrial refrigerator that dwarfed their apartment's small kitchen. Dionne shook her head then, because it hurt too much to think that she wouldn't get a call from Taneisha that morning, which always began with the same question, "So, whatchu doing?" She wanted to forget Taneisha's kindness in believing that she might actually be doing something interesting, rather than "nothing" or "watching TV," like she usually said. That, and the fact that Taneisha always waited for Dionne to say something about her mother, instead of asking, was just part of what had made them such good friends.

"Eh eh, but it look like you real watching whatever movie you playing in you head," Saranne said, pulling Dionne out of her reverie.

"Huh?" Dionne said, and then looked up to see Saranne was already halfway out the door of the changing room. She hustled, and trailed slightly behind Saranne as they edged farther down the beach, in the opposite direction of the Bird Hill picnickers.

The girls eyed and then circled their prey, a group of boys who sat on boulders that made the sea a calm lake around them. Dionne and Saranne could tell from the boys' crisply pressed designer jeans and fresh haircuts that they were from town. They felt like their practiced coquetry had finally found a worthy audience.

Meanwhile, down the beach, the Bird Hill children and teenagers swam under the watch of a lifeguard while the adults napped in the shade. Hyacinth busied herself gathering aloe vera for sunburn and the women's teas she made at home; she finished by collecting sea grapes, her favorite things on the beach. Nothing gave Hyacinth more pleasure than rolling the sea grapes' seeds in her mouth so she could taste the sea and salt and fruit flesh all at once. She had her fill of them while the kids played in the radius of sand and water she'd circumscribed.

Looking at Phaedra and Chris, at first glance some people might have said they were both boys, Chris in his navy trunks and Phaedra in a pair of shorts and a sports bra and tank top Dionne had handed down to her. Phaedra felt a bit self-conscious at first, watching the other girls in their frothy-colored bathing suits with frills and ruffles. But it wasn't long before Chris won back her attention with a challenge to see who could find the most sand dollars. That day, the sea was choppy, the waves bashing the shoreline like an angry god. The children swam just to the edge of where the lifeguards and their parents said they could go. White sea foam sprayed high above their heads, wetting and cooling them down. Phaedra was reminded of watching her father in the bathroom mirror in the morning, the dollop of cream that he put on her nose that she didn't wash off until he was finished shaving.

It was easy to think about Avril in Barbados, but Phaedra had a hard time placing her father there. Errol never talked about Barbados much, always saying that you had to leave old-time things behind to get ahead, as if the key to surviving leaving home was to pretend it never existed. Phaedra wondered if Errol felt the same way about the life he'd left behind with Avril and Dionne and herself. Did he think of them, talk about them, or did they live in the shadows of his heart, along with his memories of home?

A few minutes before yet another round of eating was set to begin, when Phaedra's and Chris's pockets sagged with sand dollars and seashells, they emerged from the water and plopped on the sand in front of Hyacinth.

"Where's your sister, P.?" Hyacinth asked.

"I don't know," Phaedra said, and shrugged.

"I don't know, who?" Hyacinth said.

"I don't know, Granny. I think she went off with Saranne."

At the sound of that girl's name, Hyacinth sprang into action. Hyacinth knew that Saranne had been sent to Barbados from Trinidad for the summer by her mother, who hoped that a dose of time at home might cool the fire beneath her clothes. Rumor had it that Saranne was pregnant when she came to Barbados, that she had stayed at a private clinic on the west coast to take care of it. Hyacinth didn't know whether to believe the story about Saranne's pregnancy, having never seen the girl for herself until she showed up one day at her house walking arm in arm with Dionne. As soon as she saw Saranne, Hyacinth noticed the way she walked, her chest and bottom thrust in opposite directions, an invitation to boys and trouble. Hyacinth didn't like the way that Saranne was always brushing her bangs out of her eyes, either, because although she could see the heat bumps that the hair was hiding, she didn't trust anyone who couldn't hold her gaze. Having raised Avril, Hyacinth knew what she was looking at when she saw Saranne and she didn't like it at all.

With all that in mind, Hyacinth walked across the sand to the cove where Saranne and Dionne stood up to their thighs in the calm, clear water so that the parts of their bodies that would most interest the boys were on display. A couple dips in the cold water made their nipples poke through their flimsy bikinis, and Hyacinth was horrified that neither girl had enough shame to cover herself.

Phaedra and Chris walked behind her, taking small, fast steps for every one of Hyacinth's determined strides. Hyacinth stopped behind the boulders and looked up at the boys sitting on top of them.

"Tell your sister to find herself here now," Hyacinth commanded.

"Yes, please," Phaedra said. She and Chris scrambled up the rocks. In less than a minute they were back.

"Dionne said she can't come right now. She said she'll see us after the picnic," Phaedra said.

"I'm sorry?" Hyacinth said, not believing her ears.

"She said—"

"You stay here," Hyacinth commanded. She hauled herself up to the table of slick, gray boulders. She had started bellowing Dionne's name when she lost her footing and fell down into the shallow water, a few feet below where the boys sat, looking on.

The boy whose hands were resting on Dionne's exposed shoulders laughed. And Dionne—who wanted nothing more than to be wanted by him, who had just finished asking whether the phone number he'd given her was really the number to his very own apartment—laughed too.

"Oh, so you think it's funny. You're going to see what's funny when I fix your business," Hyacinth said.

"You might want to fix yours first," Dionne said and laughed again, pointing to where the white fabric of Hyacinth's skirt pressed against the front of her big white panties. The gaggle cackled with her.

Hyacinth walked through the water like she was on land. She slapped Dionne in her mouth, and the laughs that were once with Dionne turned direction against her.

Dionne looked at her grandmother once she'd composed herself. A cold glare emptied out of the girl she had been when she arrived. "I don't have to be here, you know," she said.

"Oh, you don't?"

"No, I don't. My mother is in New York, and I could go home anytime. Besides, I have other places on the island I could go to."

"Oh, is so grown you be? Well, when you find your mother,

tell her hello for me. In the meantime, if you know what's good for you, you will find some clothes to put on and come." Hyacinth shook with anger, not fear; the water rippled as she moved through it.

Saranne stood smirking where she'd watched the whole scene unfold.

"I ain't finish with you yet. You stay there, keeping company like that and watch what going to happen to you. Dionne, I don't know how many times I have to tell you that you lay down with dogs—"

"You get up with fleas," Dionne said.

"Well, all right then, you can say it but it don't seem like you know it. I'm not telling you again to come."

Dionne motioned to one of the boys to throw down the bag where she'd stuffed her clothes. She didn't turn back to say good-bye to Saranne or the boys, just walked out of the water in her grandmother's wake, wishing the sea would swallow her whole.

PHAEDRA'S BODY PULLED at the light, testing the softer side of midnight. Hyacinth usually slipped out of bed in the middle of the night, careful to fit her rustle inside Phaedra's dreams. This time, she troubled the quiet with the whoosh of her matchbook and then the sound of her oil lamp lighting. The flames' shadows danced across the plywood walls and bounced off the zinc roof before coming down again. Phaedra stirred and looked through the sleep shrouding her eyes to see her grandmother standing at the foot of the bed, fully dressed in the indigo blue she wore to births, her kit slung over one shoulder.

"Well, you say you want to learn how baby born."

"Huh?" Phaedra asked, wiping the cold from her eyes' corners. She coughed on the thick smoke of the mosquito coil that was burning at the foot of their bed.

"Phaedra Ann, you have exactly five minutes to put on your clothes and come. You think Ms. Husbands's baby going to wait on you to wipe the yampie out you eye?"

"Ms. Husbands?"

"Your friend Donna, her mother."

"Oh." Phaedra did not initially take the bulge beneath Donna's mother's clothes for a baby. When she asked her grandmother how she knew she was pregnant, she said that even with a fat woman, you could always tell by her ankles and sometimes by a darkening at her neck whether she was in the family way.

"Time waits for no one," Hyacinth said, turning toward the door. "If you learn anything, you must learn that babies come exactly when they're ready, not a minute later and not a minute before. There's no such thing as rushing them out. Or pushing them back in once they come."

"Back in?" Phaedra asked. She was still sleepy but curiosity got her out of her nightie and into her street clothes, which were folded neatly on a chair between the bed and the window. Even Phaedra, who was a lover of sleep, knew that this was something worth waking for.

The hush of the night enveloped them. With her grandmother by her side, Phaedra felt safe, sure that she knew where she was going, and that no harm would come to them when they were together. They walked for fifteen minutes before they came to a fork in the road and followed it to the right. Up ahead, three houses in, a light was on in the front room. On the gallery, a man sat smoking, the glowing ember of his cigarette the brightest thing in the darkness.

"I thought you would never reach. I called Ms. Zelma's phone looking for you hours ago," he said, his voice a grumble laced with relief.

"Everything in its own time. Find yourself somewhere to catch for the night and come back in the morning."

In the dark, Phaedra couldn't see the man's face, but the voice's commanding cadence put her in mind of someone she knew. She started to ask if the man smoking on the veranda was Father Loving, but thought better of it. Phaedra had learned that asking too many questions made grown-ups remember her age. As she was mulling over the identity of the man on the gallery, a groan unlike any Phaedra had heard before came from inside the house. Hyacinth took the three front steps gingerly, her walking stick stretched in front of her to ward off any sleeping dogs.

When they reached the scratchy welcome mat, Hyacinth said confidently, "Inside."

Donna came to the door and turned on the porch light. She looked three shades paler than usual, her t-shirt stained with rum raisin ice cream, her hair uncombed. She who was usually so full of chatter opened the door silently and led them to the front room, where her mother was beached on a mattress on the floor. Phaedra was distracted momentarily from the hulking mass at the center of the room by the photographs that lined the walls, old-time pictures of black people, some posed in a photo studio, some with horses and donkeys, some in front of the church, all variations on Donna and her mother. Phaedra compared these images to the ones that lined the walls of her grandmother's house, all graduation photos from kindergarten onward for Avril, Dionne, and Phaedra, a kind of shrine to their education, because Hyacinth said that even though she didn't reach high school, every one of her girls would go to college.

"Get your nose out of your behind, child. Go boil some water and bring me clean towels," Hyacinth said.

Phaedra did as she was told, backing out of the room with Donna in tow.

"There's water on the stove," Donna said.

"Did you boil it already?" Phaedra asked.

"No."

"Why?"

"Mummy said it wasn't time," Donna said.

"Wasn't time for what?"

"Time for the baby to come."

"Why are you whispering?"

"It's just this week I find out."

"This week? You mean to tell me your mother was pregnant for nine months and you just now realize it?" Phaedra reveled in assuming the position of expert.

"How would I know?"

Phaedra stopped at what she thought was a fair question. She used a long match to light the pilot like she'd seen her grandmother do, and set the water to boil. Donna crumpled into herself, leaning into the relief of someone more capable taking over, feeling the demand for her false competence subside. Phaedra moved past the kitchen and found the linen cabinet exactly where she expected it, just above her head on the right-hand side of the hallway outside the bathroom.

"Phaedra," Hyacinth called with urgency from the front room.

"Yes, Gran," she said, as she struggled to mount the step stool and pull the towels down from the cupboard.

"Bring those things now."

Phaedra hustled toward the front of the house. She nudged the kitchen door open with her shoulder, then placed the towels next to the mattress.

"Oh, God," Donna's mother moaned over and over again, her breath coming hard and ragged.

"That's right. Only He can help you through this. Now if you want this baby to come you have to push."

Donna's mother's body dwarfed the mattress, the sheets a rusty red river of blood and shit. Having been in labor for three days, she was beyond tears, the shine on her moon-shaped face a kind of beatific exhaustion. Hyacinth grabbed two of the clean towels and placed them beneath Ms. Husbands's body. Then she motioned for Phaedra to squat and hold Donna's mother beneath her right shoulder while she took the left shoulder, as the woman's strength had all but gone out of her. Something about the way that Donna's mother flopped her sweat-slick body around reminded Phaedra of the unit they'd done on whales in fourth grade, ending with a film on how they gave birth. All the boys had *eww*-ed and the girls had covered their eyes, everyone except Phaedra, who said that the way the calves slid out of their mothers was beautiful. The girls at her school counted this as just another way in which Phaedra was strange; but having seen that film, she was unperturbed by what she was being called to witness now.

Donna, who had been watching from the sofa, went to fetch the boiling water from the stove. She poured the water carefully into a bowl and held the sides with a towel so as not to burn herself. Without being told to, she went to look for clean sheets in the linen closet. Before she returned, there was a whimper and a scream. Her mother collapsed against the mattress, spent.

After the baby boy was cleaned and the cord cut by Phaedra, the sheets changed and the floor mopped, Hyacinth held the child to her chest, rocking him and singing him a morning song. As the minutes and then an hour passed, black-and-blue marks bloomed on his tiny body, mixing with his original jaundiced color. Donna's mother slept with her back turned, her breath a symphony of sighs. Donna busied herself with making a new bed for the baby in the room she shared with her mother, padding a bottom dresser drawer with blankets and towels.

"Take good care of your mother and the baby, y'hear?" Hyacinth told Donna before she left.

"Yes, Ms. B., I will. Hold on a minute there. Mummy said she had something for you."

"All right."

Donna went inside the house, and came back with a thin airmail envelope filled with red, green, and blue Barbados dollars, a set of three carbolic soaps, and a loaf of sweetbread. Hyacinth accepted the gifts and she and Phaedra stepped off the gallery.

"Open your mouth then, child. I know you're full to bursting with questions," Hyacinth said to Phaedra as they made their way back home, this time under a sun that was pushing the silver out of the sky.

"How come the baby came out all black and blue?"

"He had a long fight to get out."

"Why wouldn't she hold him?"

"Just wait. She will hold him yet."

Phaedra had other questions, and she tried to hold on to them, to let the quiet lead them into morning. But when they reached the final turnoff before their house, Phaedra turned to see the church and the top of the hill, and the question inside her barreled forward.

"Gran, what do you do with someone else's secrets?" Phaedra asked.

"It depends, darling. Who tell you to keep secret?"

"It's not that anybody told me. It's just that I wonder about Father Loving . . ."

"Delivering a baby is one of the most sacred things someone can ever ask for your help in. Our job is not to judge or jabber our mouths, just to do the work we were made for."

"But what if the secret is hurting someone else?"

"It's not our job to fix that kind of hurt. The only kind of work we worry about is the kind we can do with our hands."

Phaedra watched the sun rise, and realized that the boy Donna's mother gave birth to was the one her dreams of fish had pointed to. The summer had taught her that no amount of prayer could make the summer go by faster, or her mother well, or her sister kinder. Dreams were a bridge between the waking world and the sleeping one, but prayer, prayer was something else entirely.

DIONNE BOUNDED INTO her grandmother's house with a netball cradled in her forearm and a red singlet plastered against her chest. Hyacinth could see beneath her shirt the imprint of not one but two bras that melded Dionne's breasts into an undifferentiated mass. Hyacinth wanted to say something about it, but she knew that criticizing Dionne would invite her prickliness. Just the week before, Hyacinth had asked Dionne to go see Jean and have him make new clothes for her. There was a standoff in which Dionne insisted that her clothes still fit. What Dionne had said exactly, below her breath, was that she didn't see why she had to let some buller man ruin her clothes like he'd ruined her hair on her birthday. Hyacinth, who believed that calling someone outside of their name was a grave offense, pounded her foot on the ground so that the few pieces of good china and crystal in the hutch shook. "What did you say?"

"Nothing, Granny."

"I know you couldn't be talking that kind of nonsense in my house. I beg you to leave whatever slackness you pick up in those streets when you wipe your feet on these steps. Jean isn't a buller man. And I won't have you going about here saying so. You hearing me?"

"Yes, ma'am," Dionne said to the floorboards.

The compromise was that Jean would mend the places where her thighs had rubbed holes into her pants and let out her tops and skirts and dresses. Never mind that Dionne's clothes were in need of replacing well before she'd come to Barbados, a fact that Hyacinth lamented when she and Phaedra unpacked their suitcases, asking if "wunna mother think that it's a department store she sending you to," ranting about the sad state of their wardrobes until Phaedra's face flushed and she tried to snatch back a t-shirt pocked with pills and holes that her grandmother held up with one finger. Hyacinth did not tolerate rudeness from children. When Phaedra tried to wrest the t-shirt from her that evening, she pulled the little girl close and said, "I know Avril ain't teach you to grab things from grown people. If that's what you did in New York, you won't do it in my house. That can't fly in here at all."

Hyacinth could tell from looking at the girls when they arrived that shame was not something new to them. Each of them wore it differently, Dionne with a bravado that belied what she knew about herself and her family, which was that neither she nor they ever had enough of what they needed. Phaedra had taken the teasing from the girls at school in Brooklyn and turned it against herself; she sometimes wondered if she wasn't the dirty, worthless girl her classmates called her. One particularly rough week, Phaedra had to wear the same two tops to school because there was no money to go to the Laundromat. Never mind that Dionne made Phaedra take off her clothes as soon as she got home, then washed them in the bathroom sink and hung them to dry on the shower curtain rod each evening. Phaedra knew that the safest response to these kinds of assaults was silence, because although she wanted to say that at least she didn't smell like Mercy, whom the other girls called an African booty scratcher, she knew that wouldn't get her anywhere. As time passed that summer, Phaedra could feel herself standing taller, as if she could tap into the better parts of herself more readily in Bird Hill than she could in Brooklyn. Dionne, though, felt her armor clink into place more securely in Barbados, felt each passing day as evidence of their mother's betrayal.

Hyacinth learned to pick her battles with Dionne, and it was for that reason and because it was the end of the day and she was tired from Ms. Husbands's delivery the night before, that she didn't remark that it looked like it was time for Dionne to get some new brassieres.

"Good evening," was all Hyacinth said, looking up from her newspaper.

"Evening," Dionne huffed. She went to put the netball on the coffee table, inside the crystal bowl that never had fruit in it. But then she felt Hyacinth's eyes on her, and placed the ball on the floor.

"So, what you find yourself in the street doing this time of night?"

"I was exercising."

"Well, I can see that."

Hyacinth watched as Dionne walked to the kitchen and then leaned over the refrigerator. The door stayed open for several minutes, the fridge light illuminating Dionne's red, sweaty face, the sound of its motor harmonizing with the rhythm of her panting.

"There's a plate on the stove for you," Hyacinth said.

"Thanks, Gran."

Dionne went to unwrap the plastic from the plate and was putting the food in a saucepan to heat it up when she heard Hyacinth.

"You're not going to bathe your skin? I bet that food would taste even better once you're clean."

Dionne knew this question to be a command, and so she dragged her feet to her bedroom where she pulled her clothes off and threw them on the floor. When she was bathed and dressed, she sat down at the table with a heaping plate of cook-up rice. Dionne slammed the food into her mouth and was sucking the marrow from a chicken bone when she felt her grandmother's eyes on her again. She put the bone down and wiped her teeth clean of the marrow, not sure whether Hyacinth would be proud of or horrified by her imitation of her mother's lusty way of devouring meat.

"Come sit with me, darling," Hyacinth said. Dionne's head grazed the wooden archway that separated the dining area from the front room; Hyacinth sighed at the sight of her first-born grandchild who was growing faster than she could keep up with.

When Dionne was close to her on the couch, Hyacinth said, "You know, sometimes I look on you and I can only see your mother."

Dionne smiled, because even though the woman Avril was now wasn't who she had been, Dionne still thought her mother was the most beautiful woman she knew.

"Did any letter come from Mommy?"

"One came last week."

"Why didn't you tell me?"

Hyacinth raised one eyebrow, and Dionne knew not to ask this question again. Dionne, more than her sister, found it hard to abide by the hill's stringent rules of respect, which meant never questioning adults. It would take more than a few months for her to adjust from being in Brooklyn, where she thought for herself and for Phaedra and for her mother, to being on the hill, where she was expected to act as if she were an innocent and incapable of making decisions for herself.

Hyacinth pushed her reading glasses further up her nose and set her newspaper aside. She motioned for Dionne to bring her purse from where it hung on the front door's knob. She rifled through it until she produced a plastic bag tied tight around a stack of papers.

"You know, your mother used to play sports. That must be where you get it from."

"Well, it's not like I'm any good. I think the girls only asked me because I'm tall."

"That's a start," Hyacinth said, wresting the bag's tight knot free. "When your mother was in school, she played everything—football, netball, track and field. You name it, she did it. When she was about your age, she went to England on some exhibition tour for the best netballers from the Commonwealth. She begged and cried to go, and when she came back she wasn't the same. Everything was 'in England, they eat baked beans with breakfast,' and 'I quite liked Tower Bridge.' It was like she left Barbados one person and came back completely different. From then, she had a hot foot."

"I never knew Mommy played sports."

"There's a lot you don't know, dear heart," Hyacinth said, pulling a few sheets of paper from a white airmail envelope. "Will you read it for me? Tonight I'm feeling my age."

Dionne didn't believe her grandmother, whom she'd never known to be any less than fully alert or mobile, but she took the letter from her and started reading anyway.

Dear Mummy,

I know I've been remiss in writing, but things here have been quite hectic of late. Looking for work keeps me busy and between that and the heat and trying to find a place to live for me and the girls, most days I come home and I'm bone-tired. I just want to eat and then fall into the bed in the same clothes I had on all day. So, all that is to say, I was writing this letter to you in my mind well before I sat down to put pen to paper. I'm glad to hear the girls are doing well and that they ask for me. It's so strange being up here without them. Sometimes I feel like this apartment is too big and quiet for just me alone. Well, give the girls my love. If you check the bank on Monday, you should see something there for you. And of course I'll let you know as soon as I can when I'm coming.

Love, Avril

Dionne turned over the last sheet as if expecting something more, a postscript at least. When she saw there wasn't anything, she read the letter again silently to herself, and then handed it back to Hyacinth.

"Sounds like she's doing well," Dionne said with forced cheerfulness.

Hyacinth said nothing to confirm or deny Dionne's pronouncement, just piled the newest letter atop the others and fussed with the plastic bag and rubber bands that held the letters together. "Well, then," she said.

"Don't you think she sounds happy?"

"You don't really want to know what I think."

"Yes, I do," Dionne said, her voice softening.

This was what bothered Hyacinth most about teenagers, the way they swung so quickly from sharpness to tenderness, sometimes in the same breath. Hyacinth knew the best way to deal with them was to hold your center firm until they came around again. Hyacinth's work helping hill women in their darkest moments had taught her how to find and stay on steady emotional ground.

"I just can't understand how it's almost two months since wunna reach here, and she still hasn't picked up the phone once to say well, hello, dog, or how you doing, cat. And I don't know why she keeps saying she doesn't know when she's coming down here to collect you. School's starting back soon."

Just the day before, they'd watched the news coverage of back-to-school sales that had already started in the States. Phaedra asked Hyacinth when they were going home; her friend Donna had already been fitted for new school uniforms. Hyacinth hated having to say, "Soon," instead of the truth, which was that she had no idea. Now she turned to Dionne and said, "A child is not a toy you pick up one day, play with, and then when you get tired of it, you put it down, and go on about your business."

Dionne felt her grandmother getting worked up and watched as she tried unsuccessfully to heave herself from the low sofa.

"I found some of Mommy's clothes in her closet."

"I don't know what kind of condition those things must be in. What the moths haven't eaten, you probably can't fit."

"That's not true, Gran. This is hers," Dionne said, pulling at the sleeve of the blue Queens College Netball Invitational t-shirt she was wearing.

"Well, I guess the things she used to exercise in would fit you. She always said that sports were the one place where she didn't have to worry about what she looked like. No matter what the coaches said about how neat the girls should look, she always had her things made one size too big."

Dionne leaned back into the sofa's shallow cushions and smiled. All summer, she'd felt her mother's life in Barbados taking shape with Hyacinth's stories and the ones the hill women told her after they said she looked like her mother had spit her out. There was something comforting about wearing Avril's clothes, sleeping in her bed, walking where she once walked, hearing stories about her.

"All those girls would be itching to roll up their shorts and tie their shirts around their waists, and your mother would prefer to look like those clothes were wearing her. You think your mother's easy? She was never easy," Hyacinth said.

Dionne stretched her legs before her, readying herself for a story, the only thing sure to ease the tension she saw pulsing her grandmother's neck.

"One day, when your mother was about your age, she flew in here with her friend Jean like the devil himself was chasing her. And from that day forward, for about two months, all these children could talk about was the end-of-year dance. For weeks and weeks, all your mother would do was eat, sleep, go to school, and work on her dress. Your mother almost broke my bank with all the things she wanted. And the things I couldn't afford, she paid for from her own kitty. She was funny that way, always liked to have her own things. Back then she was apprenticing to Jean's grandmother, and so she had all of the fabric she wanted and a little pocket change Jean's granny would throw at her when she finished piecework. So, the week before the dance, she bought these shoes at Bata, ones she had been saving up her money for. I remember now that they were red, the same color as her dress, open toe and open back with a four-inch heel. Nice shoes, you know. And her father, who was not into the idea of this dance from the beginning—"

"Father? I never heard Mommy talk about her father," Dionne said.

"What, you think I just made your mother myself? Well, after you hear this story, you will understand why she never talked about him. Her father, my husband, said that no daughter of his was going to be parading herself about like a harlot in Jezebel shoes. Not while he was alive."

"Jezebel shoes?" Dionne asked.

"Wait, wait," Hyacinth said, patting Dionne's hand to hold back the tide of questions she felt welling up in her grandchild. "So, the whole month before the dance, I had been leading the campaign for her to go, not because I cared one way or the other. I personally thought that it was a whole bunch of foolishness, that it cost too much money, and that the excitement would be over before it even really got going. But I could see it was something Avril wanted, something she was probably going to do anyway, whether we said yes or not. And I couldn't in good faith know that she was making her dress already, and then tell her she couldn't go. Truth be told, I actually liked the dress. It was a pretty pretty pretty shade of red, not red like Ms. Zelma's roses, or red like a poinsettia, but red like those birds that does fly in from Trinidad. It was a beautiful color, and the whole thing was made in organza. The material was expensive, and when she was done, there was not one sliver of material she hadn't used. The skirt was full with layers and the top fit her just so and the sleeves puffed out from her shoulders like clouds. She pinned a ring of red sequins around the neckline and at the hem. I'm telling you. You couldn't look at your mother in this dress and say she was anything less than gorgeous."

"So what happened?"

"Well, my child was all dressed to go, I mean, to the nines, hair, makeup, everything. And she was just about to put on her shoes when her father came out of the room where he'd been stewing. He walked into the front room just as her date was pulling up, and started taking off his belt."

"Who was her date?"

"Oh, you know back then, Avril and Jean were thick as thieves. Jean's father had died just a few months before the school dance, but not before spoiling that child rotten. Anything he wanted, a trip, shoes, clothes, a car, he got it. It was the car his father had bought him, a fast car the same red of Avril's dress, that he picked her up in. But you getting me off track."

"So Mommy went to the dance with Buller—I mean, Jean?"

"The one and the same. But child, you missing the heart of the story with all your questions. If you'd talk less, you would hear more. Anyways, your grandfather came in here pulling off his belt. And before Avril could even buckle the strap on the left shoe, much less the right, he had both shoes in his hands. And then he threw them into the cane field next door. Now, that time was before Ms. Zelma and Ms. Zelma's house were here, and all those houses you see lined up out there were pure cane fields, and your grandfather could throw far. Your mother, as God is my witness, walked out of this house in her bare feet. I thought she was going to go into the cane to look for the shoes, but she stepped right past her father, and got into the car that was waiting for her. And from that day forward, whenever Avril and her father would see each other, it was in passing, and they never said anything to each other beyond what was strictly necessary."

"Wow," Dionne said. She looked at the front room's shut louvers and tried to imagine the scene, her mother in a red dress she'd made for herself and her grandfather chucking her high heels through the window. She couldn't really form a picture of her grandfather. It was true, Dionne had always thought of her mother as springing from Hyacinth fully formed.

"What was Granddad like?" Dionne asked.

She watched something like a curtain close over Hyacinth's eyes. What Hyacinth didn't say, what she couldn't, was that the night she'd called Avril to tell her that her father died, when Phaedra answered the phone crying into the receiver and Errol was in the background demanding to know who was on the line, she knew that Avril wouldn't come home for the funeral. Hyacinth knew it was for show when Avril begged for a few days to see if she could buy a plane ticket. She'd tried to accept the money that Avril wired to help bury her father with a joyful heart. But she wished that Avril had known that Hyacinth needed her presence more than her money. It wasn't so much that Hyacinth wanted someone to lean on, because Hyacinth was more than capable of standing upright in the face of the most difficult things, even her husband's death. Hyacinth just wanted to know that she could shift her weight to one side and it wouldn't be just the air and the force of her will holding her up, but the support of her family too. Hyacinth thought life was not just easier, but sweeter with family by her side. That's what she'd been raised up to believe, and what her heart told her was still true now. She wondered why she hadn't been able to pass this truth on to her own daughter. She wanted to know whether and how her grandchildren might learn this for themselves.

"You don't get enough stories for one night, child? Go to bed and don't worry your head with all these old-time things," Hyacinth said.

Dionne got up and felt fatigue settle over her. She offered Hyacinth a hand to get up, but she shook her head and kept looking somewhere beyond Dionne. As the time between Avril's letters lengthened, Dionne had become accustomed to finding her grandmother asleep in the colorfully patterned living room chair, as if she wanted to be there waiting the moment Avril decided to come home.

"Night, Gran," Dionne said. She shuffled toward her room, her mother's letter and her grandmother's story animating the inside of her eyelids.

PHAEDRA STOOD BESIDE her grandmother at the bus stop at the bottom of Bird Hill, praying that no one she knew would see her in the straw sun hat Hyacinth made her wear. The white elastic string tickled her chin. She'd tried to push the string under the brim, but then a strong wind lifted it up and off her head. Hyacinth stood in the middle of the road while Phaedra scurried across after the hat; she knew what was good for her, and so kept it securely, if uncomfortably, fastened after that. It was early on a Saturday morning, market day, and Phaedra was sure that the girls most likely to make fun of her were home doing their chores. Donna was helping her mother with the new baby, and had dark circles below her eyes and a new ring of fat around her belly to show for it. Christopher was probably out with his B-team of bandits, a boy named Thomas, who was constantly digging in his nose like he was mining for gold, and his twin brother, Timothy, who was his shadow, always parroting what he said and finishing his sentences. Phaedra knew that the boys were probably shooting at fruit and birds with the slingshots Father Loving made for Christopher that summer. She was sad not to be with them, but then she remembered Christopher's response when Phaedra pointed out that he played with other kids when she wasn't around. He said that he had to keep his mind off Phaedra somehow, and reminded her that she would always be on his A-team. Knowing she and Christopher were a team, Phaedra found that imagining him playing with the dumbbell twins didn't bother her so much.

Dionne stood behind her sister and grandmother in the shade of a tree whose wide, waxy green leaves made this part of the hill feel like a slice of rain forest. After they'd been waiting for the better part of an hour, the bus, blue and yellow like the colors of the Barbados flag, barreled toward them. Dionne and Phaedra walked past Hyacinth and onto the bus while she painstakingly counted out change for their fares. Hyacinth nodded at the only other passenger, a dapper man with coarse white hair pocking his jaw, wearing a suit so carefully pressed it looked as if it had been ironed directly onto him. Phaedra took a seat with Hyacinth in the front of the bus and Dionne sat directly behind them.

"Granny, was this the same bus Mommy used to take to school?"

"Not this one exactly, but one like it."

Phaedra closed her eyes and tried to imagine her mother riding the bus in the gray school uniform she'd seen pictures of Avril wearing.

"And how long would it take, Gran?"

Hyacinth craned her neck to look at the man in the back of the bus, whose eyes she could feel on her. She threw a "Morning" and then "Do I know you, sir?" over her shoulder. The man, his voice smoother than his salt-and-pepper hair would suggest, said, "I would like to think you do."

Phaedra looked at her grandmother, and tried to see what the man saw. Hyacinth kissed her teeth, and Phaedra realized from where Avril had inherited her fantastically loud and long suck-teeth.

"What you saying now, pet?" Hyacinth said, returning her attention to Phaedra.

"I was asking you how long it is from here to Mommy's school."

"About an hour, maybe more, maybe less, depending."

"That's a long way to go to school."

"It was the best one she could get into."

"Was she smart?"

"The brightest."

"Was she sad?"

"Sorry?"

"I mean, sometimes Mommy would seem so down it was like she couldn't get up if she tried, and it just makes me wonder if that's how she always was."

"Sometimes."

"Sometimes what?"

"Sometimes she was sad. There was a whole term when she was in second form that I'd have to force her to eat breakfast and then walk her down to the stop myself and watch her get on the bus." Hyacinth looked out of the bus as it traveled past an old sugar plantation where the rusted hands of a windmill stood motionless. As silly as it was, she found herself searching for Avril on the street outside the window. "Months she was like that and no amount of anybody asking her what was troubling her helped. Just when we were thinking about sending her to my cousin in England, that dark thing lifted and she was almost like herself again."

Phaedra looked out the window and saw a desert rose tree with all its flowers skirting the bottom of its trunk, as if someone had made it their business to steal its beauty.

"So there was nothing you could do to make it better."

"I wish I could say there was." Hyacinth sighed and motioned for Phaedra to move closer to her, since the bus was starting to fill with people; Phaedra let herself sink into the cushion of flesh at her grandmother's side. Hyacinth spoke again, as if Phaedra had asked her another question. "There's nothing like wishing someone you love well, and knowing just wishing isn't enough."

Phaedra nodded and felt the bus roll past the signal station at Gun Hill. A few minutes later she drew in air when the water came into view. No matter how many times Phaedra saw it, the sea exploded her sense of wonder, especially when the dense tree cover gave way to the blue-blue water lapping against the shore. Watching the women walking by on their way to run errands, the fishermen strolling along the beach, she wondered at their nonchalance in the face of such a marvelous sight. Phaedra inched toward the windows, burying her bony elbows in Hyacinth's ample lap. And then she watched as the south coast blurred by and the sea got gobbled up by the hotels and resorts, only peeking out between openings in the concrete. She turned back to stick her tongue out at her sister, but Dionne was so deep in her own world, she didn't even slap Phaedra in the back of her head like she usually would.

They got off the bus at the depot in town and Hyacinth gripped Phaedra's and Dionne's hands. Each of the girls could feel their grandmother's fingers, sharp-nailed and gnarled by bursitis. Dionne tried to shake out of Hyacinth's grip, but she settled instead on holding her head down. It was nearly impossible she'd run into anyone who knew her, but just in case, Dionne had spent hours trying on, selecting, and then ironing two possible outfits. Dionne was the kind of girl who always wanted to be prepared for the event of someone else's judgment, even a stranger's.

They crossed the street, careful to avoid the slimy hunter green sewage that snaked down the gutters between the sidewalk and the street. Phaedra shaded her eyes so she could see the boats lined up at the careenage at Independence Square. They went inside the market and Phaedra dropped her free hand from her forehead, felt Hyacinth's hold on her loosen. It took a moment for her eyes to adjust to the dark, her nose to the damp, dank smell, her ears to the sounds of people shouting prices and engaging in friendly arguments Phaedra thought were hostile until she saw her grandmother walk up to one of the vendors, inspect her pawpaws, and then start a shouting match that ended in laughter and the woman giving her extra fruit that weighed down Phaedra's left hand. This ritual was repeated at the stalls where each woman greeted Hyacinth by her first name or, more often, Ms. B. Sometimes her grandmother would walk away in the middle of a negotiation, occasionally enticed back by the offer of a good price; sometimes she moved on for good. Phaedra loved the drama of it, and seeing her grandmother for the proud, powerful woman she was there. She smiled broadly when Hyacinth introduced her as "the little one for Avril," hoping her extra teeth would make up for Dionne's sullenness. They shopped for sweet potatoes, Phaedra listening intently as Hyacinth showed her how to check for hairs on the tubers' rough brown skin, which was how you knew they'd be sweet. Hyacinth was about to pay for one when she noticed that Dionne, who had been lagging behind them, was gone.

Hyacinth and Phaedra looked around, and then saw Dionne standing at one of the stalls off to the side of the market. Its sign read HARD TUNES & TRICKS and it was blasting Jamaican dancehall music, all of which Hyacinth considered abominable, one song's beat to which Dionne was now freely swaying her behind. Phaedra walked over, leaving her grandmother talking to the sweet potato vendor, who had enough dirt under her fingernails to prove she'd pulled them from the earth that very morning. Hyacinth's head was tilted to the right. That meant that she was listening, and Phaedra knew from the way their shoulders almost touched that they were talking about something not meant for her ears. She walked past rows of christophine, eddoes, and cassava piled high above her head, all the while watching Dionne, whose elbows were draped over the glass case where cassette tapes and Walkmans were displayed and sold for three times the price in the States.

"Who's this little princess?" the guy behind the counter asked when Phaedra entered.

Phaedra drew back toward the lip of the stall that led into the market.

"I don't bite," the guy said, and Phaedra saw his gold tooth shining. She remembered Hyacinth's pronouncement on gold teeth—she still had all the teeth the good Lord gave her and jewelry was for the body and not for the teeth.

"Granny sent me for you, Dionne," Phaedra said, looking away from the spectacle of his mouth.

"The morality police calls," Dionne said, trying to throw hair she didn't have over her shoulder.

"Make sure you call me when you reach home. And take care of my princess for me, seen?" the man called after her.

Phaedra noticed the guy talking in a forced Jamaican accent, which sounded neither better nor worse than the Jamaicans in Brooklyn whose efforts to speak American slang made words like "yo" elongate and turn into something else altogether in their mouths.

"I will," Dionne shouted over her shoulder as she exaggerated the swing of her hips. And then to Phaedra, "Why are you so opposed to me enjoying myself in this lifetime?"

"Dionne." Now it was Phaedra who was losing her patience. "I was just doing what Granny told me."

"Well, bless your heart," Dionne said, imitating the signature phrase of Phaedra's VBS teacher, Ms. Taylor.

They went back to following their grandmother around on a seemingly endless circuit from stall to stall. At the butcher, where Hyacinth called out for modest cuts of pork and beef, the flies' conference around the upside-down hanging slabs of meat made Phaedra's breakfast curdle in her throat. By the time the shopping was done, they were all so tired it was all they could do to drag themselves back to the bus station. Phaedra wanted to squat on her haunches like she saw the boys do, but she knew without asking that it was better not to. She watched the orderly way people lined up around the metal dividers, and realized she'd never seen anyone queue for a bus in Brooklyn. The quiet of exhaustion wrapped itself around Hyacinth and her girls, a cocoon in which they traveled all the way home to Bird Hill.

At home that evening, Phaedra and Dionne and Hyacinth sat at the dining room table eating beef rotis that Hyacinth bought in town. Because Hyacinth was not the type to eat on the street or even in a restaurant, by the time they sat down, they were beyond hungry. Phaedra sat with her legs crossed on the plastic seat covers to avoid the mosquitoes that congregated beneath the table hoping to make meals of her ankles. They had put away the groceries, washed their hands, and heated the food in the oven. The girls' excitement had mostly dissipated, and the meal felt like fuel rather than the treat it was intended to be.

"Watch yourself, Dionne," Hyacinth said once everyone had polished off their food, and only stray streaks of curry and channa and roti skins stuck to their plates.

"Sorry?" Dionne said. She pushed her chair back from the table and piled Phaedra's and Hyacinth's plates on top of hers.

"Just as sure as I'm looking at you, I know you're hearing me," Hyacinth said. "I don't see why you need to find yourself in public grinding up yourself on grown men and shaking your behind like a thoroughfare."

"A thoroughfare?"

"The kind of woman who everybody passes through."

"Oh," Dionne said. "I was just trying to have a good time."

"You know what kind of good time that guy was looking with you? If you do know, you're more stupid than you look," Hyacinth replied.

"Mommy always said that if we misbehaved she'd send us home. So here I am. The worst thing that could have happened to me already has."

"Don't tempt the devil, darling. He'll give you the worse bits you asked for, plus what you couldn't even imagine."

"I'll talk loud enough for him to hear, then, loud enough for anyone to hear," Dionne said, her voice rising as she snatched her plate and stormed into the kitchen. Her protest of heavy feet and slamming dishes was one that still acknowledged it was her responsibility to clean up the kitchen after dinner.

"I'm sure you will scream loud enough to make the devil hear, darling. I'm sure you will," Hyacinth said, certain that Dionne could still hear her, even above the clamor she was making.

ALWAYS, IN SPITE OF EVERYTHING, Hyacinth thought that Avril would come home. When Avril said that she was sending the girls home for the summer, Hyacinth was glad to have Phaedra and Dionne in the fullest versions of themselves, as seeing the girls day in and day out was so much better than the phone calls and pictures she'd been living off of for years. What Avril had said exactly was that she needed a break so that she could sort herself out and lay a better foundation for the girls. She kept using that word, "foundation," pressing on it for emphasis the way you pound a table or a Bible, and in her mind, Hyacinth saw concrete being poured into the foundation of a house. Hyacinth thought it was no coincidence that from Ms. Zelma's kitchen, when she stood talking on the phone to Avril, she could see a house whose foundation had been poured, its walls erected, but never finished. Hyacinth had lived long enough to know that laying down roots was an illusion that made people more comfortable, secure, a pillar they could hold on to until they got shaken to the core again.

For years, Hyacinth had told Avril that any time she was ready to come home and get help with the children, she was more than welcome. She stopped short at saying that she would come up to the States and look after them, because for one, her old bones couldn't take the cold and for two, there was no way she was leaving the good-good house her husband and she had made with their own hands to go live in an apartment in New York. Hyacinth had always been astonished at the way people lived on top of each other up there. It seemed strange that people could live in such proximity, and yet still be strangers.

On Bird Hill, there was enough space so you could stretch out your arms or raise your voice and touch only yourself and your family. But still Hyacinth knew the public and private affairs of people all over the hill. She knew whose milk wouldn't come in no matter how many cups of the special teas she brewed for her, which women to expect in her yard like clockwork at the beginning of every month when their husbands drank and then brawled, painting their wives' faces with their fists. That she knew so much was occasionally overwhelming to Hyacinth. Even when she didn't want to, Hyacinth could still feel the tug of other women's worries, which she knew as well as the birthmarks on her knees, the ones that Hyacinth's mother said made her look like she'd come down from heaven after a lifetime of prayer. Still, Hyacinth preferred this small place and its difficulties to the strangeness of living some place where nobody knew you beyond what you saw fit to tell them.

After Phaedra was born, it became clear that the thin thread that held together Avril's marriage to her husband, Errol, was frayed. Hyacinth hoped that once Errol finally left, Avril would bring the girls home and they could be a family again. In her mind's eye, she saw busy mornings sending Avril and the girls off to school, having supper ready for them when they came home, watching and talking at the television together at night while she packed their lunches and pressed uniform shirts and skirts. Despite the disembodied voice that her daughter had become over the years, Hyacinth still remembered the girl that Avril had once been, the light of her life, fiercely protective of her friends and of her mother. Hyacinth had a glimpse of this life in the year that Avril spent at home after she finished college, teaching first form at her old high school. But when classes let out that year for Christmas holidays, Avril met Errol, and the next six months proceeded only in service of them leaving Barbados together.

Hyacinth blamed herself because she didn't know enough of Avril's life in New York, of the pressures that moved against her, or the way that the children stretched the precious little that she had to its breaking point. Hyacinth didn't know that Errol's imprint was still on Avril's body—not only the bruises that were slow to heal, but also the other, more insidious ways Errol had lodged himself in Avril's psyche, the damage that Avril couldn't admit even to herself. There were only pictures and letters and cards and phone calls to go by, and Avril constructed the lie of her competence so perfectly that it was hard for Hyacinth to know what was really going on. And so she could claim only her memories of Avril before she left Barbados, and then the bits and pieces she came to know that summer in her conversations with her granddaughters. Avril, according to Phaedra, was a mother who missed parent-teacher conferences, who hadn't held down a job in more than a year, who let Dionne assume responsibility for making sure that she and her sister were bathed, fed, and on time for school. This was an Avril she didn't know. But she would come to understand that this Avril was as real as the daughter she remembered.

The summer Phaedra and Dionne arrived on the hill without their mother, Avril's letters became less frequent and the Sunday phone calls she promised never came. But Hyacinth could count on the money that she sent biweekly, which allowed her to buy Phaedra the colored popcorn and cheese balls she loved, round out the meals from her garden with meat and fish, keep the water running and the current on. It was only when Hyacinth went to the bank the Monday after she received Avril's latest letter and didn't find her deposit that she knew something was really wrong.

One of the things that confirmed Hyacinth's suspicion

that America was an evil, lonely place was that people were islands unto themselves. And so when Avril drifted away, there was no friend or neighbor or pastor or coworker to reach out to and ask after her child. It was as if Avril had disappeared down a rabbit hole, never to be found again.

The call from the hospital did not come as a surprise, then. Hyacinth had already begun to fill in the gaps of what she knew with bad news. When the phone rang, Hyacinth was washing up the breakfast dishes. She heard her neighbor Ms. Zelma call her name from across the rosebushes that separated their houses and hurried over. She stepped into Ms. Zelma's kitchen and tried not to see the alarm that thrust her neighbor's eyebrows toward her widow's peak.

"Who is it?" Hyacinth asked. She wiped the water from her hands onto her apron and then reached for the receiver.

"Some white American person," Ms. Zelma said.

The fact that the man on the line said Avril's full name when he spoke of her told Hyacinth that he wouldn't go on to say anything she wanted to hear. She leaned against the kitchen sink for support. She was soon off the call, but not before committing to memory the number she needed. She put the phone down slowly, as if stopping time might shove this news back into the awful place it came from, give her a moment longer to dwell in the bliss of not knowing.

"What happened?" Ms. Zelma asked.

"I need to sit down," Hyacinth said. She eased herself into a chair that creaked with her weight.

Ms. Zelma looked at Hyacinth expectantly. Her hands were open in her lap as if they were ready to receive the news.

"Avril's gone."

"What do you mean, gone?"

"I mean, gone. She killed herself."

Ms. Zelma sucked in a breath and soon it felt like there wasn't enough air in the kitchen for both her and Hyacinth.

"Oh Lord, I don't know what to say."

"There's no thing to say."

"And the body?"

"At the hospital. I have to call and see about how to get it home."

"What about the girls?"

Hyacinth hesitated. "No place to go but right here."

"I know that, but what are you going to tell them?"

"The truth."

"That can't fly. Phaedra is still small. And Dionne has enough on her head already without this. You can't tell them that."

"I'd rather they hear it from me than out on the street."

"No, man, there has to be another way."

"Ms. Zelma, you bury any children yet?"

Ms. Zelma didn't speak.

"Right, then."

"Can I get you anything, anything I can do?" Ms. Zelma said. She spun around her kitchen looking for something to occupy her hands.

"Tea," Hyacinth said. "I would take a cup of tea."

Hyacinth leaned her elbows against the kitchen table's sun-warmed plastic tablecloth and stirred brown-sugar cubes into her tea. She looked at Ms. Zelma and marveled at the fact that they'd both grown into round, gray-haired women. When they were younger, their houses were interchangeable, their children tracking dirt and laughter through their living rooms. This was before Ms. Zelma lost each of her three children, the oldest to medicine in Toronto, the middle child to a controlling husband in England, the youngest to a singing career in New York that deepened the worry lines in her forehead. For Hyacinth the surprise was not that Avril had chosen to end her own life, but that she and Zelma had thrived for so long in a world that was at best indifferent to their survival. A part of Hyacinth wondered at Avril's pluck in excusing herself from a game she was never meant to win.

Hyacinth would have sat there for another hour, talking around the thing that needed to be done and watching her tea cool, if she hadn't remembered that she'd left a pig tail boiling down on the stove. She pushed herself out of her chair, and made her way to the door. On Ms. Zelma's back porch, she watched the sun where it was bright and high in the sky as ever. Hyacinth looked at the same sun she'd seen rise and set for sixty-three years and counting, and she felt betrayed. It seemed unfair that it shone no less brilliantly even though inside her a maelstrom raged. She could see smoke rising up from the abandoned house across the way, foul clouds billowing through the places where its windows were meant to be. Since no one lived there, it had been turned into a dump for

Bird Hill, where Mr. Jeremiah put himself in charge of burning trash. Hyacinth inhaled the horrible stench of rubbish on fire, and the smoke burned her eyes, and she told herself that that was why she was crying.

She knew that she'd never be able to smell trash burn again without thinking about Avril and what the man on the phone had told her. He said that it had happened on the subway, that her child had jumped in front of a train, that there was nothing they could do once she'd been found. It was so hard to make sense of all of it, not just her daughter killing herself. Although she'd been hearing about the subway for years, Hyacinth couldn't really imagine a train underground, and the thought of her daughter dying in a place her mind couldn't even draw a picture of hurt her keenly. And how was it possible that it'd taken so long for the news to reach her? Avril's body had been in the morgue for ten whole days before someone had found her address, and then her apartment, and then Hyacinth's phone number. She couldn't imagine anyone dying in Bird Hill so thoroughly alone.

The faces of Hyacinth's dead passed before her, and she remembered each of them, first her grandmother, then her mother, then her husband, and now, Avril. She couldn't really piece together the puzzle of Avril's face, as the pictures she'd sent from the States didn't look like her. She preferred to remember Avril as she was when she first left Barbados twenty years before, eyes shiny and full of hope for her life in New York. More so than even Avril's dying, which was bad enough, was the fact that she'd not been home in so long that there were no recent memories Hyacinth could call upon—no hugs or trips or long afternoons spent in the kitchen or the garden—so little to take the edge off her absence.

Hyacinth would have stayed with her grief for a moment longer, which was really an accretion of loss, first of the family she was born into and then of the family she made. But it was too painful. She moved on quickly to blame. She was to blame, yes, for not being able to heal her child, for not heeding her suspicion that Avril wasn't OK no matter how much she claimed she was, for letting her fear of traveling overseas overcome her good sense. And then there was her husband, Avril's father, who had tried to meet Avril's fragility with his own hardness, claiming that what she needed was a thick skin, when nothing could be further from the truth or from his daughter's reach. And then there was Errol. And the girls. The more Hyacinth thought about it, the more she became convinced that Avril, with her constitution as bright and brittle as it was, didn't stand a chance against the life she'd made for herself so far away from home.

When Hyacinth tired of the sadness and the confusion and the blame swirling in her head, she settled on the question at hand. What to tell the children? Hyacinth steeled her shoulders the way she did before any difficult thing, and then crossed back through the rosebushes toward home.

ONCE PHAEDRA PUT her mind to something, there was little that could get in the way of the bullheadedness that was her birthright. The summer before this one, when Avril was in an incredibly good mood, she'd started talking fast about half birthdays and how they should celebrate Phaedra's, which, since she was born on New Year's Eve, would be June 30th. Phaedra still remembered the catastrophe of that half birthday, and so she knew better than to court disaster by planning a half-birthday celebration for herself in Bird Hill. She appreciated her friendships with Chris and Donna, but she knew that three kids weren't really enough to make a party. Phaedra was chastened by the memory of her, Dionne, and Avril's attempt at celebrating her half birthday the summer before, and so had settled on a Bird Hill half Christmas instead.

The summer before, Avril had barely started making Phaedra's half-birthday cake when she broke down in tears and Phaedra and Dionne had to help her to the pullout sofa bed in the living room. Dionne finished the cake, following the instructions on the back of the box to a T.

The yellow cake turned out well. It was spongy and moist, and bore some resemblance to the confection on the blue box. But the morning after the cake was made, Phaedra and Dionne woke to find that Avril had disappeared, leaving no note behind and no clue to where she had gone. Phaedra and Dionne ate cake for breakfast, lunch, and dinner for three days, each of them striving to turn their meals into a joke that was funnier than the empty refrigerator. "I'd quite like some cake" and "This cake is quite smashing, isn't it, darling," they said in accents they thought were posh, borrowed from

Friday-night viewings of *EastEnders* with their mother. Avril complained bitterly that they were so far behind on the soap opera compared to what people were watching in England, but Phaedra and Dionne loved to practice their accents and watch their mother yell at the television, as if these strange British people with bad teeth could hear her. Summer, with its extended rounds of playing double Dutch and riding bikes and roller-skating up and down their block, had turned the days into an extended play party. Hunger could be a game too.

On the fourth morning, Phaedra and Dionne eyed each other across the kitchen table with the last slice of cake between them. Dionne said, "Fuck this," and then, "You can have it, P.," because she could hear her sister's belly rumbling. Dionne went on a mission to pick through the places where her mother might have dropped money, knowing full well that she'd cased those spots before and come up empty. Still, she made a show of it for Phaedra, digging around the indents her mother's body had made in the sofa bed's lumpy frame, rifling through the kitchen drawers, shaking an empty piggy bank. Finally, Dionne put on her sneakers, through which anyone with eyes could see her toes pressing. "Be right back," she said.

By dark, Dionne was home as she promised, smelling of cheap menthols and the bar around the corner where her boyfriend, Darren, worked, Liquid Love. Dionne smiled, a smile Phaedra knew meant that she and her sister were picking up their game where they'd left it. She watched as Dionne pulled groceries from her book bag: bread and milk and peanut butter and grape jelly, Steak-umms and a head of broccoli and chicken breasts that looked like permanent residents of the bodega's freezer section. For Dionne, a cherry pie. For Phaedra, yellow cupcakes crisscrossed with white icing. Ten packs of Now and Laters for them both, which Dionne pulled from the hidden pocket of her backpack like a magic trick. Phaedra was grateful to Dionne for taking care of her, but she knew how her corniness ruined things, so she resisted the urge she had to throw her arms around Dionne's neck. Instead, Phaedra rifled through the kitchen drawer for candles to top her cupcakes. Before she blew out the flames, she made a wish for Avril to get well. Phaedra was glad that birthday wishes were secret, because she knew Dionne would have said her wish was a waste.

Instead of reprising her half birthday, on Bird Hill, Phaedra became obsessed with the idea of half Christmas, insisting that they celebrate now since they wouldn't get to spend the holidays with Hyacinth. For weeks, she'd been pestering Hyacinth about half Christmas, and even though Hyacinth pretended to be bothered by Phaedra, in truth, she was already sad that they would be leaving. And it was for this reason, and because it was hard to refuse Phaedra anything, that there was a black cake soaking in rum in the pantry and salt pork boiling down on the stove for Hyacinth's special Christmas jug-jug on the day when Hyacinth got the call about Avril.

Hyacinth came home and found Phaedra where she'd left her, sitting cross-legged on the floor, stringing colored popcorn onto thread. Hyacinth knew that Phaedra was serious about this half-Christmas thing when she sacrificed her weekly ration of sickly sweet popcorn for decorations. From the kitchen, she could see the intense concentration on Phaedra's face and Dionne with her legs curled beneath her on the sofa, reading a magazine. She turned down the water on the pot and made her way into the living room.

"Well, darlings, it looks like wunna going to spend half Christmas and Christmas with me too," Hyacinth said.

Dionne saw the ball Hyacinth was making with her skirt and fist, and she knew that something was wrong, because her grandmother was never anything but deliberate in her movements. She looked up from her magazine and narrowed her eyes. "Sorry?" Dionne clutched the smooth ebony arm of the sofa her grandfather had made, and waited for the blow.

"Really, Gran?" Phaedra asked, not looking up from her project. A stray pink kernel slipped from her hand, and she reached out for it and put it in her mouth.

"Phaedra Ann Braithwaite, that is disgusting. I bet you would eat that even if it fell into the toilet," Dionne said.

"Would not!"

"Would too!"

"Stop it!" Hyacinth said, and then immediately wished she hadn't. The girls didn't know it yet, but they would need extra helpings of tenderness for what lay ahead of them. Like so much else, Hyacinth didn't know where she would find extra from to give them.

"I have something important to tell you," she continued.

"Either you're sick or Mommy's dead. Which one is it?"

Dionne said, throwing her shoulders back. She thought, wrongly, that Hyacinth's news would land more softly if she braced herself for it.

"Your mother killed herself."

"Good for her. It was a waste anyway," Dionne said. Her voice was hard, but Phaedra and Hyacinth could both hear the pain dammed behind her bravado.

"What was a waste?" Hyacinth said.

"Her life."

"How could you say that, Dionne?"

"I'm just saying what you're thinking. She stopped living a long time ago. I'm glad she finally had the good sense to let go."

Hyacinth put her right hand up in front of her, as if it could stop the flow of Dionne's invective.

"So, how'd she do it?" Dionne said. Her eyes were cold, both feet planted on the floor. Someone looking at her might have mistaken her for an animal ready to pounce on its prey.

"Dionne, I don't think we should talk about this in front of your sister."

"How'd she do it? Just tell us. You and I both know that in five minutes every one of these silly people will be talking about it."

"I want to know too," Phaedra added from her spot on the floor. It was the first thing she could say. Tears were streaming down her cheeks and her chest was starting to heave with the "ugly cry" Dionne teased her about.

"The train," Hyacinth said.

"The train?" Phaedra asked.

"Classic. Mommy always was one for the spotlight," Dionne said. She pushed on her shoes and walked out of the house with her head tie still on, no direction in mind besides away. She left the door wide open behind her, so that the full measure of their grief, and of her anger, was on display.

WHEN THE NEWS of Avril's death first spread, it was at the top of everyone's minds and on all the hill women's lips. The women held their children and grandchildren closer to them and asked, "Can you imagine?" because they couldn't imagine it, not how Avril had lived her life, nor how she had ended it. Some of them said that because of the way she had died, by right, there shouldn't be the nine-night vigil that was always held when someone from the hill passed away. But Hyacinth had never been one to live her life by right. It was she who had single-handedly led a successful campaign to stop the practice of Saturday baptisms for the children who had no fathers to sign their birth certificates. Hyacinth gave her rousing Sunday-morning testimony from the seventh pew of Bird Hill Church of God in Christ where she sat every week, speaking plainly the truth everyone knew—Easter Sunday had seen only one child baptized, while the day before, mothers had lined up at the back of the church with their children like there was a carnival ride on offer. Father Loving's father, whom the hill women called Big Loving to distinguish him from his son of the same name, tried to stop Hyacinth, saying that the sanctity of marriage had to be upheld. But Hyacinth only had to mention her deliveries of his two outside children, no less than two months apart the year before, and that was enough to settle the matter of his challenge. The next month, on Baptism Sunday, all the newborn children, fatherless and not, were dipped in holy water before the congregation.

Given her history, Hyacinth wasn't much for "should." She would accept nothing less than the nine-night vigil and the grave-digging ceremony that marked the end of it to send her child to her final rest. What she'd said exactly was that wherever a few are gathered in the presence of the Lord there He is also, which was her way of saying that she was planning to keep vigil whether anyone joined her or not. The force of Hyacinth's conviction could fell the walls of Jericho. And so, while Avril's body stayed on ice at the funeral home in town, Mr. Jeremiah opened up the church hall for the vigil and left it open so people could come and go as the spirit moved them. And the hill women, even those who had grumbled about *by right* and *mortal sin,* even the ones who had already started churning the details of Avril's death in their mouths, crafting cautionary tales for their own daughters and spreading the news of her passing from the hill to their relations in Toronto and London and New York, those women showed up.

The first night of the vigil, a cool breeze blew off the sea. Hyacinth dug inside the trunk beneath her bed for a sweater Avril had brought her from her first trip to England, the trip that she'd returned from looking down at everything and everybody on the hill, the moment that Hyacinth would mark when Avril first started her steady journey away from her. Hyacinth pulled on the white sweater with red snowflakes embroidered on its back and went outside, the musty scent of mothballs clinging to her. On the road she could see old women not unlike herself, each moving slowly and steadily, with their Bibles and hymnbooks held firmly in their hands or secreted away in their purses. There was her neighbor Ms. Zelma closing her front gate and turning on her porch light. She noticed Mrs. Loving shuffling toward her as if she were one of the older women and not Avril's age.

"Evening," Hyacinth said.

"Evening," Mrs. Loving replied. She slipped her arm through the crook of Hyacinth's right elbow and they started to walk together. "Ms. B., I don't really know how you making out. They say there's nothing worse than burying your own child."

"God doesn't give any one of us any more than we can bear."

"I know that is true. Doesn't mean that your back won't bend from the pressure."

"Mmm," Hyacinth said. She had never spent much time contemplating what might break her, and didn't intend to start now. "Tell me something. When was the last time you heard from her?"

Mrs. Loving fluttered her hand to her temples as if the answer were there. "Must be Easter now that I think about it, you know. It was Easter, because she sent me two cards, one for Easter and one for my birthday. She always said that I shouldn't let a little holiday steal my thunder."

Hyacinth laughed at that, a tinkle that started in her throat. The kind of laughter that came from her belly deserted her after Avril's passing. "She was always like that, ain't?"

"Always wanted to be on the right side of right."

"I wonder where she got that from," Mrs. Loving said.

Hyacinth batted away Mrs. Loving with her free hand. She had never been one to go in for compliments.

Even from the front steps, Hyacinth could smell the coffee brewing in the back of the church hall. She already knew what she would find when she went inside, a table laid out with Styrofoam cups, packets of Wibisco crackers and New Zealand cheddar cheese that would have sweated the saran wrap on a hotter night. If it weren't for the wooden cross draped in black cloth and the blown-up picture of Avril from her high school graduation on the raised platform, Hyacinth might have been able to pretend that it was just another after-service repast. She let Mrs. Loving go in first, then took a deep breath and walked to her seat in the circle of brown folding chairs.

Hyacinth looked up at the picture of Avril standing next to a hibiscus tree holding one of its flowers, her hair feathered around her face and shoulders, none of the fat that would become her second skin in the States yet on her. Hyacinth recognized the look on her daughter's face as joy, and remembered that she never saw that look on her face again after she met Errol. To other people, the way Avril was in her initial courtship with Errol was joyful, but what Hyacinth saw in Errol was not an ambassador of happiness, but someone who would take her daughter as far as possible away from home and everyone who loved her. As for the nice person everyone saw in Errol, Hyacinth knew, because her mother had told her and she had come to find it out for herself, every skin teeth ain't a laugh.

When Avril's body first arrived, Hyacinth didn't believe that her child was really inside the coffin. She asked Mr. Jeremiah, who picked the body up at the airport, to check and make sure it was Avril. He found the dog-shaped birthmark on the inside of Avril's left wrist that Hyacinth told him to look for and came to her house afterward with his face ashen, balling his baseball cap in his fist. The look on Mr. Jeremiah's face told Hyacinth that she didn't want to see the body for herself.

The first of the nine nights, it was Mrs. Jeremiah who started them singing. All the women who had gathered, eight in total, had their hymnals with them, and the books weren't exactly for show, but these were older women, women who had buried fathers, mothers, cousins, husbands, brothers, and sisters, women who had all the songs they needed in their hearts. It was a question not of what they would sing but in what order, at what tempo, a question of how many choruses and with what feeling. Mrs. Jeremiah opened her mouth and her nasal soprano took the first verse of the first song.

Soon and very soon, we are going to see the king
Soon and very soon, we are going to see the king
Soon and very soon, we are going to see the king
Hallelujah, Hallelujah, we are going to see the king

The women joined in, a fiery bellowing of low notes, their altos and Ms. Zelma's tenor filling the church hall so that soon it was packed to its rafters with sound. Mrs. Jeremiah started clapping and the other women joined in and then there was only song and the sounds of their hands moving. Some of the sorrow that had sunk into the room began to lift, to ride the women's voices. After they'd gone at the hymn hard and then soft, the white candles flickering at each end of Avril's picture and the evening dropping down into night, they were together, bonded by lyric and melody. When Mrs. Jeremiah felt the air begin to settle, she slowed down the hallelujahs and brought them to a close. The women sat together in the buzzing quiet, some whispering "Amen" and other sounds of assent, some dabbing their brows and necks, all retreating into the private place where their own dead were with them.

And then, Mrs. Jeremiah spoke.

"We are gathered together this night and for the ones to come to send home the spirit of our sister Hyacinth's daughter, Avril. We call upon our most high God now and ask Him to wash His faithful servant Avril in the blood of our Lord and Savior Jesus Christ. We rebuke every evil thing that stomped out her spirit in life and any evil thing that might want to trap her spirit here now. We call upon and claim this space as her final resting place. We say to our sister Avril that your workday is done and it's time now to go be with your Father in heaven. And to Hyacinth we say with heavy hearts that your tears are our tears, your sorrows are our sorrows, your fears our fears. We know as well as you do that joy comes in the morning, but that the nights can be long and hard. We will watch these nights with you."

Hyacinth looked up at Mrs. Jeremiah, at her black dress that hung loose at her knees, and the long chain for spectacles that hung from her neck. It was strange to hear the words she'd spoken to other grieving women now spoken to her. She looked at the picture of Avril again and the song that was on her heart came out of her.

When peace like a river descendeth my way
When sorrows like sea billows roll
Whatever my lot, thou has taught me to say

The hill women's chorus swelled as they sang, "It is well / It is well / With my soul."

And then Hyacinth heard a smaller voice behind her, and felt a tap on her right shoulder. She turned around to see Phaedra. She didn't shoo her home or ask what had happened to Dionne, whom she'd left at home in charge of things. She tried to draw Phaedra onto her lap, but she was too big for that. Phaedra wriggled off and settled into the empty chair beside Hyacinth. She closed her eyes and slipped into the heave and flow of the women's song. By right, children shouldn't be at a nine-night. But there was no one brave or silly enough to try to stop Hyacinth or anyone who belonged to her from doing what they were determined to do.

Phaedra felt the next song begin inside her chest. Since her mother died, melodies haunted her at odd times of the day. When she was brushing her teeth or washing the dishes, dusting the coffee table. The hardest part of losing her mother was that there were minutes and hours and almost whole days that would go by when Phaedra would forget that Avril was dead. And then she would remember. At these moments, there was the fact of her mother's irreversible absence and then also the music that her mother loved. Avril was never religious, but she loved to sing and her voice when it soared gave her flight above her pain.

"Jesus loves the little children," Phaedra started in a tiny voice that hardly passed her lips. When joined by Hyacinth and the other women, Phaedra's voice grew wings.

"Jesus loves the little children/All the children of the world," they sang, and all wanted so much to believe.

PHAEDRA TURNED HER BACK to Jean and felt his fingers and measuring tape indent her skin. Jean was the darkest shade of chestnut; he had close-cropped hair, a lanky frame with arms that stretched almost to his knees, and thick, plum-colored lips. In another place, outside the hill, he might have been called beautiful, but here he was Buller Man Jean, and the son of his mother, Trixie, and neither allowed space for anything beyond a kind of grudging tolerance. To be the son of a whore, born into sin, was one thing. To be a homosexual, to choose a life of sin, was something else entirely, a way of sloughing off the obligations of common decency and flaunting the shame that was his birthright. The hill, like every place, had its deviants, and like other small places, what it demanded of them was sublimation. Phaedra could feel Jean's sadness behind his tough exterior, and experienced it as a kind of gravitational pull. Phaedra didn't complain about the rough, quick way that Jean calculated the length and width of her. She knew that, like her mother, beneath Jean's sandpaper exterior lay a tender, bruised heart.

Before they left New York, Avril told Dionne and Phaedra to give her love to Jean. Once they were safely out of their mother's earshot, Dionne said that she wasn't giving any love to her mother's faggot friend. But the cost of making fast friends with Jean's cousin Saranne was that Dionne had to see Jean every day when she sought escape from the heat and Hyacinth's rule in Trixie's air-conditioned shop. Over time, Dionne's initial iciness toward Jean, who she thought was eccentric in a way that reminded her of Avril, thawed. Dionne still believed that Jean's problem, and Avril's too, was that they held too tightly to their status as outsiders, which Dionne couldn't understand, given how much she wanted a normal family, a normal life, and how little their being different had profited them.

Dionne and Saranne were usually the only people in the shop where Trixie sold detergent and other sundries; the hill women only patronized her when either rain or desperation forced them to produce something for her besides scorn, and even then they would make only the barest of greetings and point to the things they wanted with their mouths. Phaedra, on the other hand, visited Jean often, finding pleasure in his easy way, a respite from the demand for good behavior and idle chatter that she found everywhere else on the hill. While Jean took her measurements, Phaedra admired the bolts of fabric that lined the walls of Jean's sewing studio, which was really just his bedroom, off to the side of his mother's shop. Since Avril had died, Hyacinth's house pulsed with reminders of her—her school pictures, the clothes Dionne unearthed from her closet and hung all over her room in a kind of tribute, the rocking chair where Phaedra liked to read and into which Avril had carved her initials, in every new crease and crag in her grandmother's face. It was a relief to be somewhere with bright things, things that were not Avril's. She pointed to the fabric that she liked, yellow cotton with red hibiscus stamped on it.

"That's what I want," Phaedra said.

"That kind of thing don't wear to funeral," Jean replied.

"Why not?"

"People wear black or white or purple. You have to respect the dead."

"But Mommy's favorite flower is hibiscus."

"That's true. That makes me think. Have you ever seen pictures of your mother from when she was younger?"

"Only a few."

Jean took the needle that was parked in the corner of his mouth and stuck it on a pincushion. He reached under his neatly made bed, which became a seating area for clients during their fittings, and then opened a red faux-leather photo album over his knees.

"You went to New York?" Phaedra asked. As the summer

wore on, Phaedra had started to divide people into categories according to who had seen her city and so could understand her, and people who had not. She was surprised that Jean made it onto her short list of the highly favored. She looked at the picture of her mother with Jean's arm wrapped around her waist. To the right, almost outside the frame, a man stood by the railing, closer to the Statue of Liberty than to Jean and Avril.

"Of course I've been to New York. And not just once either," Jean said.

"Who's that?" Phaedra asked, pressing her stubby pointer finger against the Polaroid.

"You don't know your own father, P.?"

Phaedra squinted her eyes and pulled the photo carefully from its plastic cover, toward her face. "That doesn't look like my father."

"The very same."

"No, Daddy has a belly."

"That's right. I forget how wunna does go to America and get fat. I see you slim down since you come." Phaedra felt her cheeks go hot. She remembered the way that her mother would ask her when she was eating which man wanted a fat wife even as, sometimes in the next breath, she would tell Dionne that only a dog wants a bone. All summer, she'd been grateful for the fact that on the hill, body talk was matter of fact, merely descriptive and not some indication of her future, or a symptom of failure. Still, talk of her body and its doings made her blush.

Jean motioned for Phaedra to turn toward him, and began measuring the length from her hip to her knee. She giggled as the cold tape touched her bare skin.

"So did you make a lot of friends this summer?" Jean asked.

"Is two a lot?" Phaedra said.

Jean smiled. "Your mother was the same way. It's funny, because people always wanted to be her friend, but Avril said she didn't need any crowd of people following behind her."

"But you were one of her friends, right?" Phaedra said. She wanted to change the image forming in her mind of her mother as a lonely girl. All summer, she'd wondered who her mother talked to in Brooklyn since she and Dionne and her father were gone, and she didn't have many friends to begin with. Phaedra wondered who would keep her mother company now that she was dead. Death seemed like another friendless place, even more lonesome than the life Avril left behind.

"Oh yes. And I've never met a better friend before or since."

"What made her a good friend?"

"Well, some people will tell you having a good friend is about having someone to go to parties with, or someone to go shopping with, a liming partner basically. But a real friend only has to do two things. The first is to listen to you. And the second is to claim you."

"Claim you?"

"Did your mother ever tell you about sleepaway camp?" Jean asked. He pushed aside the pincushion and measuring tape, and then he patted the bed next to him for Phaedra to sit down. She hesitated, because Hyacinth always told her that she shouldn't sit on people's beds, especially not a man's. But Jean was different. He invited her again and she eased onto the edge of the comforter.

"So did she tell you about how they used to call her a buller man's wife?"

"Yeah," Phaedra said, recalling her mother's famous stories about sleepaway camp. She didn't want to let on that she didn't understand exactly what being a buller man's wife meant.

"Well, I don't know if your mother told you that she took on those girls who used to taunt her, all six of them at once."

"She said she fought them, but she never said how."

"Well, your mother was on mess hall duty one morning. On her way to the canteen, she gathered all these red ants into an old t-shirt. And when the cook's back was turned, she poured them into the mean girls' cereal bowls."

"Didn't she get in trouble?"

"Your mother hated that camp so much, the best thing she could imagine happening was being sent home early, except she didn't want to leave me there by myself."

"Wow, I wish I was as brave as she was," Phaedra said.

"Sure as you stand here before me, I know that if Avril spit you out, you have more than enough courage to go around. I'm more afraid for whoever finally makes you use it."

"I want you to make me look like my mother does in this picture," Phaedra said, bringing them back to the photo Jean had shown her of Avril.

Jean looked down at the photograph in Phaedra's hand, at the goldenrod jersey dress that Avril loved, and that he'd made for her himself. Then, he went over to the bolts of fabric and picked out one of the black cotton ones.

"So, little miss. Here's what we're going to do. I'll sew some hibiscus on this fabric for you."

"Can you make the flowers red?"

"I can make them purple or white."

"Purple."

"Deal," Jean said. He checked his notebook to be sure that he had everything he needed, and then he bade Phaedra goodbye. And although her original destination was her grandmother's house, on her walk home, something made her turn in at the Lovings' gate to find Chris.

Mrs. Loving sat on her gallery with a cassette player on a shaky card table beside her, wailers songs streaming out beneath the huge cross that dwarfed the Lovings' front door. Mrs. Loving gestured for Phaedra to come, and she did. Phaedra was grateful for the fact that Mrs. Loving looked at her with the same far-off stare she'd had before her mother's death. Phaedra found her persistent melancholy comforting, in contrast to the newfound pity that poured out of the other hill women's mouths and onto her head like hot coals. Just that morning Phaedra had looked in the mirror and wondered if people could tell just by looking at her that her mother was dead. There was mercy in Mrs. Loving's cloud of private pain that never lifted enough for her to see the people around her clearly.

"I know just the person you're looking for, but the boys are gone to see their grandmother in St. Philip," Mrs. Loving said.

She reached to turn the cassette player's volume down. Phaedra nodded, disappointed. "Why don't you sit for a bit? I wouldn't mind the company and your face is so long it looks like you could use some too."

Phaedra relaxed into one of the chair's soft cushions. The way that her bottom sank into the seat reminded her that the chairs on her grandmother's gallery were castoffs from when the church had upgraded its hall. She sat up straight again.

"When I was your age, my mother died too. Everybody was walking around talking about what happened for weeks, about the way she waded into one of the rough beaches on the east coast, and never turned back. Me and my brother were on the beach, and I was pushing the last fist of sand below his chin when it happened, burying him. I turned around and there was just the top of her hair floating above the water, that same pretty hair she brushed every night and sometimes let me brush for her. After her head disappeared under the water, I stayed stuck like that, not talking until my brother saw me frozen and got up to see what happened. Afterwards, everybody said it was my fault for not saying something, that somebody might have fished her out if I acted quicker, but the truth was that she wanted to die, and she would have, if not that day, then another. I didn't talk for a whole year after that happened. And when I did, the big voice I used to sing with on the junior choir was gone."

These were the most words that anyone had spoken to Phaedra since her mother died, not cooing or talking over her head to her grandmother or to Dionne, but addressed directly to her. News of Phaedra's singing to herself had gotten around the hill, starting with Hyacinth's whispers to Ms. Zelma that what worried her more than anything was that Phaedra had taken to dragging hymns through her throat until they were extended dirges, woeful things that cast another layer of pallor over the house. In the hill women's mouths, the tip of Phaedra's hand toward madness was another indictment of Avril. "Look how the child walking about here like she one step away from the mental. Just mind she don't come in like her mother," they clucked. Phaedra was lucky enough to be spared these pronouncements because when the hill women saw her, all they would say was "cuhdear" and ask after her granny and offer their best. But sometimes, in the thick of the songs that settled around her, even Phaedra wondered if what was wrong with her mother was not also wrong with her.

In the beginning, when Avril first took to her bed, Phaedra was always within a few feet of her mother, sensing that her presence, even if unacknowledged, was a kind of balm. Phaedra would sleep curled up at the foot of her mother's sofa bed, stand behind her, oiling and brushing her scalp, keep her cups of tea fresh, milky, and lukewarm. But over time, as the thing that got ahold of Avril dug deeper and deeper into her, Phaedra retreated into her books and solitude, angling her body away in the rare moments when Avril remembered her children and gave them awkward, short-lived bouts of attention. It didn't help when the girls from her school, who never liked her, found new ammunition for their taunts, saying that Phaedra's mother was crazy, and that crazy was catching, and if everybody knew what was best for them, they would stay as far away as possible from Phaedra. Phaedra thought about lashing out; in her mind, she dragged the ringleader by her pigtails down the glass-strewn concrete steps in the school yard. But she knew that would only make their lies seem true, and so she'd stewed by herself, counting down until the last day of school. Now, with the full extent of her mother's madness proven by her suicide, it was hard for Phaedra not to wonder whether she'd inherited Avril's madness. Maybe, if she was lucky, Phaedra thought, Avril had passed down a portion of her bravery too.

Phaedra relaxed as Mrs. Loving's reggae music took over the dreadful hymn that had been her company that day, "Rock of Ages." She let Mrs. Loving's story wash over her. And then she spoke, her tongue molasses thick, but moving.

"You knew her?"

"Knew who, sweetheart?"

"My mother."

"Of course I knew your mother. Impossible to live here and not know her. When I came here with my husband, she was the first friend I made. And when she moved to New York, I was inconsolable. I still remember when Dionne and Trevor were born, we used to walk them all over the place. You sister could cry from the time she woke up in the morning until she went to bed at nighttime, and the only thing to help was to keep her moving."

Phaedra tried to reconcile what she knew of her mother and her sister and Mrs. Loving's son Trevor with who they had been back then. It was easy to imagine movement comforting her sister, because even now, Dionne seemed most happy when she wasn't still.

"When we were pregnant, we did everything together. We said that if we had a boy and a girl, they would marry one day. Nobody could tear us apart from one another, you know. When Avril came to tell me she was leaving, I put on one piece of crying and carrying on. I didn't think I could make it in this place without her. And in a way, I didn't." Mrs. Loving gathered her dress between her thighs and turned the volume up on her cassette player in a way that indicated to Phaedra that their conversation was over.

Phaedra started to walk away, hearing this song and carrying away some part of Mrs. Loving's sorrow: "This train is bound to glory / This train don't carry no unholy . . ."

But some part of Phaedra was unhinged by Mrs. Loving's stories. When she reached the last step of the gallery, she turned back.

"Mrs. Loving, have you ever thought about what would happen if someone you loved also loved someone else?"

"Oh, darling. Aren't you a little young to be worrying your head with that sort of thing? I know that you're all that Christopher talks about." Mrs. Loving said these words wistfully, as if she wished she could borrow some of the shine her son reserved for Phaedra.

Phaedra trembled with what was beating its way from her belly and up out of her throat. Ever since she'd helped her grandmother deliver Donna's mother's baby boy, she couldn't get the image of Father Loving and his lit cigarette burning up the darkness out of her head. "You don't wonder where Father Loving goes at nighttime?"

"Dear heart," Mrs. Loving said, looking down to the valley below and the sea beyond it, "when night comes, I have my music and my boys and that is enough."

A new song was on now, with different words, but the same guitar strains and drumroll. Mrs. Loving turned up the music and started humming along in a mournful tone that swept Phaedra off the veranda and onto the road.

FOR ALL OF DIONNE'S ROMPS inside the Bird Hill cemetery that summer, when the day of her mother's funeral came, all the resources previously at her disposal—humor, indifference, denial—abandoned her, and there was no place to escape from her mother's body and the people who had gathered to see her home. Trevor stood across from her with his face so filled with mourning you would have thought it was his own mother being buried and not Avril. As the minutes stretched with Father Loving's prayers and the hill women's graveside songs, Trevor tried to catch Dionne's eye. She glanced at him briefly and noticed for the first time the way that his hairline peaked in the center of his forehead like his father and his younger brother; the intensity of their resemblance mocked her grief. For years, Dionne had looked to her mother for clues as to what she would look like when she got older. It was hard to imagine what kind of woman she would be without the road map of her mother's body to guide her. Dionne denied Trevor the gift of her gaze.

It wasn't until she saw the coffin being lowered into the ground that the fact that her mother was not coming back, not in some undefined "soon" as Avril pointed to in her letters, not next week or the week after, not when summer was over, not before school in the States started, not ever, became clear to Dionne. Dionne's eyes had been dry since her mother died and where she'd expected to cry at the graveside, she felt instead an insistent fire at her heels and then an urge stronger than any she'd ever felt before to see her mother's face. All the anger at her mother that Dionne had been holding back her whole life rushed to her throat and threatened to choke her. This last leaving was too much. Dionne thought that if she could just see Avril's face, she'd be able to tell her that she couldn't leave, not yet.

Dionne lunged from where she stood with her arms around Phaedra, her sister's tears traveling between the black lace eyelets of Dionne's dress and pressing against her skin. She strode toward the grave's open mouth. And the hill women, the same ushers she'd seen wave fans at the brows of enraptured women, hold down grown men as they spoke the unintelligible, terrible words that God threw down on them like lightning, they came for her. She'd never known these strong arms herself. But now Mrs. Jeremiah's sinewy forearms wrapped around her midsection and pulled her back. Mrs. Gumbs's bosom and belly engulfed her. The women said things she couldn't understand, things she knew were meant to calm her and keep her safe inside their embrace. And then, she wasn't sure how, exactly, Dionne was beside her grandmother and her sister, at the edge of her mother's grave. And before she knew what her body was doing, her feet were making contact with the wreath of lilies on Avril's coffin. There was a gasp as the hill women watched a group of men, including Trevor, drag Dionne up and out of the grave.

The men pulled her to solid ground, and then Dionne felt the women's fearsome power gather around her, but she wasn't fighting anymore. She fell back into them, wishing they could take her anger from her, because it was heavy, what she felt, her rage at Avril for abandoning them in this godforsaken place with a grandmother they barely knew. It seemed unfair that Avril should have it so easy, that she could die and leave them behind just like that. Dionne fell back into the stalwart arms of the hill women who held her. And it was either Dionne's feet or theirs that led her back to Hyacinth's house for the wake.

When the last mourners had taken their plates of wrapped food and said their good-byes, once Phaedra was asleep, it was just Hyacinth and Dionne sitting in the front room, leaning together into the night, which felt darker now because it lacked the comfort of the other hill women's company. Hyacinth asked Dionne what on earth had come over her to make her want to climb on top of Avril's coffin. And Dionne, of whom Hyacinth would say after this conversation that she was her mother's own child, said, "What I did was nothing worse than what my mother's done to me. If I had been able to see her even once before she died, I would have told her that she shouldn't get off that easy." Hyacinth looked at this child, at her flinty eyes, and saw how much she believed that she was not only right, but also justified. And she knew that this was the thing that would harm Dionne in the end, not her foolishness but the foolhardy way in which she clung to her own terrible ideas. She knew that this was Avril's undoing, not that she'd made the wrong choices, but that she'd been so unwilling to let anyone in to see the lie of her marriage; this masking was worse than the original mistake. Sixty-three years on this earth had taught Hyacinth that it wasn't so much the mistakes that people made but how flexible they were in their aftermath that made all the difference in how their lives turned out. It was the women who held too tightly to the dream of their husband's fidelity who unraveled, the parents who clasped their children too close who lost them, the men who grieved too deeply the lives they'd wanted and would never have who saw their sadness consume them. Hyacinth worried about Dionne because of her hard way of being in the world, the way she could only see the world through the lens of her own flawed feelings.

FOR THE ENTIRE NINE NIGHTS that the hill mourned Avril, Phaedra and Dionne and Hyacinth were together almost every minute of every day. The girls and their grandmother formed a web between them that they wanted to believe was indestructible. They ate food their neighbors cooked for them and wiled the days away in prayer. On the last night, they took long soaks beneath moonlight in baths filled with bark and berries. They tried to build a new alliance with stories about Avril. Hyacinth, who was known less for her stories than for her carefully chosen words that awed with their precision, dug back into her vault of memories from the time when she herself was young and a mother, trying to reconcile what she thought motherhood might be with the reality of her sweet, impulsive child.

Phaedra and Dionne listened as Hyacinth told them about

the time their mother had driven with the church all the way out to Folkestone for the church picnic, singing hymns and shaking tambourines the whole way. After everyone had had their fill of food, Avril and Mrs. Loving rushed out in the cold water and did headstands on the seafloor, their gangly limbs kicking up above the water, and the skirts of their dresses falling down around their necks so that all the church people could see their puffy bloomers and their legs waving above them. Hyacinth had barely recovered from the embarrassment of that incident when Avril brought home Errol. He said he was a musician, and Hyacinth knew that meant he was definitely a layabout and possibly a criminal. Dionne perked up when she heard her father's name and she asked Hyacinth what he looked like when she met him.

"Well, when your mother dragged that young man in here, I could see from the way she looked at him like he was a bowl of milk and she was the hungriest cat that nothing good would come of them. I wondered to myself what would dead them first, his dreaming or her faith in him. He was wearing a cream linen suit and he had pretty pretty pretty hazel eyes and red-red skin. But I could see it was his mouth, the same mouth you have, that your mother fell in love with."

The girls went to sleep that night with this image of their father in their minds. The next morning, Phaedra woke up upset. After her mother died, Phaedra couldn't remember her dreams. Regardless of what the dreams were about, they left their mark on her and it was not unusual for Phaedra to wake up shaken, her clothes plastered against her skin. She had taken to crawling into Dionne's bed in the early hours of the morning, which she said was because she thought Dionne might be lonely. Now, she clung to Dionne like a life jacket.

"Dress over nuh, man. You squeezing me up too tight." Dionne pried away Phaedra's fingers, which were fastened in a vise grip around her neck. Phaedra wiped the sleep out of her eyes and looked at her sister, who had wrapped her straightened hair into a kind of tornado around her head, and then tied it down with a scarf to keep it fresh, a trick she'd learned from Saranne.

"Daddy's coming to see about us," Dionne said, looking, as she often was, into the mirror next to her bed. She searched her plump, pink lips for signs of her father, but all she could see was Avril.

"What?" Phaedra said. She sat up in Dionne's bed and looked from her sister's beehive to the fuzz of hair above her own two-week-old braids, which her grandmother hadn't insisted on redoing. There was a new softness in Hyacinth since her mother died. Phaedra knew that she got her way more often with her grandmother and the other hill women because of her dead mother. She only hoped this new reprieve from hardness would last.

"What are you talking about?"

"I said Daddy's going to come look for us."

"How do you know that? Who told you?"

"I can just feel it."

"I thought you didn't believe in all that mumbo-jumbo hocus-pocus old-wife-tale business."

"Doesn't matter what I believe in or not. Certain things you just know." Dionne whipped her silk bathrobe around her, yet another thing she'd gotten from Saranne and kept instead of returning it like Hyacinth had told her to. She flicked on the overhead light and Phaedra groaned.

"Besides, do you really think that if Daddy knew Mommy had died, he would just leave us here?" Dionne continued.

"I don't know, Dionne. Maybe he doesn't even know what happened. It has been a long time since we've seen him."

"You just watch. I know that Daddy wouldn't leave us like that."

"OK, D.," Phaedra said. She sat a while longer watching her sister fuss with the lotions and potions on her vanity, and then she started to burrow beneath the covers.

"What are you doing?" Dionne asked.

"Going back to sleep," Phaedra said.

"Last time I checked, you had a bed down the hall."

"Fine, then." Phaedra stalked out of the room, and then came back to retrieve the bandana that had fallen off her head during the night.

More than an hour later, after Phaedra heard her sister slapping her soles on the linoleum tiles on her way back and forth to the bathroom, Dionne emerged in the front room where Phaedra was eating breakfast in front of the television. Dionne was wearing a tight tube top, a denim miniskirt, Keds, and a pair of leg warmers in the same neon pink as her top.

"How do I look?" Dionne asked.

"Very, very done." Phaedra noted the lip gloss and liner her sister was wearing in a shade of gold that made her mouth pop out from her face like a billboard. "You're not going to VBS?"

"Nope. Me and Saranne have plans for the day."

"But today's the last day of rehearsals and you're in one of the plays. How are you going to miss that?"

"Let me worry about that. If Granny comes home before you leave, just tell her I had to go early for rehearsal."

"OK," Phaedra said, unsure that she would lie if the time came.

"Love you," Dionne said on her way out the door.

"Love you back," Phaedra said. Ever since Avril died, they had started saying, "I love you." This time, though, it felt like a bribe.

AFTER AVRIL DIED, Hyacinth ran out of reasons why Phaedra couldn't pierce her ears. Phaedra insisted that she needed it done because she had the VBS play coming up and she wanted to wear earrings. Since she was playing a woman, Martha, in the play, it followed that her look should be a little bit more grown up. Really, what Phaedra wanted was to perm her hair so that she could start school with her hair flouncing down her back. At her old school in Brooklyn, the other girls' mothers had said they could straighten their hair for fifth-grade graduation. But Hyacinth shut Phaedra down early on in the summer, saying that if her hair was to be straightened, that was something her mother should decide. Because Dionne's hair had been relaxed before she came to Barbados, she and Hyacinth sat once a month while Jean creamed their hair, having observed a whole week of not scratching their scalps and carefully combing their hair, a ritual and talk Phaedra wanted to be part of. Phaedra came home buzzing after the second of these visits, when she'd sat in Jean's front room watching television and saw the advertisement for Brother D's, a jewelry store in town: "Barbados Women Should Be in Chains. Brother D's Chains." Before the ad went off, Phaedra noticed that they also did ear piercing. She gathered up courage to talk to Hyacinth during her best time, the late mornings when she had just finished working in her garden, and a sheen coated her face. This was the closest time she ever came to seeing her grandmother happy.

"Granny?"

"Yes, Phaedra."

"When do you think I could pierce my ears?"

"Oh, I don't know, child. Why you in such a rush to bore holes in your ears?"

"It's just that the play is coming up and all the girls are going to be wearing gold earrings."

"If all the girls went down to the careenage and jumped in the water, you would do that too?"

Phaedra shuddered at the thought of the green-gray, murky water against her skin. "No, ma'am. I just thought it would look nice, and be good for my role."

"The Lord ain't studying what you wearing." Hyacinth sat down to take off her gardening boots but was beat there by Phaedra, who squatted in the grass, pulled them off, and started massaging her grandmother's feet in a circular motion that made Hyacinth throw back her head and say, "You know what to do, girl."

"That feels nice, Gran?"

"Better than Christmas."

Hyacinth let her shoulders drop back against the bench her husband made for her when they were still young and in love. Back then the house and her garden were as new to Hyacinth as she and her husband were to each other. He would come home in the afternoons for lunch and they'd make love for so long that he'd have to rush back to his work at the mechanic shop with his belly rumbling and his full lunch tin banging against his shin. He'd made the bench for Hyacinth because he said that she deserved a place where she could relax and admire God's work. She looked at the frangipani tree, whose fragrant flowers blanketed the ground. They were beautiful, but cleaning them up was a job that strained her back now. Hyacinth smiled to herself, knowing that her husband had made this house, this garden, this bench by hand so that she'd have something of him to hold on to when he was gone.

Hyacinth relaxed into Phaedra's touch and let her mind wander. Would Phaedra keep up the house when she was gone? Or would she and Dionne leave, like Avril, the first chance they got? She knew Dionne had a hot foot, but with Phaedra there was hope she'd stay. A couple days before Avril's funeral, Hyacinth showed the girls the safe where she kept her money, her most important papers, and the simple white dress she wanted to wear to her funeral. She'd had to tell Dionne, who stood in the doorway with her fists at her waist and her lips pursed like she was sucking lemons, that if she thought death was something she could catch like a cold, she was more foolish than she'd already shown herself to be. It was Phaedra who sat down next to Hyacinth while she explained that the plot she wanted to be buried in was already paid for and then listed out the hymns she wanted to be sung at the memorial service. Hyacinth pinned her hope on the chance that Phaedra's steadiness might balance out her sister's hot-headedness, that the two of them would take care of each other after she was gone.

Hyacinth looked down at Phaedra kneading her feet. "OK, you little wretch. Don't think I don't see what you're doing. Give me time to go about my business today and then when evening comes, we'll see about you and your ears."

"But Gran, don't the buses stop running into town after dark?"

"What we going in town for?"

"We're not going to Brother D's?"

Phaedra had imagined herself seated on a pink leather stool, careful to keep her elbows off the glass cases, smelling perfume on the lady who would take a gun to her ears while she sat valiantly still, no tears. Maybe her grandmother would let her try on one of those thick gold chains. Despite being a mostly sensible girl, Avril said, and it was true, that Phaedra had flashy taste like her father.

"Oh Lord, please deliver me from these Yankee children."

"What happen, Granny?"

"You got Brother D's money?"

"No, Gran."

"Right, then," Hyacinth said, and pushed on the flip-flops Phaedra placed near her feet.

Evening came and Phaedra finished washing the supper dishes. She listened to the night frogs' song pulsing at the kitchen window and wondered what her grandmother was planning. She went to the front bedroom and saw Hyacinth sitting on the bed, rummaging through her sewing kit.

"You need help finding something?" Phaedra asked.

"I'm looking for a needle. You know Granny's eyes not so good anymore."

"What do you need a needle for? I thought you said you were finished with the whole clothes-mending business."

"You know, Phaedra, for being such a bright girl, sometimes it seems like you don't have too much sense knocking about in that head of yours."

Phaedra was quiet. Over time, she'd come to accept her grandmother's way of serving insults and love together.

"I'm looking for a needle to pierce your ears."

"Is that safe?" Phaedra had a flash of her mother, who she thought would be wary of this operation.

"You think I would do you anything?" Hyacinth asked.

"No, Gran," Phaedra said. But Avril had told her to be careful of Hyacinth, past whom she would put nothing. Phaedra knew that the truth about her grandmother lay somewhere between her mother's occasionally venomous descriptions and the sweet, hard woman she was getting to know. She picked out the best needle she could find, a short silver one that was unthreaded and, as far as she could tell, unused.

In the kitchen, Phaedra pulled the stool where she usually sat shelling peas or husking garlic, or sometimes just watching her grandmother stir the pots. Hyacinth lit the pilot and put the needle to the fire. She handed Phaedra ice cubes from the freezer and draped dish towels over her shoulders to catch the drip. Phaedra caught a glimpse of herself in the picture window, her hands clutching the ice over her extended earlobes.

"You have ears just like your mother," Hyacinth said. When the needle was hot to her liking, she pulled it away from the flame. "Maybe you might be more able to hear with them when I'm talking to you than she was."

Phaedra squeezed her eyes shut and clenched her teeth when she felt the pressure of the needle and then the string pulling through her right ear. But she didn't cry, because she wanted her grandmother to think she was brave.

NO ONE CELEBRATED the last week of Vacation Bible School more than Phaedra Braithwaite. Someone who didn't know Phaedra might have seen the way that she was carrying on—singing more loudly than all the other girls during praise song, playing Martha in the final rehearsals with such gusto—and mistaken her enthusiasm for joy and not the relief of knowing that this particular form of torture would soon end. For while her mother's death meant that she could take an entire week off from VBS, the following Monday she was back. And just as she'd feared, the girls whose disdain had previously spilled over Phaedra like Milo now eyed her with uniform pity. In no time, she'd gone from being the Yankee girl with the long hair to the Yankee girl with the dead mother. As their mothers had instructed them to do, the girls said "So sorry for your loss" and "Sorry to hear about your Mummy." Simone Saveur even invited Phaedra to have lunch with her clique at the tables in the front of the church hall. But once Phaedra knew that she was invited and Donna, the closest thing she had to a girlfriend, was not, she refused. It wasn't so much that she liked Donna, but that she held fast to her role of outsider now. And some part of her wondered about the limits of the new courage she'd earned, the true nature of the swagger that was hers now that she was a motherless child. She heard that song on the radio the Sunday after her mother's body had been flown down and the lyrics stuck in her chest, a tape whose damaged brown plastic she thought might spool out of her mouth one day. There it was, the "sometimes" and "feel" cresting when she wasn't speaking, the doleful tune stuck in her throat where she held it. If she concentrated, the song would take over; an entire day of VBS could be survived on just one extended chorus.

Having rejected the questionable charity of her classmates, Phaedra sat down to eat with Donna. During her friend's awkward monologue about her new baby brother, Phaedra took gulps of watered-down Kool-Aid and bites of the cheese and cracker sandwiches she'd packed onto a napkin, nodding at intervals to show her appreciation of Donna's stories. Phaedra found herself both bored and hungry after she'd finished her lunch. She turned to Donna and tried to redirect the flow of her chatter.

"So, is it true what they say, that you can climb trees?" Phaedra asked.

"Sorry?" Donna looked up from her third cheese sandwich.

"I said, is it true you can climb trees?" Phaedra said, watching Donna work the soft white bread from the roof of her mouth.

Donna's face brightened. "Oh yes. Coconut tree, pawpaw tree, breadfruit tree. Fig tree. Although you can't really climb a fig tree, since the figs grow close to the ground."

"You climb that mango tree outside yet?"

"Which one?"

"The one behind the church."

"Oh, sure. Last year, me and Chris had a contest to see who could pull down the most mangoes."

"Who won?"

"Me, of course."

"Of course." Phaedra smiled because there was something about finally finding the place where Donna shone that delighted her.

Donna stayed quiet for a moment, waiting for the thrill of being directly asked about something she cared about to return.

"Come," Phaedra said. Donna followed Phaedra outside where the girls from their class were taking a break from jumping rope to play in each other's hair on the church hall's back stairs. Angelique, whose hair was wavy and weighed down by the coconut oil her mother brushed into it every night, sat on one of the concrete steps, her ponytail open and her hair spread over the laps of three girls who admired it with their hands. Angelique hadn't spoken more than two words to Phaedra since she had beaten her decisively in the Bible verse memorization championship. Phaedra had won by remembering that the Lord said to Jeremiah, "They will fight against you but will not overcome you, for I am with you and will rescue you." Angelique hemmed and hawed while she tried to remember Psalm 127, verses 3 to 5. Even after Father Loving, who favored Angelique, gave her the word "arrows" as a hint, she still couldn't produce the verse about how children are a heritage of the Lord. Just that morning, when the other girls mumbled their condolences, Angelique just looked at Phaedra and said, "Morning." Phaedra was grateful for the steadiness of Angelique's spite.

Phaedra thought to say excuse me to the girls who were blocking their way out, but instead she jumped off the side of the steps, and Donna hopped down too.

"Pick some mangoes for me, nuh," Phaedra commanded. She shaded her eyes and looked up into the branches of the fruit-heavy tree.

"How many you want?"

"Donna Husbands, I know you are not going to climb that tree with your skirt on." Simone Saveur spoke from where she sat clasping a fistful of Angelique's slicked-down hair.

"I have shorts on underneath," Donna said to the crowd, which was gathering now, as it always did when she climbed.

"You don't have to explain yourself to those dusty girls," Phaedra said.

"How many you want?" Donna asked, sizing up the tree. The ripest ones were also the highest.

"As many as you can get."

"What did you say?" Simone Saveur spat from her seat.

"I said she doesn't have to explain herself to any dusty girls. If she wants to climb a tree, she can climb a tree. Go ahead, Donna."

Simone walked over to where Phaedra stood and planted herself directly in front of her. "Oh, so you think because you come from America, you can call us names? No one cares if your mother was too damn mad to know better than to kill herself. The two of you make a nice pair. The daughter of a whore and the daughter of a madwoman."

A roar started among the children who could hear the fight inside Simone's words.

"I see you have plenty chat when your boyfriend is around, and now your mouth not working so fast," Simone baited.

"Excuse me, Simone," Phaedra said, trying to push her gently aside. But the mountain of Simone Saveur, who had tree trunks for thighs like her five older sisters, would not budge. Their father had left after the last of the girls, twins with the same fierceness as the ones who preceded them, were born. The hill women had offered their condolences to the mother but no one could blame him for seeking somewhere he could be a man.

"What?" Simone spat back.

"I can't see what Donna's doing with you standing there," Phaedra said.

"I'll show you who's dusty now." Simone grabbed a handful of dirt and grass and threw it in Phaedra's face. Phaedra grabbed at the doorknob breasts poking out from Simone's shirt and turned one of them. The girls clutched each other, and then fell to the ground, rolling and trying to land licks. It was hard for the crowd to know whether to look up at Donna scaling the tree, or to look down at Simone and Phaedra rolling around in the dirt. While the girls fought, Donna defied gravity, using the parts of her body that usually jiggled and waddled in service of her task. When she reached the top of the tree, she shook the branches and mangoes rained down, sending the children running away from the tree and toward the church. Simone Saveur was on top of Phaedra landing blows as the crowd cried, "Cuff her" and "Beat her." But then Simone took three mangoes to the head, and fell off Phaedra.

Timothy, of the snot-nosed twins, was raising Phaedra's arm to declare her the winner when Ms. Taylor came outside, summoned out of the staff's lunchtime prayer meeting by the noise. She broke up the crowd and sent both girls home for the rest of the day. Simone left, and Phaedra walked down to the graveyard to spend the rest of the afternoon napping among the headstones. She wanted to sleep near her mother's grave, but the new grass scratched her legs, and she couldn't get comfortable enough to stay there for very long. She settled on her great-aunt's grave instead. When VBS let out for the day, she called out to Donna, who cautiously stepped just to the edge of the cemetery.

"You not going home?" Donna asked.

"Not just yet. You go ahead. I have some things to do here," Phaedra said.

"All right, then. See you." Then Donna turned and said, "I'm sorry about what happened."

"What do you mean? What are you sorry about?" Phaedra said sharply, on guard for any delayed condolences. She had had enough talk about her mother for one day.

"I didn't mean for you to fight for me."

"Oh," Phaedra, said, relieved. "Donna?" Phaedra called after her friend, who she knew was rushing home to relieve her mother. "Thanks, y'hear?"

"Sure."

Phaedra sat under the mango tree in the cemetery until she could feel dusk creep around her shoulders. She gathered the fallen mangoes and started sucking and biting at the fruit, until her tongue turned orange and her stomach gurgled a warning to stop. When she was done, she stretched out beneath the tree. Since her mother's passing, sleep was Phaedra's only refuge where talk and song and memories of her mother could not find her.

She woke up to her nemesis Angelique kneeling above her, shaking her shoulder.

"You don't know mango will run your belly?"

"What?" Phaedra said, wiping the sleep from her eyes with her sticky fingers.

"You sit down here alone and eat off all these mangoes?"

"Why do you want to know?"

Angelique sat down next to Phaedra, and Phaedra felt her wavy hair touch her shoulder. Feeling its softness, Phaedra understood some part of why all the girls wanted to be like her. "Who don't hear will feel. That's what my mother says," Angelique offered, stressing "mother." And then, tugging at Phaedra's grimy t-shirt, "Come." This was the most Angelique would ever say about Avril's passing. She was one of those rare humans who made it her business not to worry about the why or how of the way things were, but to accept them. It was this solid ground of meeting each other squarely, without pity or false knowing, that thawed and then prepared the ground for a friendship between Phaedra and Angelique.

But for now, it was enough for Phaedra to let Angelique help her up and then to walk home, where she knew that the news of her behavior had already reached.

SLEEP TOOK PHAEDRA to its bosom and didn't let go until the small hours of the morning, when she awoke sweating and dizzy. Hyacinth sat on the side of the bed, watching over her.

"Why are you up, Gran?" Phaedra asked once her eyes opened and adjusted to the dark.

"I was waiting to see what going to happen to you."

"What happened?"

"You tell me. You in here smelling like you eat every mango from here to Speightstown. And then I'm hearing that you were rolling around in the ground behind the church like a common so-and-so with one of the Saveur girls."

"What?" Phaedra said again, and then she remembered everything: VBS, the tree, the fight, her naps, and the walk home that felt endless because she knew what was awaiting her on the other end.

"Why do I feel so hot?" Phaedra touched the back of her neck, which was soaked with sweat, and felt the places where her nightie clung to her.

"Tell me something, P. How many mangoes did you eat?"

"I don't know. Maybe twenty. Maybe more."

Hyacinth's eyes widened and she pressed the back of her palm to Phaedra's forehead.

"How do you feel?"

"Bad. Hot."

"Oh, dear heart. Too much of even what you love can hurt you."

"I have to use the bathroom," Phaedra said, and made one of many trips down the hallway. Right before dawn, Phaedra started to cry, not for the pain that seized her belly or because of the chills, but because this was the first time she'd been sick and known that her mother could not comfort her, that she never would again.

"Granny?" she said.

"Yes, dear."

"Could you sing that song Mommy used to sing when I was sick?"

"I don't know which one you're talking about, darling."

"Of course you wouldn't."

Hyacinth decided that it was not the right time to put Phaedra in her place. "Sing a few lines for me and maybe I could pick up the tune."

Phaedra closed her eyes to search her memory. She saw her mother then, moving around the apartment in Brooklyn, trying to make Phaedra comfortable while she wrestled her yearly bout with tonsillitis. She remembered Avril saying that her tonsils were so huge they looked more like extras from Stonehenge than something that belonged in her mouth. Phaedra saw her mother's lips moving and felt her body relax, but she couldn't make out the song. And then the memory was over, and she was back in her grandmother's bed, a miserable, wet mess of a girl. "I can't remember it," she said, defeated.

"That's all right. When the time comes that you really need it, you'll find it."

"But I need it now," Phaedra whined.

"Cuhdear. What you need now is rest. Drink some water and let sleep take you," Hyacinth said, pushing a glass to Phaedra's lips.

Phaedra drank and then closed her eyes, willing the song and sleep back to her.

"Gran?"

"Yes, darling."

"Where's Dionne?"

"I haven't seen her since morning." Phaedra almost said something about Dionne's plans with Saranne, but then she thought better of it.

THE BOTTOM OF THE SUN was kissing the top of the ocean when Dionne and Saranne rumbled up Bird Hill in Chad's car. The car was incredibly old, not the slick roadster that Dionne had imagined when she first met him. Had she known what would happen that night, the way his car would wheeze on inclines and take curves on a precarious lean, she might not have dialed the number that he wrote on the inside of her wrist the day of the church picnic. All the way up the hill, Dionne, who hated heights, gripped the car door handle. Under her breath, she whispered: "Help us, Father, now and in our time of need, O Christ our Sanctifier and our Redeemer." Two months of church in Bird Hill had taught her, at the very least, how to call upon the Lord.

Dionne hoped Chad would drop her off first, but the house Saranne shared with her aunt Trixie and her cousin Jean was before her grandmother's. The whole ride, up until they'd reached St. George and needed her help with directions, Saranne slept bunched up in the backseat, her head draped over her wrists in a way that made her look more innocent than she was. Dionne was glad that the windows were down because Saranne stank of boys and vomit and the rounds of rum punch they'd downed.

When they dropped Saranne at her house, Dionne could see through the open door that the television was on, and Trixie was pacing in her housedress and hairnet. There were two reasons Trixie didn't box down her niece right then and there—because Saranne stumbled inside and fell on top of her, heaping her foul breath on Trixie, and because she could hear Chad's car engine idling outside. A lot of things could be said about Trixie, but one thing the hill women would say in her defense was that she was discreet. When the hill women's husbands found themselves in need of Trixie's services in the dry spells that followed the birth of children or the eventual hollowing out of desire between man and wife, Trixie's tongue never wagged with news of their husbands' indiscretions or the wild things they wanted, their wives refused, and she offered for a price. When Trixie traveled with her husband before he died, going on trips up to New York and even a cruise around the Caribbean to islands she'd only seen before on maps, she carefully studied the way that white people talked to their children. And so while she was not above giving a headstrong child a good thump, she did adhere to the principle of praising in public, reprimanding in private.

While Dionne was saying her prayers on the ride to her grandmother's house, Chad was humming the song that was on when they first met. The lyrics went "Country girls does be sweet sweet/Country girls does be sweet sweet sweet." When he first sang it, Dionne found it catchy and endearing. But now that she knew that she was the song's sweetmeat, it grated on her nerves; she counted the minutes until she could be away from the insistent beat of his fingers on the dusty dashboard. When they pulled up in front of Hyacinth's house, Dionne saw her grandmother sitting on the veranda. Chad tried to lean in for a final kiss, but Dionne gave his face the flat side of her palm instead.

"Not even a thank-you for driving you all the way out here?" Chad asked. Dionne slammed the car door without speaking.

Dionne got to the house's rickety bottom step and said to its splinters, "Morning."

"Oh, so the sun rose and you thought it might be a good time to come home?" Hyacinth said.

Dionne stuck out her chest, having become accustomed to using her body's maturity as a proxy for the good sense she didn't yet have. "We went to a party and then it was getting late so we decided to stay the night."

"Who is we?"

"I went with Saranne. I told Phaedra to tell you we'd gone out."

"They didn't have phones where you were?"

"You don't have a phone here, Gran."

"You could have phoned Ms. Zelma and she would have called me to come." Hyacinth looked up at the sun, which she could see stretching its face above the water now. "Look, Dionne, your mother already gave me my fair share of problems and I'm determined not to lose my head with worry over you and what you do and who you're doing it with. I can see from what you're showing me now that you are determined to try to send me to an early grave. Please move out of my face before I do something I don't want to do," Hyacinth said, waving Dionne inside.

Dionne walked up the stairs. She hugged the wall because it was cool and because she didn't want to be in the path of her grandmother's hands, which were as heavy as ripe pawpaws.

"Mind how you go in there. Your sister's sick."

"What's new?" Dionne sighed.

"What did you say?" Hyacinth hissed. When Hyacinth stood, her chin was at Dionne's chest. What she lacked in height she made up for in girth and fortitude.

"I said, what's new? Every time I turn around Phaedra's sick and somebody's running behind her to clean up the mess. At least this time it didn't have to be me."

Hyacinth slapped Dionne with a mighty blow that Dionne was glad none of her neighbors were outside to witness, although she was sure at least Ms. Zelma could hear it. When she brought her face back up to meet her grandmother's, it was with the imprint of Hyacinth's palm on her check.

"Me and your sister is the only blood you have. You can go

on with a lot of things, but I will not tolerate you disrespecting your family."

"Family? Where was family when my mother was lying in her bed day after day after day wasting away? I was the one who bathed her and cleaned the house and made sure Phaedra went to school looking halfway decent. I was the one who did the shopping and went out every day pretending like everything was normal. Every time I needed something, it was my own damn self that I had to depend on. I didn't see anybody called family coming to help me then."

"Dionne, if it's one thing I hope you learn, it's to stop blaming everybody else for your problems. When you walk past this door, nobody is going to care whether you had a sick mother or a sister you had to care for. All that is past and only you can make your future. You at a crossroads, child. I see you there. I only hope you know which way you turning next."

Dionne walked into the house, making a ton of racket as she shed her clothes. She was sure that she would never wear them again. And she didn't care whether Phaedra or Hyacinth or anyone else, for that matter, heard her.

BEFORE ERROL EVEN SET his white wingtips on the steps of Hyacinth's chattel house, Phaedra could smell the bad on him. She knew without being told that nothing good could come from her father's unannounced arrival in Bird Hill. By this time, when her skin was a deep ochre and her feet had a new layer of callus from walking outside barefoot, she could see more clearly with her heart and her eyes. Phaedra looked through the window at Errol and at the woman he had brought with him, who struggled as her stiletto heels dug deeper into the mud. Errol's woman's whole foot sank inside the wet earth, and her shoes turned the same color brown as her skin, so that she looked as if she were a part of the hill rather than temporarily stuck to it. The wind whipped her white, wide-brimmed hat into the pile of mud behind her. Once both her feet were on solid ground again, the woman tried to fluff out her hat hair, but there was still a broad band around her forehead that made her look marked.

Phaedra wasn't afraid, just alert. There was nothing, she thought, that between her and her grandmother, they couldn't handle. Dionne could help, too, although Phaedra worried about her sister more these days, wondered if there wasn't a way to make her see that the thing she was searching for was something she already had.

When Errol's foot tapped the top step, Phaedra shouted, "Granny, look trouble come."

Hyacinth, who had just wiped her gardening boots off on the back steps, heard Phaedra and asked, "What you saying, child?"

"I said, look trouble come."

"I don't know what kind of foolishness you talking," Hyacinth said. And then she went to the front door, which Errol was knocking down like the police.

A memory shivered up Phaedra's spine, the sound of her father's knocking on the front door of their apartment in Brooklyn while she and her sister cowered in the bathtub. Their mother dragged the love seat, and then a dresser, and finally the dining room table to shore up the door, which was already triple-bolted. In the bathroom, along with the sound of the water dripping from the leaky faucet onto Dionne's house shoes, Phaedra heard the pounding of her father's knuckles. If Phaedra wasn't sure before whether this man in white, fleshy around the edges of his face and with a beard, was her father, she was sure now.

Hyacinth wedged the door open and eyed the red-skinned man grinning at her in his white suit. When Errol opened up his mouth to speak and she saw the glint of gold from his front teeth, Hyacinth was sure that it was, indeed, her dead daughter's husband. When he'd first started courting Avril, Hyacinth warned her against dating any man who had more money in his mouth than in his bank account. But Avril's eyes were blinded by Errol's shine, her better judgment overcome by the songs he strummed on his guitar. When his visa to the States came through, Avril wondered not whether to leave with him, but when.

Hyacinth shifted her weight to the right, obscuring Phaedra's view. As quickly as the question of who had come to her door was answered, the problem of how to keep him away from her grandchildren filled the first question's emptied space.

"Hyacinth," Errol slurred. From where she stood behind her grandmother, Phaedra could smell the rum wafting from his mouth, which hung slightly open like a dog's even when he wasn't speaking.

"Errol," Hyacinth said.

"Well, I didn't think these would be circumstances under which we would meet again," Errol said.

"I had hoped you would dead first."

"Is that the kind of thing you say to your son-in-law after all these years? I came to pay my respects."

"Mmm. You late for that," Hyacinth grunted, and then planted her fist on her waist in a way that Phaedra knew meant business.

"So do you plan to let us in or do we have to stand outside in the sun?" Errol said. He pulled the woman who was with him close, grabbed her by the cream waistband of her white dress. Phaedra didn't know much about drinking because she had been so young when her father left, but she looked at his quaking and thought her father's grip was more for steadiness than affection.

"Anything you and I have to talk about can be discussed right here," Hyacinth replied. She clicked the padlock on the gate inside the door closed.

"Well, you always were a battle-axe. You know what they say about the apple and everything."

"My tree ain't stop growing yet. But tell me, really, Errol, what kind of business you have here. You finally see my daughter exactly where you want her, in the ground. What more you want? The nails in her coffin screw in already."

Errol swayed then, a movement that, like a personal earthquake, started in his shoes and went right up to his head. "I came to see about my girls."

"Your girls?"

"My daughters."

"Sweetheart, aren't you going to say hello to your daddy? You must be Faye," the woman in the white dress said to Phaedra, who had planted her face inside Hyacinth's crooked elbow. The scent of rum was on the woman too.

"My name is Phaedra," she said. She'd never been well-liked enough to earn a nickname at school, and the sound of her shortened name was strange in this new woman's mouth.

"And what is this, Errol?" Hyacinth asked, pointing her mouth at the woman beside him.

"This is Evangeline. I brought her along to help me with the children. She's a great cook, keeps the house together for me back in Miami."

"How you find yourself all the way down there?"

"It's a long walk from New York, a short flight from Miami."

"Errol, you must take me for a poppet or a fool. You think that you could just put down your children one day like an old toy and come back another day and pick them up? I have no intentions of handing these girls over to you. You have exactly sixty seconds to clear yourself, and this, this person, off my porch, y'hear?"

"Don't make this any harder than it has to be, Hyacinth. I have a lawyer that I consulted."

"I thought you were below the law."

"Tell me which judge would give a woman like you custody. You think obeah women make good guardians?"

Hyacinth got close enough to Errol to speak in his ear. Phaedra couldn't hear what she said, but her words pushed Errol and the woman off the gallery. Whatever spirit had dragged Evangeline down into the mud earlier now summoned the wind to reveal the red bloomers beneath her white dress.

Later, Hyacinth would tell Phaedra that women wore red underwear to ensure that their dead husbands would not visit them in the night after they'd died. Phaedra couldn't understand why she would be wearing red underwear when the person who had died was her mother, and she said as much to her grandmother. Hyacinth looked at her, and Phaedra understood that this, like so much else, was something she would only come to understand in time.

For now, Phaedra dug her knees into the crinkly plastic cover on the sofa and watched as they walked away from the house. The woman was whispering something to Errol, a thing that clearly annoyed him and which he dismissed with a wave of his hands. Before they tumbled out into the road, the woman lifted up her dress, squatted, and pulled aside her panties to relieve herself in Hyacinth's rose bed. Hyacinth, who did not deign to deal with every and anybody, especially this kind of childish behavior coming from what she would call a big hard-backed woman, responded by making a loud show of shutting the louvers. Phaedra heard but did not see the thorns tear at the woman's dress when she tried to get up.

"You see that, Phaedra? You see how common dog does bark in church?" Hyacinth said.

Phaedra nodded her head although she didn't really understand.

"That is all right, though, because the good Lord takes care of his flock and their foes. Some fights you don't need your own fists for."

"Yes, Gran," Phaedra said, and then she tried to remember what she was doing before her father came.

WHEN DIONNE CAME HOME from a day of hanging out with Saranne, the last bits of light were casting slits and shadows over her grandmother's kitchen. She used the key that Hyacinth gave her after Avril died, when she started locking up the house at night. Dionne saw the television's blue screen that meant that there was no more programming for the evening. Phaedra sat reading a book in the vestigial light even though she had been warned countless times about ruining her eyesight this way. Dionne turned on the lamp beside Phaedra and sat down on the sofa.

"So I heard we had a visitor today," Dionne started, and then waited for Phaedra to take the bait.

"Who'd you hear that from?"

"I have my sources."

"So, you know, then."

"Know what?"

"Know that Daddy wants to take us back with him to Miami."

"Daddy was here?"

"I thought you said you knew."

"Trevor said that his cousin said that she saw a man and a woman dressed in white over by my grandmother's house. He didn't say it was our father," Dionne said, leaning her long body forward so that her elbows and knees met.

"Your father."

"OK. So, Daddy was here. And he wants to take us to Miami. When's he coming back to pick us up?"

"What are you talking about, Dionne? Going to live with our father and his, his woman is not a good idea."

"What woman?"

"Some brown-skinned black American lady. She got stuck in that pile of mud behind Ms. Zelma's house. And then she peed in Granny's rose bed."

"What? So what did Granny do?" Dionne said, barely containing a laugh.

"She didn't do anything. She just shut the louvers."

"So, was she pretty?"

"I wouldn't say she was ugly, but definitely not pretty like Mommy. Daddy said she could cook."

"Huh. Fat or slim?"

"Round." Phaedra sighed. She was so tired of her sister's obsession with other women's size, which started right around the time Dionne's body turned into a riot of arms and legs and breasts.

"And she can cook."

"That's what Daddy says."

"You don't believe him?"

"Why would I?"

"How could you say that about Daddy?"

"How could I not? Nothing I remember about him is any good."

"I'm surprised you remember anything at all. You were all of five when he left. Did he look good today? Healthy?"

"He looked fat to me. Well, more like puffy."

Dionne leaned back and closed her eyes as if putting her father together in her mind. "Well, he did always have a belly. But now he's puffy? I find that hard to believe."

"Well, that's what I saw. And there's no way that I'm going to live with him."

"What are you talking about? He's living in Miami and clearly has enough money to buy a plane ticket and come down to Barbados to look for us. So, he must be doing well. You would rather stay here with Granny and go to school with these backwards children instead of going home?"

"Miami is not home."

"Don't you remember what Mommy used to say about how home is between your teeth? Daddy is the closest family we have left. I'm going."

"You would leave me here?"

"Do you really think that you could stay here if you wanted to? Exactly what would be your defense? That you have more spells to learn before you start school again?"

"I'm staying here with Granny."

"Suit yourself. I'm leaving," Dionne said.

And with that, Dionne went to her room. From where she sat in the living room, Phaedra could hear her sister opening and closing drawers, as if she were already packing.

THE NEXT DAY, early in the morning, when the cocks were conferring in the front yard and the sun was not yet high in the sky, Errol returned. Hyacinth rose while Phaedra and Dionne were still asleep and went outside in the cool of the morning to speak with him. This time, he was clean-shaven. And the scent of rum was gone, although there was sourness on him that Hyacinth smelled and knew to be the sign of a greater sickness. He came alone, with his head bowed, to make a simple request. He only had a couple days left in Barbados, and wanted to take the girls to the beach and to Kiddie Kadooment, the children's version of the Grand Kadooment parade that marked the end of Crop Over season.

Hyacinth agreed begrudgingly, mostly because Phaedra had been whining about how badly she wanted to play mas. Hyacinth was not up for taking the children to Kiddie Kadooment, as the heat and the crowds and the money to buy costumes was more than too much. Besides, she thought that the celebrations were just an excuse for slackness and getting on bad. According to Hyacinth, the whole business of planting crops and harvesting them and the slavery on which the island's wealth was built and her ancestors' lives were lost was forgotten in the revelry. All summer, in spite of her grandmother's grumpiness, Phaedra stopped whatever she was doing whenever anything about Crop Over came on the television. She would sit transfixed, watching the children her age in fabulous costumes parading around the stadium, imagining herself among them. After a while, she knew better than to ask Hyacinth if she could play mas, as not even she could bear her grandmother's tirades and her corny line about how she couldn't wait for Crop Over to be over. While Hyacinth was not holding her breath about Errol making good on his promise, a part of her was happy to see Phaedra excited about something again.

After Errol left, the morning passed by slowly in the way that hours do when a thing deeply dreaded or longed for looms. Hyacinth hovered over a steaming pot of pelau, trying to tease the chicken off the bone and salt from the beef she'd bought at the market. Phaedra counted her mosquito bites; she had reached 103 before she had to start all over again because she missed one on her collarbone. While she ran her pointer finger up and down her body, the clock passed one, when Errol was expected, and then it was two o'clock. Phaedra remembered that Hyacinth had told her and Dionne not to get their expectations up about their father. What her grandmother had said exactly was, "Don't take a six for a nine." Dionne rolled her eyes when Phaedra said she didn't understand and Hyacinth explained that you have to learn to see past the face people showed you. Phaedra was about to take off her swimsuit when she heard the car honk outside.

The swimsuit she was wearing that day was red and brand-new. Mrs. Loving had bought it on her monthly trip into town to shop for Father Loving and the boys. Since Avril died, Phaedra had become accustomed to the hill women, who channeled their initial judgment of Avril into the task of mothering Phaedra and Dionne, offering her things. Hyacinth was proud, and therefore a stranger to charity, but Mrs. Loving was Avril's old friend. And Phaedra showed such delight in the sporty swimsuit with the trademark swoosh on her chest that Hyacinth couldn't bear to tell Mrs. Loving "No, thank you" as she'd said to the other women and their gifts. The day that Mrs. Loving brought the suit by, Phaedra wore it around the house nonstop; she ate dinner in it, watched TV in it, and was only convinced by the threat of an extra dose of cod-liver oil to take it off and change into her nightie.

Hyacinth shook her head at the whole affair, which reminded her how poorly equipped she was for the task of raising this pair of strong-willed girls. Her hands, which swelled when it rained, were no match for Phaedra's unruly mountain of hair, and she wondered how she would deal with Dionne's determination to face her time in Barbados like a prison sentence and Hyacinth as her jailer. There was something else, too, about the way that Christopher looked at Phaedra when she tried on the suit—from which Mrs. Loving had smartly removed the price tag—in Hyacinth's living room. Slack-jawed, his admiration of Phaedra on full display, Christopher's face told Hyacinth she'd be worrying about him chasing at Phaedra's skirt before too long.

When the rental car finally pulled up with Errol and his woman in the front seats, Dionne waved a heavy hand to them. She had her beach bag packed and had been sitting on the steps the whole morning on her hands, which at first moved too much and then fell asleep from the pressure. She ran to the car, shaking the pins and needles from her fingers.

Dionne went to kiss her father. Earlier in the summer, when they were closer, Dionne and Trevor had practiced drinking with Father Loving's secret stash of hard liquor, which he kept in the linen cupboard behind his vestments. They passed bottles back and forth in Father Loving's study, waiting for the warmth to spread across their chests. When Dionne leaned over to kiss her father and shake his girlfriend's limp, lotioned hand, she recognized the sweet halos of Mount Gay rum that hovered above them—and also what two people looked like when they knew each other's bodies well. They waited with the engine running while Phaedra and Hyacinth locked up the house.

Hyacinth huffed her body into the backseat and spoke to Errol before he had a chance to drive off. "How far we going?" she asked.

"Just down to Pebbles Beach," Errol said.

"All right," Hyacinth said. She made sure the girls were strapped into their seats and then turned to watch the familiar houses on the hill pass by as they rumbled downward. At the bottom of the hill, the girlfriend, who looked as if her stomach might heave from the turbulence, turned to face the backseat.

"I don't think we've officially met," she said.

Dionne had been studying the woman, especially the way her weave was expertly attached to her real hair so that the tracks didn't show. She spoke first.

"I don't think we have. I'm Dionne. Phaedra, have you said good afternoon?"

Phaedra glared at her sister and then mumbled a greeting.

"I'm Evangeline."

And Hyacinth said, "Of course."

At the beach, they parked among a seemingly endless row of other cars. The gray rocks that gave Pebbles Beach its name were piled up, creating a barrier that made people work hard for the privilege of touching their feet to the sand. The beach was mostly empty, with the exception of a few bathers. A family was speaking in guttural tones that could have been Dutch or German. The children, a boy and a girl with hair the color of straw, were building a fortress and moat with their shovels and pails. Phaedra looked at the children's pile of toys and thought that this must be what it was like to be rich, to have toys for home and toys for vacation. She looked down at herself and was suddenly less excited about her swimsuit. She wished Chris were there to tell her it didn't matter. Knowing him, he'd probably make a joke about how he didn't know white people got whiter than white when he saw the sunscreen the mother was smothering in thick layers onto her children. That made Phaedra smile a little bit, and she tuned back in to Hyacinth's lecture about being safe on the beach. "The sea ain't got no back door," Hyacinth huffed. When Hyacinth asked for the third time if she and Dionne were wearing panties beneath their bathing suits, she simply said "Yes, Granny," and tried not to roll her eyes.

When they made it near the water, Errol's girlfriend slipped out of her cover-up to reveal a two-piece bathing suit that showed off her large breasts, the sight of which made Hyacinth draw in her breath. Something about Evangeline's breasts seemed like a call to competition for which Dionne was woefully underprepared, and for the first time that summer, Dionne saw a woman she considered more beautiful than herself, almost as beautiful as her mother. Dionne felt newly self-conscious in the polka-dot bathing suit she'd so proudly worn at the church picnic a few weeks before. She kept her t-shirt on, claiming that it was cool in the shade of the sea grape trees where they parked their beach towels.

In spite of the tension that drew them together on its taut cord, no one could maintain enmity in the face of sunshine and water. Eventually, after Dionne and Phaedra digested the food that their grandmother made them eat before leaving the house in case "wunna father decide he not coming again," Hyacinth let them go into the water. She and Evangeline watched as Errol entertained the girls with underwater cartwheels. Phaedra stayed close to the sea's edge, jumping with each new wave and searching for sand dollars and seashells to add to her collection.

Dionne pretended to be a weaker swimmer than she was so that Errol would show her how to float and how to breathe between strokes. Floating with her father's hand beneath her back, Dionne wondered if the sky was this pretty in Brooklyn, since she'd never taken the time to look up at it and see for herself. Barbados, with no apartment buildings or office towers blocking her view, was beautiful. She marveled at the vastness of the sky and sea, and at her smallness in relation to them. She would have stayed floating like that forever, admiring the clouds. But he let go without warning, and she went under. Dionne's heart raced when her feet couldn't find the ocean floor. The moments that she flailed beneath the surface stretched like infinity before Errol dove under and hoisted her onto his shoulders.

Hyacinth watched Errol dunk and then rescue Dionne; she calmed an urge to go in and drag her granddaughter away from him. She tried to laugh with Evangeline when Errol and Dionne emerged from the water spitting and coughing between guffaws, but the best she could do was to purse her lips and take note that this kind of behavior was exactly the reason she'd decided to come down to the beach with the children.

A breeze teased the hem of Hyacinth's long white skirt and a memory was conjured in her mind's eye. Hyacinth noted that the last time that she'd had a real sea bath was forty years earlier, when she thought baptism might cure her of her destiny, or at the very least secure the love of her husband, Kenny, who was a member in good standing at Bird Hill Church of God in Christ, and courting her then. Kenny insisted that he wouldn't marry any woman who wasn't baptized in the church, and then waited patiently for months while Hyacinth decided whether or not to do it. He listened as Hyacinth explained that she was mad at God for taking her grandmother from her, that her church was getting quiet in the grove of guava trees just past her house, where she retreated to on Sunday mornings while all the other hill women and some of the men were praising the Lord. He heard all of Hyacinth's grievances against God and the church and organized religion, but still, he maintained that his heart couldn't cleave properly to a woman who hadn't been washed in the blood of the Lamb.

When she met Kenny, Hyacinth didn't trust her heart. What she'd thought was love with the first man who courted her turned out to be that man's desire to consume her; the fire of what Hyacinth thought was first love had burned her. But Kenny was patient, happy to chip away at her defenses one day at a time. Maybe it was the fact that he didn't want to change her, or that he kept all his promises, from the time he said he would pick her up when they went out together to the way he'd built the house they lived in by hand, just as he'd said he would. And so even though there was so much that was difficult about him, there was so much that Hyacinth was willing to forgive in her husband because he loved her as she was and did exactly what he said he would do.

When she was young, Hyacinth believed that she had a choice about whether or not to heed the call that beckoned her mother and her grandmother before her, to work roots and deliver children as she'd been taught. Hyacinth, who was not given to doing things because people recommended them, who in fact was least likely to do the things recommended to her, needed to have a reason besides Kenny's insistence to be baptized. She settled on her belief that maybe baptism in the church might change the course of her destiny. Never mind that none of the women in her family, saved or not, had been able to sidestep the heritage that was theirs. Hyacinth thought she would be the first. Hyacinth's mother's and grandmother's work and their aloneness—their men barely lasted long enough to see their children born—were two fates Hyacinth wanted to avoid. And so, she was baptized on Easter Saturday 1949, in the water just at the bottom of the hill. By Palm Sunday of the next year she and Kenny were married.

But no amount of holy water or determination to resist her destiny could turn Hyacinth's feet from the path on which her steps had been ordered. Kenny died soon after Avril's thirtieth birthday, a few years after Phaedra was born. The work that Hyacinth had been ambivalent about all her life would be the thing that sustained her once she no longer had her husband or her child to depend on. Within a few months of her husband's passing, Hyacinth was delivering babies and handing out advice and tinctures to the hill women who sought her out, as the women in her family before her had done. Just as she was trying to remember what song they'd sung when she was dipped into the water that Easter Saturday, she found that she couldn't, and the lost memory bothered her.

A few feet away from Hyacinth, Errol's woman sat with her breasts and exposed belly button turned up toward the sky. She spoke first.

"I never had a chance to meet your daughter, but from everything Errol says, it sounds like she was lovely."

"You clearly haven't known Errol long enough to know when not to believe his lies."

"It all seemed true to me. He said she was a great mother before she got sick."

"Sick?"

"Errol said that she suffered from depression, that he'd wanted to stay with her but then she turned away from him. He said that eventually he just couldn't take it anymore."

"I'm sure you would believe any version of history that makes Errol a hero."

"I don't see why he'd make that up. He said that for days and days she could barely get out of the—"

"Why are you so interested in my child?" Hyacinth said sharply.

"I don't know, really. I guess it just seems like I'd know Errol better if I understood why his last relationship didn't work out. She's always been like a ghost haunting us. I guess she really is one now."

Hyacinth sighed, remembering that this was what she liked least about Americans, their desire to pry open shut doors. They liked unearthing things. And the silence where Hyacinth spent most of her time unnerved them.

"Well, I guess we all have ghosts, don't we?" Hyacinth said.

"We do."

And with that Evangeline saw the shutters of Hyacinth's openness close and felt their conversation come to an end.

ON THE DAY Errol was to take the children to choose their costumes, the sun was hot, the kind of hot that had over the course of the summer turned Phaedra's scalp a deep, dark brown, imprinted the crisscross of her jelly sandals on her feet and the underside of her Cabbage Patch Kids watch on her wrist. Hyacinth knew that seeing Errol meant a break from the children running in her garden, singing the VBS songs they knew by heart so blasted loud she was sure even the good Lord would shush them, and making weapons out of Pine Hill Dairy juice boxes. Because while Trevor and Dionne's relationship had soured, Phaedra and Chris still got on famously and were always giving either Hyacinth or Mrs. Loving a headache with their enthusiasm for everything from salting slugs to chasing lizards to stealing ackees from the Jeremiahs' tree. Donna rounded out their crew, and it wasn't unusual to find her at the top of a fruit tree, taking instructions from Phaedra and Chris about which ones to shake down. Still, Hyacinth would take the children bothering up her head any day over the questionable parenting of her former son-in-law.

Hyacinth was glad when she saw that Evangeline wasn't in the passenger seat, even though it meant she had to referee an argument between Phaedra, Donna, and Chris, who each wanted to ride shotgun. Errol decided that Chris would ride up front with him first, Donna would switch seats with him at the petrol station, and Phaedra would have the honor of riding in front the whole way back. Phaedra was already tired of her father calling her his little princess, but after their day at the beach and now, with him taking her and her friends to the band house, she hated Errol a little less than she had when he first showed up. That said, she still was rankled by Chris's unabashed admiration of her father, from the jeans that he sported to his encyclopedic knowledge of automobiles that enriched their game of "that's my car" once they were on the road.

"I really like those glasses, Uncle Errol," Chris said, referring to the aviator sunglasses Errol was wearing, which even Phaedra could tell were expensive.

"Thanks, big man," Errol said, punching Chris affectionately on the shoulder.

When Donna and Chris changed seats, Phaedra turned to Chris and rolled her eyes at him. She said, "If I didn't know you better, Christopher, I would say that you have a crush on my father."

"Ewww," Chris said.

"Now that's not the sort of thing I would expect from my little princess," Errol said.

"Maybe I'm not your little princess," Phaedra said, low enough so only Chris could hear.

They drove for what seemed like hours, first dropping down to the bottom of the hill where they watched the rough waters smash against the old train tracks at Martin's Bay. When they zipped past the cane fields in St. George, the kids stuck their heads out of the car windows to feel the wind against their faces and the stalks against their outstretched palms. In Oistins, they crept along in the late afternoon traffic and watched the fishermen's wet, dark faces as they chopped and sold dolphin, marlin, and flying fish. Phaedra and Donna called to the birds that strutted along the edges of the fish market hoping for a stray meal.

Just past the first beach on the south coast road, they pulled into a driveway with streamers and balloons that declared this spot to be the Legendary Mas Camp band house.

A girl stood outside crying while her grandmother talked loud enough so that anyone passing by could hear. "I don't know why you would want to go up there and embarrass yourself, as tall as you are. You would be towering over those children. You want to go up there and look like a poppet? That's what you want? Wipe your face, y'hear." Phaedra watched as the girl tried to stop her tears; she felt grateful for the fact that her grandmother never spoke to her with that kind of harshness.

Errol called "Inside!" to the house where a radio announcer was talking excitedly about the finals for the soca monarch competition, which was happening that evening at the stadium. Ten days before Grand Kadooment, Barbados was pulsing with Crop Over fever. It was hard to have a conversation about anything else, and everyone had an opinion about who might be crowned champion of the singing competition that night.

An older woman with a spritely air greeted them. "You come to look about costumes?" A coral necklace the woman wore shook against her wizened skin as she spoke. Phaedra's grandmother told her that in the same way she could tell a woman's pregnancy by her ankles, you could read a woman's age from her neck. This woman's neck was definitely older than Hyacinth's, Phaedra thought.

"Yes, we did. It's Mrs. Alleyne, right?" Errol asked. He cupped both her small hands in his large ones and gazed into her eyes.

"That's me. But you can drop the 'Mrs.' Mr. Alleyne was my father and he's gone on to better pastures."

"All right then, Ms. A.," Errol said. Phaedra watched the woman's smile widen, and it made her remember how women acted around her father. One of the cashiers at Allan's Bakery in Brooklyn had given Phaedra extra currant rolls for months, thinking that her stomach was the way to her father's heart. During the brief period when her father, mother, Dionne, and Phaedra all went to church together, Errol caused such a stir among the women, who started fighting to set aside the largest slices of sweetbread for him at bake sales and finding excuses for Errol to work with them on various projects. Phaedra watched this older woman fall under her father's spell, and wondered exactly what it was made of.

"And who do we have here?" the woman asked Errol, bending down to look at the children in a way that bothered Phaedra.

"This is my daughter Phaedra. And her friends Donna and Chris."

"That's funny, we don't have many fathers coming in. Mostly mums."

"Phaedra's mother just passed away," Errol said, pressing the meaty flesh of his palms into Phaedra's shoulders.

"I'm so sorry for your loss," the woman said mechanically, and Phaedra felt another spark fly from the woman to her father.

"Well, children," the woman said, "the hour is late, but I can show you what I have left. We still have some ixora and flamboyant and birds-of-paradise for the girls. And for the boy . . . we'll find something for the boy."

Where the front room would usually have been, half-made sculptures of chicken wire, fabric, and sequins stood. Phaedra expected a dining room right past the arch in the living room, but instead there was a long worktable covered in costumes in various stages of progress. Two women and one man sat at the table, gluing, sewing, and cutting, their heads all bent in concentration.

Ms. Alleyne showed them to one of the back bedrooms, where the finished costumes hung on racks. Phaedra and Donna fingered the soft fabrics, the reds and oranges and pinks.

Ms. Alleyne let the girls look around before she said to Donna, "I have a girl from New York who was supposed to be a desert rose, but she's not coming down again. What do you think of this costume?" she said, picking up a stretchy fuchsia top, a matching skirt, and a headpiece of petals made from painted cardboard.

Donna, who couldn't resist the idea of having something made for a girl from the States, said excitedly, "We could wear that, right, Phaedra?"

Phaedra was awed by the costumes, their colors and then her imagination making them come alive in the same perfect design as her grandmother's garden. She nodded and then went with Donna into the next room to try on the costumes. She could hear Ms. Alleyne speaking to Chris. The band house, like Hyacinth's house on Bird Hill, was small, and sound carried over its plywood room dividers. "I've been waiting for a boy like you. My king costume is a royal palm tree, and it needs just the right person to wear it. Would you like to try it?"

Just then Phaedra and Donna came out in their costumes. Phaedra's face was a perfect oval peeking out between the petals; the dusty pink color of the costume popped against the brick red of her arms and legs. Donna was eclipsed by the shine that radiated off Phaedra. Chris couldn't speak, but Phaedra's father did.

"I don't know how you get to be so lovely, but I can see it, Phaedra, I can see you getting your looks," Errol said.

Phaedra blushed in spite of herself. She looked down at

her sandals and at the layers of ribbon and fabric that lined the floor of the band house.

"We'll take them," Errol declared.

Chris and Donna each pulled out tight wads of cash their mothers had given them, but Errol shooed them away. "This is my treat, kids. I know you all are going to be fantastic. If you win, I'll take you out to Chefette."

"What if we don't win?" Phaedra asked.

"We can still go to Chefette," Errol said.

"Yes!" the kids shouted, already placing their future orders for chicken and ice cream, not sure which was better, playing mas or the promise of afterward.

In the car on the way home, Phaedra took the passenger seat next to her father while Donna and Chris slept in the back. Just as they passed Miami Beach, where cars whose inhabitants thought they were parked away from prying eyes lined up facing the sunset, Phaedra turned to her father. She liked him better when it was just the two of them. She admired the ramrod posture he'd tried and failed to instill in her. "Daddy?" she said.

"Darling?" he said, turning down the radio, which was blasting one of the same five songs that played on a seemingly endless loop.

"What happened that day you came to the house?"

"What day, P.?"

"The day that you came and you were knocking down the door and Mommy wouldn't let you in."

A cloud settled over Errol's face as he searched his memory. He heaved a deep breath and then spoke. "You mean, days."

"Sorry?"

"You mean, days. It was four days that I came to see about you-all. Your mother had you locked up in there and every time I called she wouldn't answer the phone."

Phaedra remembered how the phone's shrill ring filled the otherwise quiet apartment. Eventually her mother took the phone off the hook, but not before picking up and telling the person on the other line to stop harassing them, that they didn't do anything to deserve this.

"Why wouldn't she answer the phone?"

"Your guess is as good as mine, Phaedra. Your mother was a strange woman. She had her ways. She was always convinced that somebody or something was trying to hurt you or hurt her."

"So you weren't trying to hurt us?"

"Nothing could be further from the truth. All I wanted was for her to let you and your sister leave the house. I didn't think it could be good for you girls to be cooped up in there like that."

"And the police?"

"You know you and your mother are the same way; once you set your mind to something you're not turning back no matter what."

Phaedra smiled a half smile. "So, you were the one who called the police."

"I thought that was the only way I might get her to see sense," Errol said in a small voice. His back curled over the steering wheel like he was trying to protect his heart, or the memory.

"Did it work?"

"They came and she opened the door. You would know better than me whether it worked," Errol said.

Phaedra's head spun as she tried to reconcile the version of events she thought she'd known with what her father told her. She wanted to sleep, but every time she closed her eyes, all she could see was her mother and that day, the phone and the bathtub and the sirens, her father's knocking, her mother finally caving and moving the furniture that barricaded the door. When they arrived home, Phaedra had never been happier to see her grandmother's front porch and the question, "Why worry?" written in script at the top.

IT WAS ONE IN THE AFTERNOON, and the sun was beating down on the children from Legendary Mas Camp, who were made up to look like flowers and plants from Barbados. The heat was threatening to wilt them all. There were a few Legendary mothers who kept ginger ale and smelling salts in their fanny packs for the occasional stomachache or fainting spell. Their job was to keep the stragglers moving in time with the music, break up squabbles, and try to make sure the kids kept themselves distinct from the other bands. Donna's mother was home taking care of the baby. So Chris's mother kissed each of the kids good-bye, wished them good luck at the drop-off point, and promised to meet them at the north corner of the stadium when it was over.

That morning, Errol drove the children and Mrs. Loving to town and then went to find a seat with Dionne in the stadium. Some part of Phaedra leapt up, knowing that her sister and father would be watching. It was too soon to say that Phaedra trusted Errol, but he was growing on her, in no small part for having finally made good on her parents' promise to let her play mas. Every West Indian Day parade on Eastern Parkway in Brooklyn when Errol was still around, Phaedra sat on her father's shoulders and cried when the men dressed as blue devils came by. She wanted desperately to be one of the children masquerading with troupes like Sesame Flyers and Burrokeet. But her parents said she was too small to play mas, that she'd be tired from jumping up and dancing before the parade even got going. Once she was big enough, Errol was gone and her mother was definitely not up for that kind of thing.

The bass line and trumpets of that year's road march blared through the speakers, and Legendary Mas Camp was called onstage. Phaedra started to dance to the music that she'd been committing to memory for this very moment. A solid month of memorizing lyrics from the radio finally paid off as she sang "Leggo I Hand" along with all the other children. She looked back at Chris, noting the way he loomed over everyone with the beanstalk height he'd grown to over the summer, carrying the weight of his royal palm tree costume with a majesty she'd never seen on him before. Phaedra and Donna chipped across the stage in their desert rose costumes, and soon their faces were covered in sweat, sequins, and glitter. They danced proudly, slowing down and then making their movements bigger when they neared the judges' bandstand. Phaedra and Donna both looked to it as if it were the promised land because their feet were aching in the old tennis shoes they'd dyed to match their costumes. All the kids put on their best smiles and flew across the stage, and then it was over, a rumble of chat and an echo of applause filling the stadium, and offstage the sound of somebody's child crying.

The winners of first, second, and third place were called and took their awards. No one called Legendary Mas Camp for any of the prizes. Phaedra was overcome by guilt, thinking that maybe if she had danced harder, kept her energy up, they would have won. She held her breath as they gave out the awards for best costumes, hoping her band would be called. Phaedra looked at the sea of gloating children who crowded the front of the stage, the sun's rays bouncing off the fake gold of their trophies. Her face began to crumble in pieces so that by the time Mrs. Loving met her, Chris, and Donna, she had devolved into a full-on sob.

"But Phaedra, what happen to you?" Mrs. Loving asked.

Phaedra shook her head, hardly able to speak for the tears that flooded her mouth. "I thought we would win. We were good."

"Of course you were good. So were the other kids. You think it matters who won?"

"It always matters," Donna said in the knowing way of a girl who had never been inside the winner's circle.

"I thought you-all came here to enjoy yourselves."

"I know we did. But we should have won. It would have been better," Phaedra said.

"I know, I know," Mrs. Loving said, burying Phaedra's dirty face into her skirt.

Phaedra looked up finally and asked, "Where's my father? He said he was coming."

"I'm not sure where he is. I haven't seen him or Dionne since we dropped you off."

"Why is everything so wrong today?" Phaedra said. Now she wondered whether Legendary might have won if her father had kept his promise to watch them.

"Stop worrying yourself, Phaedra. I'm sure Uncle Errol will turn up," Chris said. He tried to put his arm around Phaedra's shoulder, but she shrugged it off.

"Nobody ever shows up for me. Nobody. And you. Christopher. Stop calling my father Uncle Errol," Phaedra seethed. "He's no more your uncle than Father Loving is Donna's father," she blurted, and instantly wished she could take the words back.

Donna, Chris, and Mrs. Loving backed away from Phaedra as if her anger were contagious.

"This day can't get any worse," Phaedra said.

With that, the sky opened up, and the rain the clouds had been holding back all morning was unleashed like an answer.

ONCE THE STADIUM had cleared and the cleaners started sweeping up cotton candy sticks, soda bottles, and wax paper from Kiddie Kadooment, it was clear that Dionne and Errol were nowhere to be found. The scent of popcorn hung in the air, and the empty food carts were strewn near the entrance like forgotten toys. Mrs. Loving packed up the children and went to the church in town where Father Loving was meeting with his old boys' club from seminary. Called out from the cocktail party, he was alarmed to see his wife and the children. He handed his wallet to Mrs. Loving and waved them off to have dinner somewhere without him, shaking the ice in the drink that was in his hand as a farewell.

Even though they'd all been excited for Chefette, the children's gusto was considerably subdued when they finally got there. They sat eating their chicken and chips in silence, no one taking the bait each time Donna tried unsuccessfully to strike up a conversation. Donna got sick after the second cup of her favorite cherry vanilla ice cream, and Mrs. Loving ushered her to the bathroom. Chris's mother nodded when he and Phaedra asked permission to go to the play yard.

Outside, strong winds whipped up off Accra Beach; heavy rains had turned the sand beneath the plastic swings and slides into a thick sludge. Still, the cool breeze was a relief from the stagnant air inside the restaurant. Phaedra was getting onto one of the swings when Chris inched toward her. Phaedra moved back. Her mother's death had made her wary of closeness.

"Phaedra, I want to ask you something," Chris said.

Phaedra looked up at him, noticing the specks of glitter that sparkled at the corners of his eyes. "OK."

"So, you know I like you, right?"

"OK."

"And I was just wondering if maybe I could kiss you."

"You don't have to like me because you feel sorry for me," Phaedra said. She was glad that the waves were crashing so hard against the shoreline because it meant Chris couldn't hear her heart thump.

"I don't feel sorry for you. At least that's not a reason to kiss somebody." Chris shook his head and looked down at her again. "So, can I?"

Phaedra shrugged her shoulders and held on to the swing's seat. She let Chris rock her back and touch his lips to hers. She closed her eyes because even she knew this was what you were supposed to do when someone kissed you. And then she felt a strange tingle that started in her tongue and then traveled down her back. When she opened her eyes, she looked around Chris's long torso to see Donna and Mrs. Loving standing in the doorway to the play yard.

Just then Father Loving honked his horn. Chris let Phaedra and Donna each have a window seat, even though all of them wanted to avoid the middle seat's bumps up the gravelly roads outside the city. The car was quiet except for the earnest strains of a program on family radio. Phaedra hated the Christian shows that Father Loving played in his car, but with her thigh touching Chris's, she sloughed off her annoyance and almost forgot about all the terrible things that had happened that day.

PHAEDRA HAD HOPED THAT when she got home, Dionne would be there, but she wasn't surprised when she was not. After Hyacinth finished interrogating Phaedra, even though she didn't think it would do any good, she called the police station from Ms. Zelma's house. She didn't like having to share her business, even with Ms. Zelma, whom she'd known since they were both little girls running up and down the hill. Hyacinth had her own pain pulsing behind her eyes, and she only felt her worry magnify when she heard the concern in Ms. Zelma's voice, saw the way that she kept shaking her head and talking about how you can't trust people these days and fussing over Phaedra more than she usually did, offering her a cool drink and biscuits, which Phaedra knew better than to accept. Since a few minutes after she'd gotten off the stage at the stadium, Phaedra had felt a thirst in her throat that several soda refills at Chefette couldn't quench. But Phaedra knew that it was more than enough to expose that her sister had gone missing; Ms. Zelma didn't need to know that she was thirsty too.

As Hyacinth expected, there was nothing that the police could do, given that Dionne had not yet been missing for three days. Hyacinth sucked her teeth hard at the officer who suggested that a girl gone missing during Crop Over didn't register as a missing-persons case until a couple days after the parties died down. "Sir, I beg you not to pass your place," Hyacinth said when the man asked if there was a friend's or boyfriend's house where her granddaughter might be staying. She thanked the officer for his time, hung up the phone, and bade Ms. Zelma good night.

When they were back inside their house, Phaedra opened the windows to let in fresh air while Hyacinth dished the pudding and souse she'd made especially for Phaedra to celebrate after Kiddie Kadooment. They sat down to eat, the shadows of Avril and Dionne hovering above the dining room table's empty chairs. Phaedra pushed the pig feet and sweet potato pudding around on her plate, afraid to tell her grandmother she'd already eaten at Chefette.

"Your sister say anything to you about leaving?" Hyacinth asked Phaedra once she'd tucked away enough food to satisfy her.

"She said she wanted to go to Miami with Daddy."

"I know that. But did she say anything about when?"

"I heard her packing, but then I didn't really think she would leave. Dionne's always threatening to do things."

"That girl have her mother on her. From the first time I see that child, even when she was a wee little thing, her mind was made up about life and she wouldn't hear another word about it. If she sees something shining, she just picks herself up and goes to it."

Phaedra jiggled a piece of pork onto her fork, and thought for a minute about this reading of her sister, which she didn't think was entirely untrue.

"Well, the only thing we have left is our work to do."

Hyacinth took out a bottle of rum, and Phaedra raised her eyebrows, a reflex she'd acquired upon seeing her father and mother under its influence, their eyes and mouths turned wilder, as if a cork at the edges of their personalities had come unscrewed.

"But watch your face, Phaedra. If somebody was looking in here right now, they would think that you were the old lady and not me."

"I'm not old. It's just that I don't like to see people drinking." Phaedra frowned.

"It's not everybody that turns their lips to a bottle is a drunk. Sometimes we have to coat the throat and wet the eye so we can see more clearly the road ahead." Hyacinth twisted the bottle open and offered a thimble-sized shot to Phaedra, who shook her head no.

"That's my girl. Sometimes people will come to you and

ask you to do things you don't want to do. And the only right answer is no. You start using your head now, it will see you through hard times."

Phaedra nodded as if she knew what her grandmother meant; she watched Hyacinth tip the bottle to her lips, and then followed the rum as it slid down her throat.

They went into the yard where the moon, almost as brilliant as it was full, shone down on them. Hyacinth gave both herself and Phaedra baths scented with Florida water and jasmine and other herbs Phaedra knew the names of now. The water had been out in the yard all day heating up under the sun, and now it was shot through with a coolness that goosed Phaedra's flesh and made her shiver as the night's cool breeze moved around her. When they were clean and dressed, Phaedra and Hyacinth made their way up the hill to the church. At the edge of the cemetery, Phaedra hesitated.

"What frighten you?" Hyacinth asked.

"I don't want to go in there with all those dead people." All summer, Phaedra had run and jumped and played among the gravestones, but now, with her mother buried there and her grandmother beside her, things felt different.

"So you think if you don't walk in there, you won't see dead people? Do you know how many spirits we passed on the road between our house and here? Before time, people used to bury their family in their backyards so they could go talk to them whenever they want."

"It's different, though. I know someone dead now."

"Even better, then. You'll have more to say. And someone to help you from the other side."

Phaedra hesitated, but then quickly followed her grandmother once she realized it was better to keep walking with Hyacinth than to be left alone.

They made their way toward Avril's grave, which was positioned in a way so as to receive the full light of the moon. A fresh bouquet of Avril's favorite hibiscus sat at the head of the plot. Phaedra and Hyacinth admired the flowers and then sat on the ground, which was damp and still slightly raised. There had been no money for a tombstone, just a small cross made of poured concrete, with Avril's name and dates of her birth and death. It cost Hyacinth a small fortune and the indignity of begging a distant cousin to make the cross at a deep discount. But she thought that Avril deserved at least this.

Phaedra sat at the edge of her mother's grave, boring her eyes into the cross as if by deciphering the numbers and letters she might crack the code of why and how she'd died. Phaedra remembered what her grandmother had told her about Avril's suicide. But this image, of a woman brave enough to take her life, didn't match up with the mother Phaedra had left in Brooklyn. A lot had changed in the last few years, when Avril had gone from being a woman who was vibrant and full of life, writing children's books for Dionne and Phaedra, taking them to every free event she could, making elaborate birthday celebrations for them, to someone else, someone dull and slow moving, burdened by the world. Maybe this woman could have killed herself, although Phaedra suspected that in the end her sadness wouldn't have allowed her to go through with something so terrifying as jumping in front of a train. Phaedra remembered how tightly Avril held her hand when they stood waiting at the Sterling Street subway station, how many times Avril warned her not to ever walk between the cars. Still, so much had changed about Avril in the last few years, and Phaedra considered that the Avril who'd waved good-bye to her and Dionne at JFK airport in her slippers might be capable of doing anything that she thought might relieve her pain.

Phaedra held out hope that the end of summer might wipe clean the slate of what had come before, that one morning she would wake up and still have her mother and her sister, be back in Brooklyn, and none of the bad things that summer brought would be true anymore. In this moment, Phaedra felt as far as possible from this vision of the future as she could possibly be. She dug her hand into the dirt and felt her mother there, and some part of her ached less violently than before. With an anchor to the land, she felt steadier, safe.

"So what do we do now?" Phaedra asked. Her grandmother was bathed in the pale brilliance of the moonlight and starlight. Phaedra looked at Hyacinth's face, the lines around her mouth and forehead that had deepened from creases into valleys in the weeks since Avril's passing. Phaedra thought then, though she'd never thought it before, that her grandmother had been beautiful once, and was now too.

"Nothing to be done different now than if your mother was standing in front of you."

"But she's not!" Phaedra shouted. She looked down into her lap, at the way that the front and back of her palms were almost the same color now, equally coated in dirt.

"I know that, Phaedra, I know. Come," Hyacinth said, and stretched open her arms. Phaedra went toward the now-familiar musk and starch of her grandmother's clothes.

"Cuhdear. You need something to loosen your tongue and say the things that need saying. You hold on too tight to something that you don't need and your hands won't be open for the thing that you most need when it comes along."

"But I don't know how."

Hyacinth reached into the white canvas bag slung over her shoulder and pulled out a flask. She tipped a bit of the liquor onto her index and middle fingers, and then pressed them to Phaedra's tongue.

"Now, speak, child. Talk as if everything you want to say can be heard."

Phaedra dug her knees into the earth and stared at the swirl of dates and names to which her mother's life had been reduced. When she felt her words come, she spoke.

"Mommy, I don't know what happened to you. One day we were getting ready to get on the plane, running around trying to find this and that and you were running behind us, telling us not to forget our toothbrushes, and our sweaters for the cold nights. When we didn't hear from you, we thought that maybe that meant you were so busy getting your life together that you didn't have time to call us or to write. Mr. Jeremiah says that you can't be living your life and talking about living your life at the same time, that if you are, it's not really living you're doing. So we thought maybe that's what you were doing, living. But then I realized that wasn't what you were doing at all, that while we were running around here and playing and getting in trouble, you were back in Brooklyn, and moving further and further away from us. You were dying there. And once you were dead, there was nothing we could do to bring you back to us. Well, not alive, anyway. When I was little, you used to laugh at the same knock-knock jokes I told you over and over again, and you'd laugh every time as if it were the first time. What I've wanted to tell you all this time more than anything is that I forgive you. And that I understand why you might have had to leave us. Granny's teaching me a lot of things. I bet some of the things you don't even know. And Dionne, well, Dionne is Dionne. She ran away with Daddy, and I just want her to be back here with us, so it could be the three of us again. Or the four of us, really, because I still count you even though you're not exactly with us. Mommy, I'm not sure if you can hear me. Or what you might be able to do if you can. But if you can, if there's something you can do about it, please send her back to us."

Phaedra was close to the headstone now, her ear pressed to

the cool earth, her head just above where she thought her mother's head might be. She stayed there for a while, listening for the sound of Avril below the hill. She would have stayed longer, had Hyacinth not nudged her and told her it was time to go home.

ASK A BAJAN where their navel string is buried and you will get as many answers as people you ask, and all of them will have to do with home. Hyacinth, while a believer in the medicine that her mother and grandmother had passed down to her, also knew that there was more than one way to skin a mongoose. So, after she and Phaedra called on Avril to help them, she decided to turn over one last stone. Whenever she needed something, it was nothing for Hyacinth to drop in on someone she had delivered, and find them either in their garden or in their house, at their work site or in their office. And even if they were a big man or a big hard-backed woman, there was none that could resist doing a favor for the woman who had seen their naked bottoms before even their mothers, who had bound their bellies and given them a tether to this world.

So on the second day Dionne was missing, while everyone else was busy putting the final touches on their costumes for Grand Kadooment Day, flapping their mouths about which man or which woman they would be working up on while they went down Spring Garden, finalizing their party plans, stirring batches of rum punch with heavy hands, Hyacinth paid a visit to Inspector Joseph. The inspector was a burly man whose grumbling so thoroughly frightened his subordinates into doing their work that he'd built a reputation for running the most efficient police station on the island and become the go-to man for anything criminal in Barbados. Never mind that Hyacinth hadn't seen the inspector since he was wearing short pants and going to Bird Hill Primary School, before his mother had the terrible business with his father that required her to flee first to the west coast and then to the States. The year before Phaedra and Dionne arrived, when women started turning up dead in the wells in St. George, it was Inspector Joseph's face that flashed beside a news story about a crack-down against sexual violence in Barbados. And Hyacinth, who couldn't understand how a country that could get so up in arms about elections and Crop Over and cricket barely sounded off about the phenomenon of their daughters and granddaughters and nieces being disappeared, felt some pride in knowing she had something to do with Inspector Joseph being a voice of reason and, more important, a man of action in response to the gruesome murders. Within two months of declaring that the island would not tolerate this kind of violence against its women, the wells were full only of water again.

With Dionne gone, the inspector was the first person Hyacinth thought to call upon.

Hyacinth could not imagine any safer place to bring a child than a police station, and so Phaedra was in tow when the secretary told Hyacinth that the inspector was a very busy man and asked her what business she had with him. Hyacinth announced herself as Mrs. Braithwaite, midwife, and told the inspector's secretary that he would know what her business was. In no fewer than the four minutes it took him to finish up a phone call, Inspector Joseph was hugging up Hyacinth as if she were a long-lost aunty, pinching Phaedra's cheeks in a way that she expected that an uncle might if she had one. After listening to Hyacinth's story, the inspector put out an all-points bulletin and dispatched his available men, with a special detail to the airport, where he thought Errol might try to leave with Dionne.

By the time the six o'clock news came on, a picture of Dionne from her eighth-grade graduation appeared alongside her name on the CBC, along with instructions to call with any information regarding her whereabouts. As soon as the news went off, neighbors started streaming into Hyacinth's house, offering their condolences, stories about the time they'd last seen Dionne, offering to pray or cook or both. Phaedra watched her grandmother carefully, and tried to make sense of how this woman, whom she'd taken for granted as part of the backwater her mother always complained about, had been able to make the search happen. She concluded that there was so much about Hyacinth that she still didn't know.

WHEN ERROL SUGGESTED they sneak out of the stadium before the end of Kiddie Kadooment, Dionne hesitated. She reminded her father of the promise they made to Phaedra and the other kids to stay until the end and take them out after. It didn't take much convincing, really only Errol glancing down at the tennis bracelet he'd bought Dionne at a duty-free shop in town, to get her to go along. What he'd said—"I ain't know that one summer in Barbados could turn you into a real grandmother's child"—shut down Dionne's protest. She tripped as they squeezed past the other people in their row, her head turned to see if she could spot Phaedra in the band that was being called onto the stage. She and her father took deep breaths once they got to the stairwell, because it was free of the press of people in the stands, but Dionne regretted it once she inhaled the rank odor: the pee smell from people who'd relieved themselves beneath the stadium all Crop Over season was at about the same volume as the music onstage.

They left the stadium and went to the hotel where Errol was staying with Evangeline. Dionne thought to call Ms. Zelma's house for her grandmother. But years of watching Taneisha and Saranne and other popular girls had taught her not to assert herself until she'd seen what the dominant girl, or boy, or man, in this case, would do. And so, once Errol took off his heavy gold watch and placed it on the nightstand, pulled a bottle from the mini fridge, and turned on the television, all without any mention of Phaedra or Hyacinth, she was sure they were in for the night, and didn't dare ask to use the telephone. I'm with my father, she thought, trying to convince herself that everything was fine.

Dionne watched Errol pour three glasses of wine, then set one in front of her and another in front of Evangeline. She sipped hers slowly, unused to the bittersweet taste.

"You don't like it," Evangeline said.

"No, I like it," Dionne said too quickly to be convincing.

"It's OK. Certain things take getting used to," Evangeline said.

Dionne watched her father pour himself a second glass, all before she'd gotten halfway through her first.

"Dionne, you know, you really starting to get your looks. I deal with a lot of pretty girls in my work, and I can see now that you could go toe-to-toe with any one of them," Errol said.

"Thank you, Daddy," Dionne replied. She wanted to ask exactly what kind of work her father was doing now, but she knew that it was better to have Errol offer details about his life than to pry.

"When your mother was your age, she was the prettiest girl."

Dionne watched the bulge of Errol's belly move up and down as he talked.

"And when I'm saying the prettiest, I'm not saying the prettiest for Bird Hill, I'm saying the prettiest girl in Barbados. And she was smart, too, almost too smart for her own good."

"So what happened to her?" Dionne surprised herself by asking.

"Life is a funny thing, you know. Just when you think you know what you're doing, which way you're headed, the target moves. At first we thought all we had to do was get out of Barbados, and everything we wanted would fall into place. You couldn't tell us that everything we dreamed for wouldn't rain down from the sky the moment we set foot in New York."

Errol took a big gulp from his wineglass, and then he leaned down to scratch a lesion on his ankle. Dionne watched Evangeline watch her father, noted the way that she hung on his every word and movement, noted the fact that she was now fetching lotion for his dry feet. Dionne wondered if this kind of deference was what a relationship with a man required.

"As soon as we started to get ahold of things there, you came barreling along. And I couldn't say I was sorry. When you were born, everyone we knew in New York, all my partners from my band, even a couple aunts I didn't know your mother had, they came to see you. I sat up in the hospital all night holding you. I wouldn't put you down no matter what.

And when they came to take you to the nursery, I bawled bloody murder until one of the nurses brought you back to me. Your first morning, it was my face you opened your eyes on."

Dionne relaxed into the story she'd heard her father tell so many times; hearing it again stitched back a piece of her heart she didn't know needed repair.

"So what happened to Mommy?" Dionne asked again.

"You know, Dionne. That is it. That is the million-dollar question. The only one that needs answering. Your mother was hard to know. Twelve years together, eleven of them married, and I couldn't begin to tell you what was going on in that woman's head half the time."

Errol slid open the door that separated the hotel room from its balcony. Dionne heard the sound of the sea rush in, and she followed him outside, where the waves were crashing against the boulders. They stood there, inhaling the brine and listening to the sea's chatter. There was so much Dionne wanted to say, to ask, but she didn't want to disturb the moment, the first time she'd been alone with her father in years.

"You want a next drink?" Errol asked, and then turned to go back inside.

"No, please," Dionne said, feeling the wine hit her head like the waves. She wanted to ask her father why he left them, had been wanting to ask him since he'd showed up at Hyacinth's house. She stumbled over the metal grating of the glass doors, thrown off kilter by the drinking and her questions and her cowardice. She saw Evangeline, who'd changed into her nightgown and was pinning up her hair when they got back inside, and knew it was a question she didn't want to ask in front of her.

"You all right?" Errol asked. He pressed a meaty palm against the small of Dionne's back to steady her.

"I'm fine, Daddy," Dionne said. And although she wanted to say more, the simple gift of her father's hands, exactly what she'd missed most of him since he left, stopped her. She was afraid that asking Errol why he'd left might mean he'd never hug her again, and she didn't want to do anything to lose another parent's touch. And so she said again, "I'm fine" and then, "Good night," and crawled into one of the double beds.

Dionne pretended to be asleep when she heard Errol moving on top of and then inside Evangeline. She felt ashamed by the heat that swept over her body as she listened to them, and then a new wave of shame washed in when she wanted to know if the sounds they made were like or unlike the sounds Errol had made with her mother. Dionne couldn't get to sleep after that and so she was happy to be shaken awake from what was really just a nap to get on the road for the Grand Kadooment parade.

All Kadooment Day, Dionne and her dance partner, Isaiah, Errol and Evangeline, and the rest of the people in their band danced and drank, and sometimes stopped to eat snacks from the food vendors on the parade route. They didn't have any fancy costumes like the other revelers, just beat-up shorts and t-shirts. By the end of the day these rags would be better thrown away than tossed in the laundry, soiled by sweat (their own and others'), baby powder, paint, and all manner of other grime. Every once in a while Dionne looked out of the corner of her eye at her father, and saw him dancing, waving a rag in the air that was steadily turning from white to gray as they progressed. Errol was enjoying himself, dancing with Evangeline with abandon. Dionne realized she hadn't seen him that happy in a long time. Something had shifted between Dionne and Errol, and he seemed less like a father to her that day, more like a friend.

Dionne was sure that her dance partner's crotch would soon be imprinted on the back of her shorts. His full name was Isaiah, but he'd told her to call him Izzy. She was glad that the music and people were too loud for her to call him anything, much less that nickname, which she thought was odd for a boy. At one point, when the liquor made the muscles in Dionne's shoulders tighten and her head feel light, she mused to herself about whether she'd be able to clean him off her like the dirt she felt graveling her skin, and which she'd long since stopped trying to wipe away. She ground her behind into the hard pants front of Isaiah, who was not unlike Chad or Trevor or Darren, winding her waist like Taneisha had taught her to do on Sunday nights when they listened to Dahved Levy's radio show, collapsing with laughter every time he interrupted the music with his trademark "Rocking you, rocking you, rocking you" tagline.

Like the others and like her father, Isaiah was tall and red-skinned. Other girls would have called Dionne's suitors cute, but it was their flaws that drew Dionne in. In the case of

Trevor, it was his razor-sharp widow's peak. With Darren, a lisp he hid by not talking much, which only made him more mysterious and attractive. When Isaiah walked up to her that morning holding a cup of orange juice like an offering plate, she noticed that one of his legs was shorter than the other, and this endeared him to her.

"You have to keep up your strength once we get going," he said. She wondered how Isaiah would manage with his mismatched legs on the long parade route, but by the late afternoon he had, as he promised, not let her out of his sight, and he didn't show any signs of slowing down anytime soon.

All the shops along the parade route were closed, and some of the more cautious owners boarded up their windows, lest they become the victims of overzealous revelers. Because while most of the partying on Kadooment Day was in good fun, it wasn't unusual to see people whose quarrels had been brewing since the year before use the day to settle scores. Most of the brawls ended soon after they started, but sometimes blood mixed in with the other residue of the day. It was no more surprising to see drunk, injured people taking breaks on the side of the road on Kadooment Day than it was to see children in their uniforms on their way to school on a Monday morning.

Crop Over was a chance to see and be seen and, for some, to tinkle a little extra change into their pockets. People were lined up three deep along the road, cheering on the masqueraders, singing and dancing and eating, making jokes about which fat women did not belong in their costumes, which guys and girls were fit and ripe for the picking, judging for themselves which bands had the best music and the most beautiful costumes. Some opened up their houses for parties, and other, more enterprising folks made their money by charging to use their bathrooms, or selling water and cool drinks.

By the time the band Dionne and Isaiah were dancing with neared the turn onto Spring Garden, it was four o'clock, and the parade was almost over, and everyone was wondering when the rain that came every Kadooment Day would pour down on their heads. If you asked a reveler, they might have told you that God was holding his water back stingily, making them beg for relief from the heat and the reassurance that this year was like any other year.

The turnoff from Black Rock Main Road onto Spring Garden Highway was a tight one, barely wide enough for the two lanes of car and foot traffic it usually fit, much less the trucks with their outsize speakers and respective masses dancing beside and behind them. The music was turned down so that the truck could turn without injuring anyone. And it was into that cavern of relative quiet, over the echoes of music from the bands ahead and behind them, above the DJ's awkward small talk and bad jokes, that Dionne heard the unmistakable sound of fists landing on flesh.

Dionne's drink turned over with the commotion. The coconut cocktail slicked her wrist, and she looked up. Just a moment before, her right hand had clasped a length of rope that distinguished their band from the crowd of onlookers. Her beverage was at a precarious lean in her left hand. Dionne's entire midsection was plastered to Isaiah as they marched in time to "left right/left right/in the government boots/the government boots." She felt the rain in the air and she wondered what her hair looked like. She was sure that so many hours of dancing had sweated out her perm.

Now, Dionne felt the crowd push her and Isaiah forward, and they were, impossibly, closer than they had been before. The motion lifted Dionne off her feet, and she felt Isaiah's hands at her hips, trying to hold her down. Her father, who just a minute before had been sweating next to her, and working up on Evangeline, was beating on someone whom she took at first for a woman, until the crowd joined in. She could see Errol's sweat glistening on the roll of flesh below his blue baseball cap. And then suddenly his cap was up and off his head, propelled by the men who had jumped in to pound their victim. Some threw punches, others branches, and then rocks of all sizes. Finally, clouds that had been holding rain back all day broke open. Dionne could hear shouting and rocks whistling through the air and breaking glass and the deafening roar of rain. Above the underwater feeling of rum sloshing against her skull, Dionne made out the words: "You nasty buller man!"

And then she saw the signature band of hair ties on Jean's wrist.

"So I see you come back determined to destroy every last thing Avril had. I always knew you wouldn't rest until you tore her down to the last bits," Jean shouted.

"You want me to shut your blasted mouth?" Errol said,

leaning in to Jean, whom he had pinned on the ground. The men were close enough that they could see each other's eyes, but Errol was still talking loud enough for the crowd to hear. "I knew from the first time I saw you, all you wanted was my cock in your mouth. If that is what you want, I could give it to you, you know," Errol said, making a motion to unbuckle his pants.

"From what Avril said, it wasn't much to write home about," Jean replied.

"Looks like I'm going to have to shut your fucking mouth since you won't do it yourself." And with that, Errol landed blows on Jean's head and shoulders, pummeling him until Jean's lips were both the size and color of plums. Jean tried to fight back, but his punches were no match for Errol's heft and thick fists.

Dionne surged forward, toward the trouble, and Isaiah pulled her back. His hands felt different from the men and women who'd held her away from her mother's grave. This time, she wouldn't relax into his arms; she didn't want to, even though his strength was more than that of the entire Usher's Guild. She writhed out of his grasp and tried to peel back the hulk of her father, and the men who'd joined him, off Jean. She felt blows land on her shoulders and forehead and one that she thought would take her out, on her lower back. But even that wouldn't stop her.

Errol forced himself back into the melee to stop people from throwing their confused, tired blows at Dionne, which was easy, because by then they were full on the meal they'd made of Jean's humiliation. Once the crowd thinned, Errol puffed out his chest and yelled, "This nasty so-and-so get what he deserve. I don't know what kind of place Barbados is turning into where a buller think he can dance on me and it's all right. It could be Crop Over or Christmas, but it could never be right." The people around Errol murmured in agreement, and Dionne looked at her father, and then at Jean, and then at her father again. She could see the fire in Errol's eyes, the same fire that had burned her mother, and she knew that the smolder was what the women and the men saw in him and what they thought they wanted, before it scorched them too.

Dionne stopped looking to her father for an answer she knew wouldn't come, and focused instead on Jean. Because there, lying beneath the pile of revelers that dispersed once the truck's engine coughed into action and the speakers blared a gospel song, there, as the MC made platitudes for peace and a return to all that was Christian, there, beneath it all, in threat of being trampled, but still breathing, was Jean.

Isaiah, who Dionne could now see was a man and not the boy she'd taken him for, helped her carry Jean to the doorway of a pharmacy. Space opened up for the three of them, as if the crowd, which had been thick just moments before, didn't want to catch whatever it was they had.

"Mind he don't give you that AIDS business, y'hear," one woman said, and Dionne wanted to take her on, but she was too focused on getting Jean to safety to respond.

When they reached the pharmacy, they laid Jean down on the pavement. Dionne looked at Jean's pulpy, bloody face, and then at her own reflection in the glass. For the first time that she could remember, Dionne didn't care about whether or not she was beautiful. Her only concern was that the ragged breaths Jean took would deepen, that somehow he, she, they would be made whole again. Isaiah looked at her, his eyes asking her permission to keep going, to catch up with the band that was edging down Spring Garden now, her father and Evangeline with it. She knew he was going to leave, and so she nodded, the same way she did when her mother would leave, to make the leaving easier on him. Isaiah knelt down to kiss her on her cheek, but she wouldn't give him this. She edged closer to Jean and eased her weight back onto her heels, trying to figure out what to do.

There were several bands behind the one that swept away Evangeline and Errol and Isaiah. The music went on and people danced and drank, and Jean and Dionne blended into the parade route. In the same way that she couldn't summon the courage to ask Errol why he'd left them, Dionne was afraid now to ask for help, unsure whether the crowd that had pounced upon Jean would rally to his aid. And so she sat, trying to devise a plan, shrinking away from the stares of the people who occasionally squeezed by her and Jean, scrutinizing them but not helping. A couple of women her mother's age asked if she was all right, and Dionne nodded yes. She thought that maybe once the parade was over, Jean would be feeling strong enough for them to walk to someone's house and ask if they could use the phone. In the meantime, she sat with Jean's head in her lap, letting the people and music and food smells swirl around her. The whole time, she kept talking to Jean, asked him questions and told him stories, anything to keep him alert until they were able to get help. She settled for Jean's one-word answers, and then, when he was too tired to talk, his fist's strong grasp.

Just as the last band was turning onto Black Rock, an older woman seemed to appear out of nowhere. She was, not unlike Hyacinth, dressed in white. Dionne could only see the whites of her eyes and her teeth as the sun had already set by then, the darkness come to swallow up the shadows. The sunsets in Barbados, which Dionne sometimes watched from Hyacinth's gallery, were a marvel, a fantastic light show of oranges and pinks and reds, and on days when it had been stormy, purples. Such a contrast, that dance of color to the pitch black that followed it, as if God wanted Bajans to appreciate the portion of abundant sunshine He granted them in the daytime. It was into that darkness that sirens blared. Having gone for so long without help, Dionne didn't really believe the woman when she offered to call the police from her house. But she did. And then she returned with a bucket of water and rags to clean Jean's face. And once she'd cleaned him up, she waited with them, and then watched as Jean was put onto the stretcher and Dionne climbed into the ambulance behind him.

Dionne, who couldn't rightfully claim to be Jean's family, made it to the reception desk of the Accident and Emergency Department at Queen Elizabeth Hospital before she was told that she couldn't go any further. Dionne would have stayed there longer, trying to figure out a way home by herself, had she not remembered Clotel Gumbs bragging that a relative of hers worked at QEH. Clotel's aunt, a nurse in a starched uniform and a pointy cap whose officiousness echoed Mrs. Gumbs's, was paged and came downstairs. She sat Dionne down in the waiting room with a packet of stale corn curls and went to the nurses' station to call her sister. From where she sat, Dionne could hear the woman's loud voice. "Yes, we have the girl," she said loudly, confirming the details of Mrs. Gumbs driving into town to collect her. Something seemed righted by Dionne being referred to as a girl, and the logistics of her return home being taken care of for her. Because right then, adrenaline was draining out of Dionne like air from a blown tire, and what she wanted more than anything was her bed and sleep. For the first time that summer, Dionne thought of Hyacinth's house with longing. Errol's behavior had made it clear that Bird Hill was the closest thing she had to home.

Dionne wondered what exactly had set her father off, because the trouble between him and Jean seemed to have roots that were planted well before Kadooment Day. She resigned herself to the fact that she might never know. Something Avril had always said made her feel more at peace. "You get exactly what you need when you need it," Avril had told her, trying to tamp down Dionne's longing for better and more—clothes, friends, boys. Dionne didn't know how badly she'd needed to see the truth of who her father was, and now she wasn't quite sure what to do with what she knew.

"Apparently everyone's been looking for you," the nurse said to Dionne when she got off the phone. Dionne felt the woman's intense scrutiny and drew her head back in like a turtle. She stared into the bag of chips that was smeared with salt and oil, grateful for anywhere else to place her attention besides herself.

And then the receptionists and the nurses and some of the patients looked at Dionne, as if seeing her for the first time. One of them said, "This is the girl in truth." Dionne shrunk away from their attention. She knew that being "the girl in truth" was just a prelude to whatever judgments they would make of her or her grandmother or, worse, her mother. More important, Dionne knew that the fact that her eighth-grade graduation photo had made its way onto the CBC news meant that Hyacinth would likely be in a state beyond anger when Dionne saw her again.

Dionne settled into the hard blue seat in the waiting room, and tried to drown out the women's clucking. She fixed her ears instead on the ticking clock above her head.

"EVENING," DIONNE SAID when she'd made her way from Mrs. Gumbs's car to her grandmother's front steps.

"Evening," Hyacinth said, more fact than greeting.

Dionne looked up at her grandmother and held her gaze. She'd never really noticed the blue-gray rings around Hyacinth's irises before, and she thought the cataracts had their own kind of beauty. She could tell that Hyacinth was too tired to argue. Since Mrs. Gumbs was in the car idling behind her, Dionne knew that Hyacinth wouldn't say much of anything, lest she give the self-righteous cow any material for her performance of Dionne's downfall. Dionne put her dirty sneaker on the whitewashed front step, as if to come inside the house.

"Eh eh. If you think you coming in here with those filthy clothes, you must have left more than your good sense out in whatever place you washed up from," Hyacinth said.

Dionne stood with her head hung low, awaiting instruction.

"Go behind the house and take off those clothes before you come in here." And Dionne, who now knew every inch of her grandmother's property in the same way that she knew the apartment she'd shared with her sister and mother in Brooklyn, walked to the back, past the chicken coop and the hydrangea and the rosebushes and the goats watching her from their perch beneath the house. She stripped down to her underwear and put the rags in the rubbish bin. When she'd finished bathing and put on the nightclothes Hyacinth had laid out for her in the bathroom, Dionne went to her room and was startled to find her grandmother there, sitting on her bed.

"Sit down, pet," Hyacinth said, patting the bedspread.

Dionne eased onto the bed, wary because her punishment was so long in coming.

"Granny, I—"

"Don't start, child."

"It's just that, if you let me explain—"

"I already heard everything I need to hear."

Dionne was quiet then, because even though what had happened had happened in town, she knew that the island was small, and news traveled fast, and Hyacinth had eyes everywhere.

"So you know what happened to Jean?"

Hyacinth nodded.

"And you're not mad at me."

"You did the most honorable thing you knew how to do."

"Daddy left."

"Did you think he would stay?" Hyacinth said. She went to smooth the thin cotton of Dionne's nightdress against her knee, and Dionne jumped a bit with surprise, so rare was the gift of her grandmother's touch.

"I thought he was going to take me with him."

"Of course you did, darling. And now?"

"I don't know. I mean. Seeing him do what he did, it's like I hardly knew him."

"Or at least you only knew the side of him you wanted to know. You know that they say that everything done in darkness—"

"Will come to light. I know that. But I didn't think he'd do something like that."

"I knew that you would have to learn for yourself. Your sister, now, she can watch and wait, and see how things go. But you, you're not taking anything to be the truth unless you have the living proof for yourself."

Dionne smiled and then squirmed a bit. It was strange to be so clearly seen, no judgment, just description.

"Maybe the next time you might listen."

Dionne went to protest.

"Or not," Hyacinth said, and wearily heaved herself up and off the bed. "I'm just glad you made it home. Night, darling."

"Night, Granny," Dionne said. She lay down and closed her eyes, though she knew it would be some time before sleep found her.

THE LAST FEW WEEKS of August came and went quickly, the end of summer passing by in a blur as Hyacinth called upon her army of hill women to help her get the children enrolled in and then ready for school. There were uniforms to be fitted for and sewn, placement exams to be written, headmistresses and teachers to be met with, bus routes to be drawn and tested.

On the Sunday night before Phaedra and Dionne were set to start their new schools, both girls were in bed by seven, where their grandmother had sent them. Hyacinth bustled about the house, double- and then triple-checking their uniforms, which were pressed and hung in the hallway outside their bedrooms, looking to see whether their school shoes needed another polish. She was in the kitchen washing the dinner dishes when she heard Ms. Zelma call to her.

"Look here a minute, Hy-cee," Ms. Zelma said. Hyacinth smiled at her friend's pet name for her. Since Avril died, Ms. Zelma's living room had become an extension of hers, the girls going back and forth to bring herbs from Hyacinth's garden or return a dish. Weeknights, they watched television together until the signal went off. During the day, Phaedra and Chris flew kites in the field next to Ms. Zelma's house, the same field that made Dionne think about her mother's red shoes landing and taking root there. Now, as they each lay in their beds imagining different versions of their first day at new schools, Phaedra and Dionne felt darkness press down on them, but they couldn't sleep.

Hyacinth heard Ms. Zelma's feet shuffle across her kitchen floor and she smiled at the fact that her friend had never learned to pick up her feet when she walked, a habit no amount of nagging or teasing could break.

"Hy-cee, you ain't hearing me? I said come," Zelma yelled. Hyacinth wiped her hands on a dishrag and went next door.

"Only the good Lord knows what has you screaming bloody murder," Hyacinth said when she came through the back door of Ms. Zelma's house. Her friend patted the sofa beside her but Hyacinth wouldn't sit down.

On the TV screen there was a police car chase along the south coast road just past Oistins. The same clip played over and over again, a white car leaping over the promontory at Miami Beach, before falling straight into the sea.

A man with a snorkel pushed off to the side of his face,

spoke into a microphone. "We're all experienced divers," he said, pointing to the men in wet suits behind him. "We still haven't found anything yet, but we're not giving up hope that we might find something soon."

The news cut back to the CBC studio where Taryn Weekes, a woman whose neon lipsticks always matched her scarves, filled the screen, her brow furrowed with practiced concern. "An attempt was made today to arrest Errol Rose, a Bajan national living abroad in New York and Florida for many years, on charges of exploitation of minors. Rose, a onetime jazz guitarist, is accused of throwing several parties during the Crop Over season at which girls as young as thirteen years were made to have sexual encounters with much older men. Upon being found at his cottage hideaway, Rose tried to escape in a rented vehicle. The police gave chase as you saw in that last clip at Miami Beach, and divers are still searching for Mr. Rose and an unidentified woman. The police apprehended several of the men who attended Rose's parties today, many of them prominent members of Bajan society who were arrested at their homes or places of work. They are being charged with various crimes, including indecent sexual assault and having sex with a minor."

The newscaster's eyes twinkled as the names and pictures of the accused men appeared on the screen beside her.

"Divers continue to work around the clock to find the car and the bodies of Mr. Rose and the woman who was said to be with him. We'll have more news on this story for you as it develops. For now, good night and God bless."

Ms. Zelma turned down the volume on the set and the weight of what they'd seen bore down on them.

"Well, then," Hyacinth said, rooting around in her mind for something meaningful to say.

"The Lord works in mysterious ways, don't you think?"

Hyacinth just nodded and then said finally, "Yes. Yes, he does."

Hyacinth turned to leave, but was pulled back by a question. "When was the last time you saw Errol?" Ms. Zelma asked.

"Maybe a month ago, when he came to pick up the kids for Kiddie Kadooment. I ain't lay my eyes on him since then, lucky for him." Hyacinth knew there was more her friend wanted to ask.

"Well, everything comes to its own righteous end," Ms. Zelma said.

Hyacinth grunted her assent. And then she said good night. On Ms. Zelma's steps, the moon where it shone above Hyacinth was brilliant. She stopped to consider the way her life was so thoroughly changed by the last few months, and marveled that although she'd watched as the moon waxed and waned, it was still the same. After her grandmother died, Hyacinth had gone on a kind of strike against God. A fragile truce was heralded by her baptism and broken again by her husband's, and then Avril's, death. Something seemed righted by Errol's passing. She could feel the weight of her child's absence differently now, feel it settling on her in a way she could bear.

"I KNOW what happened, you know," Trevor said.

Dionne looked up from the bowl of rice on her lap. She was so intent on separating the pebbles from the grains that she didn't notice Trevor walk up or hear him mount the steps to Hyacinth's house. She'd found solace in being Hyacinth's shadow in the kitchen, staying so close and quiet that her grandmother never moved too quickly lest she run over Dionne at her elbow or underfoot. Dionne didn't say anything to encourage Trevor, but he stood there, his gaze intent on a green lizard that was racing across the gallery, a safer place to rest his eyes than on Dionne, where they'd been just moments before.

"I said, I know what happened," Trevor tried again.

"Well, if you know that, then you also know that I'm not deaf," Dionne said, still looking down and sifting her hands through the rice.

"Do you know what I'm talking about?"

"For the love of God, Trevor, stop talking in circles, man."

"They say Jean's healing nicely."

"Oh," Dionne said, surprised that Trevor, whom she'd heard dismiss Jean as a nasty so-and-so in front of his friends, didn't take the chance to rail on about how Jean got exactly what he deserved.

"He's better now. Maybe we could go see him one day."

Dionne didn't say anything, hoping that Trevor, who was practically allergic to silence, would eventually become uncomfortable and go away.

"Your friend Saranne's gone back to Trinidad."

"I know," Dionne said.

"T&T." Trevor moved closer, to the top step where Dionne sat. He stretched his long arms up to the gallery's awning. From where Dionne sat, she could see his stomach. If she wanted to, she could have leaned in to sniff the scent of the English laundry soap Mrs. Loving used, and she had once loved to smell on Trevor's clothes.

"I know that T&T stands for Trinidad and Tobago."

"You think you'll miss her?" Trevor invited himself to sit next to Dionne on the front step. She didn't move over; his legs dangled over the side of the steps.

"Not really."

"You guys spent so much time together."

"You could spend a lot of time with someone and still not really know them."

"That's true," Trevor said, and then stood. He noticed Dionne squinting up at him and he stepped to his right to block the sun for her.

"All those years with my mother, and I never saw what she did coming. Sometimes people have bombs ticking inside them, but you can't hear them until they go off."

Trevor nodded, and for the first time in a long time, Dionne didn't dismiss him or think him stupid, but was actually grateful for his visit. It was a relief to have someone to talk to who wasn't inscribed in the same circle of grief she shared with her sister and grandmother.

"I'm sorry."

"What are you sorry about?" Dionne craned her neck to get a closer look at Trevor. She could see that he was taller since she saw him last.

"I'm sorry about what happened to your mother."

"It's OK."

"Not really."

"You're right," Dionne said, and for the first time she felt something soft land where her rage had been before.

"I mean, you don't have to pretend it's OK, at least not with me," Trevor said.

Dionne nodded.

"Well, anyways, I was just passing by. Maybe I'll come check you tomorrow."

"I'd like that," she said.

"Look, I know you didn't plan to stay here after the summer

was over. I don't know how you feel about it, but I'm glad you're here." Trevor took the three steps down from Hyacinth's house in one leap. "All right, then," he said.

"All right," Dionne said, and then returned to the rice in her lap. Contemplating the whys and wherefores of her new life was easier when her hands had work to do.

BY THE TIME ADVENT ARRIVED, the long hair that Dionne had when she arrived in Barbados was falling in thick clumps, which she left behind her everywhere, like bread crumbs on a trail back to herself. At the desk where she studied and where her mother had studied before her, she scratched a bloody patchwork into her scalp and plucked out her straightened hair strand by strand. On the back steps where she shelled peas and cleaned rice, on the gallery near the chair where she always sat, Dionne's hair dusted the ground like the snow she knew was starting to fall in New York. It was a nervous condition even Hyacinth didn't have a cure for, because she couldn't follow Dionne to school and around the house, couldn't force her to stop this new habit of picking at and pulling out her hair. Hyacinth figured that in time, as Dionne settled in to her new life on Bird Hill, this, too, would pass.

Every first snow, Avril let Dionne and Phaedra stay home from school. It was a welcome respite from her ironclad rule that only children on their deathbeds could miss a chance to learn. As soon as the warmth burned off the air, right after Halloween burst through their neighborhood with rotten eggs hurled against bus windows, the girls would start to study the weather forecast, hoping that they could will a snow day to come simply by watching for it. That day usually came in November, but sometimes not until the first or second week in December. On the appointed day, they roasted marshmallows on the stovetop, drank hot chocolate and ate pancakes, and snuggled up on the couch together, telling stories as the city's white coat fell around her shoulders. Avril would tell them about what it was like when she was in Girl Guides, and the girls would pretend that they'd never heard these tales before, not the one about the time when she didn't have a bowel movement for a whole week during sleepaway camp because she had a "shy bottom," or when she gave a girl a black eye for calling her a buller man's wife, the nickname Avril earned once it was clear she would not succumb to pressure to scorn her gay friend, Jean. Without fail, Avril would tell them about the first time she'd seen snow in New York, how she hid under the covers in a cold-water flat in Bed-Stuy, terrified as she counted the hours until Errol came home from work.

Dionne wondered what had happened to their winter clothes, the jackets and coats and boots they'd packed away in plastic bins before coming to Barbados. Hyacinth said that a distant aunt, one who the girls never heard of, had gone to clean out their apartment and give their things to a church. Occasionally, Dionne wondered who had ended up with her things. She was particularly curious about a cream peacoat with brown leather buttons that her father bought her the year she turned eleven, right before he left. Her last winter in Brooklyn, her arms were already too long for the coat, but she wore it anyway, fashioning a pair of stockings into arm warmers; she was glad that her mother was too dazed then to protest. Every evening now, when she watched the news broadcasts from the States and saw clips of people rushing around Rockefeller Center doing their holiday shopping, Dionne scrutinized the screen, looking for a girl wearing her coat.

This winter was the first that Dionne found herself somewhere other than Brooklyn but not the first time she'd welcomed the first snow without her mother. The girls' last winter in New York, when the snow came, Avril was gone. The flakes started falling just before daybreak and Dionne, who'd never been able to sleep when her mother was out, was up when it began. She coaxed Phaedra awake to watch the snow fall slowly, then with more fervor as the sun pressed through the gauzy sky. They watched all morning as the snow made beds on the windowsills, and they tried their best to resurrect the ritual without their mother. Dionne made pancakes from mix that she poured out of the plastic bag that protected it from cockroaches that came out at night in Brooklyn like the field mice that rustled the sugarcane next to Hyacinth's house after dark in Bird Hill. Phaedra sat at the kitchen table her mother had rescued from the Dumpster and painted a hopeful shade of yellow, her knees pulled up to her chest. She watched as Dionne burned the pancakes, and then pretended that she liked them crispy.

Night fell, but Avril still wasn't home, and the marshmallows Dionne took down from the cabinet were starting to sweat the plastic bag on the counter where she had laid them. When the kitchen's clock radio read ten, Dionne was sure that her mother wasn't coming home. She felt overcome by a sudden thirst. The tropical temperature that the building was set to in winter dried out the lining of her throat. She perched on the lip of the open window in the living room and pulled back the security gate. Dionne called Phaedra and asked her to hold her hands as she leaned out of the window. She opened her mouth and let the snow tumble past her teeth, savoring the feeling of being suspended above the courtyard below. She leaned back more and more until Phaedra wouldn't let her go any farther. Dionne sensed her sister's fear in her tense grip, but she stayed supine, feeling the silver glow the moon cast above her and the cold wet falling onto her skin and into her mouth. When she finally came out of the window, she brushed past Phaedra and opened the marshmallows. She ate the entire bag in silence before going to bed.

Now Dionne was in Bird Hill on a Saturday morning in December when she was sure kids in Brooklyn were outside making snowballs and snowmen. Somebody else was kissing her old boyfriend Darren, some other girl wearing his varsity ring and letting him give it to her in one of Erasmus's abandoned stairwells. Dionne tried to conjure what she'd felt for him when she'd first arrived, but there was no tingle between her belly and legs anymore. The part of her that needed a boy's eyes to be seen was steadily dying, and she knew it would be a long time before she let herself be touched in that way again.

The sun beat down on the back of Dionne's neck as she hung clothes to dry on the line behind the house. She felt the sweat collecting in her pits and between her thighs as a kind of betrayal of what she knew December should feel like. All summer and fall, she'd held out hope that something would change, but with the first snow falling without her and the blue sea and sun shining as brightly as they had been when she and Phaedra first arrived in June, the truth of this as her home now clicked into place. She finished pegging the clothes to the line and went back inside through the kitchen door.

Dionne was chopping okra for her grandmother's cou-cou dish when the memory of leaning out of the window in the old apartment in Brooklyn came back to her. She remembered that when she finally came inside, Phaedra was crying. She pushed past her sister, thinking it was stupid for her to be afraid that she'd fall. In Dionne's mind's eye, her shoulders were brushing past Phaedra's wet face. She could almost feel the cold at her back, the snow melting into her hair, her t-shirt plastered against her breasts, which were so much smaller then. Dionne was a stranger to apologies, but now she walked up to the edge of regret about how she'd treated Phaedra then.

It was no wonder that the knife in Dionne's hand slipped.

Behind Dionne, Hyacinth was sitting on a stool, snapping

the heads and legs off okra and watching her granddaughter. She noticed the patches where Dionne's hair once was, the way she stood with her toes turned out, the same way Avril had. And so, just a split second after Dionne's hand was cut, Hyacinth was out of her seat. By the time the blood started to soak into the cutting board, Hyacinth was by Dionne's side, running her hand under cold water, fashioning an old white dishrag into a compress that brightened and then darkened as Dionne's blood soaked it. Dionne was shocked into silence by the intensity of the pain; she drew in sharp breaths as her grandmother helped her.

When her blood stopped flowing, Dionne pulled back the rag and saw the white of the bone between her thumb and index finger. She knew the okra had been solid beneath her hand, their insides slick and white, just before she cut herself. She was reminded again of the snow she'd been dreaming of just before her accident, and of her mother.

Without warning, the tears that Dionne had been holding back since Avril's death came, the ones she'd gritted her teeth against, thinking that if she ever started crying she would never stop. She let the tears form a salty river in her mouth and splatter her housedress. Hyacinth saw the dam she'd been watching for months finally break. And as she went to comfort Dionne, something dislodged from the high shelves of her own heart. Hyacinth's mother had told her that grief was a funny thing, not put to bed before its time, and that not even a nine-night would still a soul that isn't ready to come to rest. Hyacinth remembered her mother often over the weeks and months she'd waited for Dionne to shed the prickly shell she'd gathered around herself, to release Avril's spirit from the tight, small place where she tried to keep it captive.

Hyacinth knew the way it was with a story. She held Dionne's unharmed hand and led her into the front room. They sat down next to each other in the way that two people who know each other well only need to hear the sound of each other's voice to know the look on their beloved's face. Hyacinth waited until her voice steadied, and then she began.

"Well, child, the old people say that it was a morning just like this when wunna great-great-grandmother was doing laundry, beating the white clothes with a rock. Her shirt was still wet from the child the master had sold away a few days before. That time, her husband, your great-great-grandfather, was always behind her telling her to clean herself up. That was the thing that mashed them up in the end, you know, that he couldn't understand she needed to see and smell the milk, that there was no sense in trying to erase the only thing she had left of the baby.

"She'd let others go before. But this one, for some reason, maybe because she knew it would be her last, this one was harder. After she had my great-grandmother, every Crop Over saw her tumbling big. One by one they all went away. There were more than a few she was happy to bury before they got to know this place. But then there were four that survived and came quick-quick, all boys that she raised until they were out of short pants, only to see them sold away. Everything Bertha knew should have told her not even to look on this new baby and think love or stay or lifetime, but that's exactly what she did. And so when they took this one, and didn't even let her nurse him, it was like something inside of her broke open. The least of her worries was the milk.

"The old people say that back in those days you would never see a body crying, because the body that starts crying, that body wouldn't ever stop. But that's not what I'm wanting to tell you, because you already know that things does start and then end even if you want them to go on forever.

"It was a morning like this when your great-great-grandmother, her two big bubbies leaking down on everything, brought one of those big rocks, big like what you see by Bathsheba, down on her hand while she was doing the washing. People say that they could hear her scream all over the hill, from those that was working in the fields to the people working in the big house, all the way out to the sea. They say that the fishermen who heard her scream pulled up their nets, no matter that they hadn't yet caught fish nor fowl. They say that every man, woman, and child who heard that scream knew that what had been broken couldn't fix. And everyone, from the little boys in the plantation yard to the old man who couldn't hold his penis to go to the bathroom by himself, everyone knew the pain behind that scream. And they went to look in on her, all who could walk, to see who had felt that kind of pain and lived.

"They say that her hand was never the same again, neither her mind. They say that from the time she start screaming until the next time she spoke was the three days the master let her take off from work. You would think that was generous, but the crop had already been taken in and he could spare her. On the fourth day, she got up before cockcrow. She said to her daughter, my grandmother, that the next blood shed would be bakkra's. And she never said another word to her husband again.

"If you think this life you have is hard, you have to imagine those days. No television to watch. No electric iron to turn on. No curling iron to fix up your hair. No inside bathroom. Nothing like everything that you know to be true now, nothing like what you call your life now. Every day the children that you call your own, the husband that you call your own, the wife that you call your own, everything that you call your own, you knew it wasn't yours in truth. You knew that any tie to what you thought was yours could be broken just so. And so this thing people call grief, this thing that people call sadness, this thing that people call darkness, that was what we were living in all the time. There was joy, yes, a dance here and there, a boy who catch your eye, the babies before they grow big enough to have value. But that part of your life that was light was small and this dark thing, this ugly thing call slavery, it was big. This big ugly thing had a hold on you strong enough to make you feel like nighttime was constantly grabbing at your neck.

"Before time, there was a whole heap of confusion about renaming this place Seven Man's Hill. And that's because people can only remember the men who went into battle for our freedom and not the women who made it possible for them to be there. Because even though Bertha herself didn't even have two strong hands to fight, it was she who gave the young men the courage to make up their mind about what they had to do. It was she who said the prayers over them, she who put the pouches next to their hearts that protected them. And beside her every step of the way was her daughter, a girl with strong, long legs like you, about your age, your great-great-grandmother I'm talking about now, and she was a warrior too. And so even as the men were already puffing out their chests at what it was they managed to do, there was your great-great-grandmother among them, fierce and taking in everything she needed to know to make a life. That is the people you come from, child. Not a sad-sack kind of people that does sit down and let life blow all the air out they chest.

"The same way that your father's people blood run through your veins, you have a strong line of women behind you, Bertha and her mother and her mother before her. If they could still stand up after what they did and what had been done to them, you have more than enough legs to stand up on now. Your heart is going to heal, you know. Your hand too."

"What did they do to make their masters set them free?" Dionne asked.

"Oh, dear heart. They didn't ask for their freedom. They took it."

"But Bertha was an old woman then. What could she do?"

"Being old and being dead isn't the same thing. She was a wise woman. She never turned her back on the things her mother brought over with her from Africa. So even though she wasn't in battle herself, she cleared the way for the people who could fight."

"You mean to tell me that it was some spells that took down the planters?" Dionne said. She turned to look at her grandmother. From this angle, she could see the wiry gray hairs that sprouted like wildfire at Hyacinth's temples after Avril died.

"It was some spells that brought you back here after your father took you away."

"Spells that drowned my father too?" Dionne said, straightening her back the way she'd seen Errol do.

"You already know the answer to that."

Dionne searched Hyacinth's face, although she wasn't sure exactly what guilt would look like when she found it.

"I don't practice the kind of magic that hurts people. And if you think that I killed your father, then you don't know me half as well as you think you do," Hyacinth said.

"Apparently you don't practice the kind of magic that helps people either," Dionne said.

"What do you mean by that?"

"Exactly what I said. All these years you've been helping all these women on Bird Hill. And not once did you say to yourself, well, let me go check on my child and see how she's doing. Or I wonder how my granddaughters are."

"You don't think I thought about you?" Hyacinth asked.

"Thinking about someone and helping them is not the same thing. That's the problem with all you old-time people here. You believe that if you just pray for something, 'watching and waiting' for it, then it will appear. But the world doesn't work like that. Don't you remember what Father Loving said about how when you pray you have to move your feet?"

Hyacinth went to hold Dionne, as the tears her story had dried were back. She said something that she'd never said to Avril, though she'd always wondered if saying it might have brought her home. "I'm sorry, Dionne. I'm so, so sorry. If I could bring Avril back or go back and change the way things were for you, I would," she said.

"I know," Dionne said. "I know."

And they stayed there like that for a while, feeling the newness of embrace and apology until the pressure cooker's whistle called them back to themselves.

"Well, child, this food is not going to cook itself. I'll let you finish the cou-cou. Your cooking is getting so good I just want to lay back with my two long hands now," Hyacinth said.

"Yes, Gran," Dionne replied. She followed her grandmother into the kitchen where neat piles of okra and cornmeal lay on the counter. And then she went back to making the meal that was so close to Hyacinth's heart it was like second skin.

OLD YEAR'S NIGHT IN BIRD HILL found the new moon with a copper ring licking its edges. Watch night service started at seven o'clock, and by eleven, low notes and a hum of hymns were laying the ground for Father Loving's sermon, the words that would carry them over into a new year. At home, black-eyed peas that had been cooking all day stood cooling on the stove. The black cake that wasn't eaten at Christmas was wrapped carefully in waxed paper. Oranges that would be passed around at midnight, to give the bittersweet taste that the year ahead would certainly bring, were in coolers by the baptismal font. All who could come had come, because the people on the hill thought that if the new year found them on their knees, the months that followed might bring what they prayed for.

In the pews, hill women tried to keep their minds on the

Lord, but their thoughts strayed. Hyacinth wondered whether her jug-jug would keep. As they were saying prayers for the church they had adopted in a country in Africa whose name Hyacinth could never pronounce, all she could think of was how long she'd spent making the dish even though she was sure only the old-timers would eat it. The young people were corralled into the church hall, a couple teenagers left to keep watch, because the five-hour church service was too much to ask of a child.

While Hyacinth and the other hill women and some of its men tried to stay focused on the Lord, Phaedra sat in the church hall with Donna, Chris, and Angelique Ward, who, after the mango-eating incident, had joined their crew. They ate sweetbread Hyacinth made and Phaedra tried to avoid getting her birthday licks by reminding everyone that her birthday was technically almost over. Something about turning eleven in Barbados made the fact of Avril's death real for Phaedra. This time there was no hope for her mother's arrival, because Avril was where she would always be now, silent and below the ground. And this fact, rather than saddening Phaedra, settled in beside her, the way that the hill's red dust filmed her white clothes, the way that sand lined her pockets days and weeks after she'd come home from the beach. It was always there, a reminder of what had come before.

They were all on their third and fourth cups of Fanta and the feeling in the air was one of sugar-fueled giddiness, of sitting on the precipice of the unknown. The children, who were too young to be fearful or resigned about the future, were considering what to do next, when Simone Saveur left her roost at the center of her girlfriends to approach Phaedra and her friends.

"So I hear you have a birthday?" Simone said.

Phaedra nodded.

"Congrats," she said, and Phaedra knew not to accept at face value either the question or her goodwill. "Wunna tell she already about the fire hag?" Simone asked Donna and Chris and Angelique, as if Bajan were a foreign tongue Phaedra could not understand.

"Oh, don't start with that nonsense," Angelique said. Despite having broken off from the clique of Simone Saveur and her henchwomen, Angelique retained her favored status because of her beauty and the trips she took to England each year to see her father. She could brush off Simone with a confidence the others didn't dare.

"What story?" Phaedra said, leaning forward and directly addressing Simone, which was easier to do now that they'd spent an entire term together in school.

"How old you say you turning again?" Simone asked.

"Eleven," Phaedra said.

"Well, if I were you, I would be careful walking home tonight. The fire hag does like to take girls on their eleventh birthdays."

Angelique touched Phaedra's shoulders, trying to smooth the curves alarm had etched into them. "It's just an old wife's tale. They told me the same story to try and scare me on my birthday," Angelique said breezily.

Donna, a notorious frighten Friday, was edging out of her seat and toward the snack table. Phaedra grabbed Donna by the wrists and pulled her down to her seat.

"I want to hear it," Phaedra said. She felt for the braids her grandmother had plaited for her, loose like she liked, and tucked under so her neck could stay cool.

"I don't know why you want to hear that foolishness. All it's going to do is get you worked up," Angelique cautioned.

Tanya Tompkins had assumed her place as Simone Saveur's yes-woman in the power vacuum created by Angelique's defection. She walked over in her new low-heeled patent leather shoes from her clique's spot below the cross. "Well, it can't be total foolishness if everybody says it's true. My cousin said that she knew a girl who knew a girl who had a friend who had a cousin that it happened to," Tanya said.

"That certainly sounds believable," Angelique said, throwing her hair over her right shoulder.

"Nobody ain't ask you, Angelique. Phaedra, you want to hear the story or not?" Simone said.

"Yes, please," Phaedra said, and leaned back into the folding chair around which Chris had draped his arm. The smell of his underarms was pleasant to Phaedra. It was funny to Chris, the weird things she liked about him. Her affection for him always came as a surprise, and he cherished it more for the ways in which it was unexpected, peculiarly Phaedra.

"You want to tell it then, Pokie?" Simone asked. Angelique furrowed her lips at the sound of her nickname. The sixth-formers called her Pocahontas because of the two braids that ran thick and glossy down her back. Phaedra looked at Angelique's hair and wondered at her friend's confidence in wearing her power openly.

"Fine, then, I'll tell it," Angelique said. She stood up and started in a voice that was so smooth it sounded like she'd just drunk her nightly dose of cod-liver oil.

"Back in the old, old times, the Arawaks and the Caribs roamed Barbados. They mostly lived peacefully but occasionally a fight would break out among the tribes and then they would go to war. There was one Arawak woman who was a witch doctor. She was the sole survivor of an attack on her village in which everyone was killed."

Phaedra looked at the children who sat cross-legged around Angelique, the ones who had just moments before been racing the length of the church hall, running the hems of their shirts out of their pants and unraveling their freshly done hair from its barrettes. When she'd first come to Bird Hill the other children had all seemed the same to her, but she could see them more clearly now. There was Samson, the middle child of seven Rastafarian children, whose locks were wrapped in two mounds the size of footballs at the nape of his neck. There were the identical twins Timothy and Thomas, inveterate nose-pickers despite teasing, and Donna's cousin, Kaylin, whose seizures had stopped after her mother finally gave in and let Hyacinth see about her. Knowing these children, their families, and their stories made Phaedra feel like she belonged, and being among them made the story feel less scary than it was.

"Once she'd buried the last of her people, the witch doctor was thirsty for revenge. The devil knew that he needed to make a pact with her to stop the war. The fire hag, as she was known, was given three powers. She would live forever. She could shape-shift into any animal or human being. And she could fly in a ball of fire as far as she could imagine, leaving her skin behind her. The fire hag was greedy. And so she asked the devil if there was no blood for her in her new power. The devil agreed that as payment for her people that had been wiped out, she could make her own sacrifices.

"Now people say that the fire hag preys on the night of their eleventh birthdays. If she finds these girls alone, she wraps them up in her ball of fire, takes them back to the cave where she lives in Chalky Mount, and cooks them. People say that when the fog is thick over Chalky Mount, it's the smoke from girls the fire hag is cooking that you see." A shriek went up among the younger kids. Angelique paused until they simmered down, and then she continued.

"Once the fire hag has your daughter, there are only two ways that parents can get her back. Both involve going to her cave at night. If she's taken flight, they can burn the skin that she leaves behind. When the fire hag feels her skin burning, she will return to her cave and give the people's child back to them. Or, if they find her in her skin, they can drop a bag of rice on the floor. The fire hag has to count every grain, and start again if she drops even one piece. While she's counting, the parents can rescue their child."

Angelique turned to Phaedra, whose skin had blanched.

"Satisfied?" Angelique asked, and looked around for an answer in the crowd that had gathered.

Phaedra jumped when the door between the sanctuary and the church hall banged open. She fully expected the fire hag, and not her grandmother, to be standing there.

On the walk home, Phaedra turned to Hyacinth. "Granny, did you ever hear the story about the fire hag?"

"Yes, why?"

"They said she comes for girls on the night of their eleventh birthday."

"Phaedra."

"Yes, Gran?"

"I ain't teach you well enough to know when somebody is pulling your leg?"

"But the things she was talking about sounded real. Tanya Tompkins said her cousin's friend's cousin had it happen to her and her parents had to go looking for her."

"So, what would you do if the fire hag came for you then?"

Phaedra looked down at her hands, hoping they might somehow hold an answer for her. She remembered a night when her mother, in her cups, her eyes gone glassy, had told her, "The one mistake I made was in thinking that someone could save me. First it was England, and then it was your father, and then it was you girls. You girls are the only things that ever came close. But still. I can tell you for sure one thing. You can't wait for someone else to save you from the life you made for yourself. If I teach you girls anything, I hope it's how to gird up your loins and face the fate that's yours." Her mother moaned then, and even now, Phaedra could hear Avril's voice trembling with tears.

"Phaedra Ann Braithwaite, don't you know enough to keep yourself well?" Hyacinth asked.

Phaedra nodded, wanting to be sure. She looked up at the stars and the red-ringed moon for an answer but all she could hear was the sound of her mother's voice, and in it the sea of regrets she'd lived and then drowned in. What she wanted more than anything was to believe what Avril had told her, and the summer had taught her, was true, that she could save herself if she needed to.

"There's nothing that can come for you that between me, you, your sister, and God we can't handle. You hearing me?"

"Yes, Granny," Phaedra said.

"Right, then," Hyacinth said, considering the matter settled.

Acknowledgments

Shari Jackson Oyefeso, my sister and first friend, has been an unflagging supporter of me and my writing. I thank you and Ademola for being so kind and for making beautiful children, Aaron Adejola and Ella-Adeniké, who I hope to write books for one day. Neil and Kim Harvey, I'm so grateful to have you as my brother and sister-in-law; I can't wait to see who Emmanuel grows up to be.

My parents, Reginald and Sadie Jackson, have shown me how big their love is. Thank you is just a start.

My mother, Cheryl Rose, first unlocked the world of literature for me, for which I will always be grateful.

My grandmother Ruth Jackson taught me so much about life and generosity. I'm not sure this book would be here if she hadn't kicked me out of her room and back into the world.

Thank you to my grandmother Oriel Brewster, a woman of infinite wit. I pray she is looking down from above with a wry smile.

Thank you to my godmother, and number one fan, Evelyn Meade.

To my JA family—Shauna and Jason, Shav and Shamar, Deidre, and the extended clan—thank you for the jokes and inspiration.

To the Jackson family, my cousins Jeffrey, Nikki, Vincent, Rodney, Michelle, Michael, Maurice, Haniff, Marlon and Raquel, all my aunts and uncles, Tanty Chrissy, Vincent and Erin, Patrick, Cynthia and Morris, and Janet, I hope you see some of yourself and the summers we spent together in this book. Uncle Carlton, I'll never forget how much you taught me about loving and living with a big heart.

Friendship has made walking this path bearable by making it less lonely. I am deeply grateful for the literal and figurative shelter provided by my dear friends Jaynemarie Angbah, Vanessa Agard-Jones, Tisa Bryant, Sunu Chandy, Celeste Doaks, Shamaine Francis, Rhashidah Hilliard, Ronak Kapadia, Jason King, Thomas Lax, Brinda Maira and Chad Jones, Ayanda Mngadi, Kamilah Aisha Moon, Ariadne Papagapitos, Ra Ruiz Leon, Nicole Sealey, Shante Smalls, Glenn Solomon-Hill and Sara Whetstone, and Andrea Williams. I am grateful for all the little ones who were born around the same time as this book, especially my godchildren Tessa Pearl and Langston.

Thank you to the friends who helped me see Barbados anew. Lisa Harewood, your guidance shaped this book more than you'll ever take credit for, but I still want to "give Jack he jacket." Sasha Archer, Tammy Jacyna, and Lisa Marshall, thank you for showing me a magical time in Bimshire. Arquita Cunningham, your resourcefulness allowed me a soft landing so I could do my work. Shout-out to my neighbors in Fairholne Gardens. Love to Mrs. Pauline Gittens and family, Beresford Yearwood, Marva Forde, and Ethnie Weekes. Sheena Rose, thank you for the gift of your artwork and your irrepressible spirit.

Shout-out to my Philly crew, Asali Solomon, Jos Duncan, Essence Ward, Pooja Mehta, Nina Ball, Anya Dennis, Tsitsi Ella Jaji, Deborah Thomas, John Jackson, and Duarte Geraldino, who helped me get to work and play during the last round of writing. A special thanks is in order to Jessica Lowenthal, Alli Katz, and

Andrew Beal at the University of Pennsylvania's Kelly Writers House, and the fantastic Literary Boot Camp participants.

Thank you to my agent, Julia Masnik, for her unwavering belief in and tireless work on behalf of me and of this book. You had me when you summoned the specter of the shiv.

Many thanks are due to Andrea Walker. You set this dream in motion and brought me in from the literal and proverbial cold.

Thanks to the incredible team at Penguin Press for your manifold efforts in support of this book. First, deep gratitude to my editor, Virginia Smith-Younce, for her grace, eye, and care. Thanks to the entire Press staff, especially Sofia Groopman, William Carnes, Sarah Hutson, Juliana Kiyan, Matt Boyd, Caitlin O'Shaughnessy, Darren Haggar, Ted Gilley, Ann Godoff, and Scott Moyers for their work to bring this book to the world.

This book would not be what it is without all-star readers. I am especially grateful for the women of my writing group at Powder Keg, Sharon Lerner, Holly Morris, Kelly Zen-Yie Tsai, and Lorelei Williams, as well as Samantha Thornhill, Kamilah Aisha Moon, and Wura-Natasha Ogunji. Susannah Shive made me see this book's ending in an entirely new way. Mya Spalter's razor-sharp eye and magic whipped early drafts into shape, and got me righted on course.

I treasure the community of talented writers and friends at Iowa who brought light and levity to my time there, especially Susannah Shive, Chinelo Okparanta, Alexia Arthurs, Stephen Narain, Yaa Gyasi, and Nana Kweti. Sylvea Hollis and Reinaldo, thank you for keeping me in good humor and health. Marcus Burke and Mary Coats, thank you for your friendship and for making your home in Iowa City an extension of my own. Michael Hill and Sandra Sousa, thank you for the education and your kindness. Modei Akyea, thank you for the dances, meals, and laughs. Sydne Mahone, thank you for being an ecstatic reader and mentor, and reminding me that my destiny was intact.

Thank you to all my colleagues at the Russell Sage Foundation, Rockefeller Brothers Fund, and the Studio Museum in Harlem, especially Aixa Cintron-Velez, who looked the other way when

I started writing at work; and to Ben Rodriguez-Cubenas, Doreen Wang, Haki Abazi, Shenyu Belsky, Betsy Campbell, and Ben Shute. A special thanks to Carolyn Caddle-Steele and Leona Hewitt for their encouragement.

Thank you to all my writing teachers, especially Kimiko Hahn, Tyehimba Jess, ZZ Packer, Marilynne Robinson, Ayana Mathis, and Sam Chang, whose phone call changed everything. Special thanks to Connie Brothers, Deb West, Jan Zenisek, and Kelly Smith for your support when I was at the Workshop. And thanks to the writing communities where my words first formed—Cave Canem poetry workshops in New York City, the Frederick Douglass Creative Arts Center, and Tongues Afire writing workshop at the Audre Lorde Project.

I am grateful to the remarkable writers whose work informed this book, especially Toni Cade Bambara, Paule Marshall, Jamaica Kincaid, Edwidge Danticat, Tiphanie Yanique, Marlon James, and Chimamanda Ngozi Adichie.

The financial and moral resources of several institutions underwrote the writing of this novel. The University of Iowa and the Iowa Writers' Workshop gave me the gift of three years to write, through the Maytag Fellowship for Excellence in Fiction, the Dean's Graduate Fellowship, and the Stanley Graduate Award for International Research. I wrote portions of this book during the ArtsEdge residency at the University of Pennsylvania's Kelly Writers House. I am especially grateful for two residencies at Hedgebrook Writers Retreat, where this manuscript came to life, and for Amy Wheeler's cheerful leadership there. I'm grateful for support from the Point Foundation both in graduate school and beyond, especially from Vince Garcia and Scott Arneson.

And lastly, thank you and love to one-in-a-million Lola Flash. I couldn't have chosen a better companion and champion for this journey's last leg.

For anyone whom I've forgotten to mention here, but who knows that their story, mine, and this book's are deeply intertwined, thank you.